A SILENT DISCOVERY

Tawnya Torres

This story is for the underdogs. To all the people who feel unseen:
I notice you.

IN THE SHADOWS

1

During spring, the sound of a flower blooming can be heard. Pop, it goes. Of course, only someone like me notices. The garden to the east of the castle has the best roses. Their blossoms are exaggerated compared to the other one facing west. Our home is surrounded by a tall wrought-iron fence. It has sharp tips to discourage the crows. My mother hates birds. Finds them to be noisy creatures. Which is odd because she boldly resents me for my inability to speak. She is an unpredictable woman, behaving as five or fifteen separate people in a single day.

My three sisters are having tea in the courtyard. They have smooth flaxen hair. It has an iridescent sheen when the light hits it. I'm the oldest, but get treated like an unwanted guest. I often spend my time pretending I don't exist. It's a bizarre predicament. To be naturally quiet but feel too obnoxious to be palatable.

I take a fistful of my hair and examine it in the afternoon sun. It's unruly—a curly, copper mess. My sisters throw back their pretty heads and laugh. They make a racket. I think they do it on purpose. Adrian is the most beautiful and second born, which is unfortunate for her. Mother drones on about how terrible it is to marry me off first. Adrian has had several proposals but can't accept them until I'm betrothed. I stick out my tongue and wince at the thought of marrying the man my mother chooses.

They are twice my age, hairy, and come with poor manners. Royals

2

don't always act as such. Especially upon learning about my condition. Just because I can't talk doesn't mean I'm stupid. They speak slowly and stare at me like a dessert. I'm lucky they find my muteness distasteful.

Last month, I was rejected by the Duke of Lorendale, a medium-sized kingdom with several allies and mines filled with precious crystals. He wasn't bad looking or too old, but his arrogance made him unattractive. At first, he was interested in touching my hair and doting over the freckles that litter my face and the tops of my arms. Mother says they are hideous and make me look "dirty." He expected me to make conversation with him. When he learned I couldn't, he scowled and walked out the door.

My middle sister is the kindest to me. Her name is Penelope. She is as pretty as Adrian, but not as confident. After our mother and sister abuse me, it's Penelope who brings me tea or offers to sit with me. She slips me notes under my pillow. They say nice things like "Good morning." Or silly stuff like "Doesn't Adrian walk like a pregnant horse?" Mother nearly strangled me to death after the Duke of Lorendale left. Penelope stayed in my room and read to me. She is the sister who reaches out to me in small ways.

A breeze moves through my hair and the green ribbon comes loose. I try to catch it but I can't. It's on the other side of the fence and out of my reach. I've never been beyond the castle's fence. My sisters have attended balls and banquets, but not I. As the family shame, I hide among the rose briars and poppies. I walk up to the fence and hold the iron bars in my hands.

My youngest sister gets up and goes into the castle. Margaux is Mother's favorite. She has the perfect nose with a pointed tip and big brown eyes. I want my little sister and I to have a relationship, but she is estranged from me. Mother does her best to keep her from me, since she is convinced my affliction is somehow contagious. I don't blame Margaux for the way things are. She is too naïve to know any better than what our mother tells her. Margaux is like a flower pot being filled with poor soil.

The knights are leaving. Their horses make loud clip-clop sounds on the cobblestone. They pay no mind to me, but I'm in awe of them. I wish I was a boy. If I were a boy, I wouldn't have to worry about marriage. It wouldn't trouble me to have such a mean sister. My mother couldn't hurt me physically anymore. In fact, it would be of no inconvenience to be mute as a boy. They hardly speak anyway. It seems they communicate with grunts and exclamations.

I can't see their faces and I wonder about them. It's a girlish idea, but it crosses my mind. I'm on the verge of twenty-four. Too old to be unwed. Mother is worried that by the time she finds someone to take me off her hands, Adrian will be past her prime. All she cares about is making sure Adrian gets whatever she wants.

Adrian has her eyes set on the Prince of Arwin. He is handsome, wealthy, and owns land in the west near the sea where it is said to be nothing but tropical paradise. I don't like his smug smile. His teeth are straight and pearly white. It hurts to look at them. Mother makes sure to have Adrian attend every event he's at so he doesn't forget her. Too bad she has to deal with me first.

The last knight is approaching. His horse is black with white speckles across its back. The armor the knights wear is high grade metal. It gleams as the rays of sun touch it. To my surprise, the knight stops for a moment to look at me. The stallion rears up, and the knight kicks him in the sides. I give him a small wave and even though I can't see his face, I know he's looking in my direction until he exits the castle gates.

***

A stream of light peeks at me through the curtains. I get out of bed and brush my hair. The maids and I have an agreement: I'll do things by myself. They don't tolerate my tight curls and brush it too hard, yanking out clumps of it. If they wash it, they use too much soap and not enough conditioning product. They do it to offend me. I can't imagine them ripping out Adrian's or Margaux's hair.

I've learned how to do many things a lady shouldn't do, like how to lace up my own corset. I can tie the laces of my boots and style my hair. It's not so difficult anymore. I usually braid around my crown and pull it to the back, where I secure it with a ribbon. I pick my dress for the day. Before I go anywhere, I put my lucky charm in the bosom of my corset.

It's ridiculous, but I like it. When I was fifteen, I found a rainbow crystal right in front of the fence by the east garden. It was like it was waiting for me. I haven't shown anyone. They might steal it, or worse, break it. People in this castle seem intent on ruining my things or taking them away.

I had a dog when I was eight. Her name was Vix. She was a good girl and followed me everywhere around the castle and accompanied me in the garden. We played all day and I cry when I remember her slobbery, happy face. Mother took her when I was nine. She said I can't have something I couldn't control and blamed it on my inability to speak, but she is a cruel woman.

"Amadeus, breakfast is ready," says one of the maids. Not only is my mother open about the fact she loathes my condition, she parades around her resentment that I wasn't a boy by giving me a man's name. I take another look at myself in the mirror and make my way to the dining hall. My sisters all have big brown doe eyes, but mine are almond-shaped and pine green, almost reptilian.

I sit down and pretend I'm not here. A servant brings me a small portion and a cup of water. I sip politely and avoid eye contact with my mother. She sits at the head of the table. I know it caused her great suffering when Father died, but I can tell she enjoys being the sole ruler of Syrosa. Her hair is styled up in braids and adorned with flowers. The crown sits on top as an afterthought.

I miss my father. He was the one who accepted me the way I am. He would pick me up and spin me until I got dizzy. We would laugh all the time. He told me it's okay to be silent because then it's easier to see what's important. I'm not sure what he meant, but I hold his memory with respect and admiration. Every day, I try to piece together the little things he tried to teach me in our short time together.

"I want a new dress," says Margaux.

"Of course, dear," says Mother in a soothing tone.

"When can I see Lancelot again?" asks Adrian in her throaty voice. She never stays off the topic long. The Prince of Arwin is a big fish for her to reel in. In a sense, I pity this man. If I were the object of my sister's desire, I'd be petrified.

"Soon. You have to let him miss you. Stay mysterious and never be too giving," says Mother.

A cold-hearted woman would give such an answer. Penelope makes eye contact with me but doesn't participate in the conversation. It cheers me up. For the rest of the meal, everyone acts like I'm invisible.

Not existing is better than being the subject of torture.

I'm still hungry, but no one offers me another serving and I don't bother going through the hassle of getting more. I wait for my mother and sisters to finish and we excuse ourselves. It's another nice day. I make my way to the garden. Penelope grabs my elbow before I make it too far. She slips a note in my hand and walks past me. Once I'm in the garden among the red flowers and away from prying eyes, I open the folded piece of paper. My sister's handwriting is soft and flowy:

Adrian's desperation smells of horse manure

I laugh to myself, glad I can have moments like this to break up the monotony of my life. Penelope's sense of humor is a bit brash, but its truthfulness makes it more hilarious. She acts reserved around our mother and sisters, but I know the truth. Her secret is safe with me. It's a wonderful thing to share a secret with someone. I long to have a friend or a mother who loved me to experience it with.

Mother didn't treat me as poorly until Father died. I wonder if she thinks my affliction killed him. He doted on me, picked me up, and played with my hair. His death was tragic. He died battling against the chimeras. My mother didn't want him to go, but he was an honorable and stoic man. He believed he should fight alongside his people.

The war was over sixteen years ago. Our people haven't been to war since. The king's death has altered our ways. We now outsource other kingdoms to aid us. The knights fight the smaller battles on their own, but there have been times when we paid for someone else's army to fight for us.

I take my lucky charm out and let it shine in the palm of my hand. If Father was around, would I be this lonely? Sitting in the grass is unladylike, but I don't care. They don't treat me like a lady of the castle, anyway. I glance out between the bars of the fence. My green hair ribbon is gone. Probably carried away by the wind.

***

If I'm not in the east garden, I spend my time in the library. I read book after book with hunger, unable to reach satisfaction. Even if I read four books in a single day, I'm not content. My need to consume is insatiable.

I can go anywhere in the world when I'm in the library. I can be in jungles, on top of mountains, and roaming exotic lands. Sometimes I'm in a temple or praying with native people. Occasionally, I visit the badlands on my way to the sandy beaches of the coast. I can feel everything, too. There are hundreds of emotions I've never experienced myself. Through the characters I can know what is to be adventurous, to be strong, and to be loved.

My favorite stories involve men competing for a kiss. There is something wild and romantic about it. Apparently, in the desert countries men will go to war and bring back the heart of a soldier as a victory present for the empress, who would then give them a kiss on the lips in return. I read about a knight who trained for seven years to win a jousting competition to kiss the princess.

In the southern continent, the warriors are greeted with a bride upon their homecoming. The women wear white dresses and hold baskets of goods out to the men as their ship touches the sand. The Island of Rithe holds an event where twenty-two men fight to the death to claim the princess. It is considered an honor to enter such a competition.

The arctic aisles of Mosako allow the duchess to choose her husband. It is more modern there. The men are expected to bring her a gift. The one she likes the best is the winner. I found this custom unusual, but delightful. At least there are women out there who get to choose for themselves.

"Amadeus, you always have that frizzy head in the clouds," says Adrian, as she steps out from behind a bookshelf. I roll my eyes and continue reading. She strolls with wide hips in my direction. Her smooth hair falls over her shoulders. She twirls the strands in her fingers to mock me. She knocks the book about birds able to sing in human voices out of my hands. I shrug and give her a defeated look. If I act cool, she grows bored quicker than if I lose my temper.

"You are so bizarre. What man will possibly want you for a wife? I'm doomed because of you!" she shouts and rips a big leather book off the shelf and throws it onto the ground. I put up my arms to block her. She grabs them, fingers strained. Her big doe eyes stare into me with unadulterated hatred.

"I bet you can speak, but do this to vex me," she snarls and throws me back into the chair. For as long as I can remember, I've been mute. I don't recall saying a word as a child. Adrian thinks I exist to ruin her life. She looms over me with her hands on her hips. "I hope Mother finds someone dreadful for you to marry," she whispers as she glides out of my sight and into the maze of shelves.

I'm sure my mother would love to marry me off to some hideous creature. She'd give me to an ogre or goblin if she had the chance. I lean back in the cushy chair and sulk. Adrian's rudeness is a daily occurrence. It wears me down.

Maybe being married wouldn't be awful. Anything might be better than this. It is lavish and cozy, but I'm uncomfortable in every corridor, in every room. Who knows, maybe the man wouldn't be bad. I've had to put up with my mother and Adrian all my life. How could any man be on their level of petty cruelty? I sigh with annoyance and lean on my elbow.

"Psssst," Penelope is hiding behind the chair. It makes me smile and she giggles. "Adrian is in a bad mood because she heard the Prince of Arwin is attending this year's spring banquet with Princess Morello," she whispers. I'm smug with this knowledge. Adrian is having a tantrum like a child. I relish in her misery.

"You're my favorite sister," says Penelope. I give her a look of shock. We have fun together but I didn't think she felt close to me. She holds my hand for a moment and walks into the shadows of the library. I get out of the chair and pick up the book Adrian threw on the ground. It's hefty with a red ribbon attached to the black leather as the bound bookmark. Sitting on the ground with my legs crossed, I open to the first page. It's a story about a mercenary who kills thirteen types of monsters so he can marry the princess.

It takes him three years to complete the tasks. The mercenary travels to a dense bamboo forest with serpents of all kinds, then he gets the head of a griffin and takes down a dragon. There is hardship but he prevails. No one believes he would because of his low rank, though. He gets enough gold to buy her a ring. The princess chooses him over the nobleman her father picked for her.

I like this story the best and finish it as the sun is readying itself to set. When it's over, I feel hollow and go back to the beginning. I don't know why, but the mercenary's character resonates with me and I find it haunting my thoughts. How someone could love so brutally and beautifully captivates me.

THE OTHER DEER

2

Today I'm supposed to meet the Duke of Erving. I'm not looking forward to it. Erving is a dreary little kingdom with nothing to offer but wool from their thousands of sheep. That's all Erving is. Eerily small, with too many hills, and not enough people. A false land. It doesn't matter though. My mother wants to be rid of me by any means possible.

Looking at my reflection, I wonder what he will see: a princess, a person, or an imbecile? I'm not beautiful like Adrian. All my sisters have clear complexions and hair the color of gold. I take after my father with fiery hair and high cheekbones. If he were here, I wouldn't have to do this. I miss him.

There's no way to hide my dappled skin. The freckles take over my forehead and the bridge of my nose. I have them all over my arms and back. The dress I'm wearing isn't revealing, but the tawny splotches can't go unnoticed. Mother chose the white and yellow dress for me this time. It has gold filigree and ruffles. I think she is trying to make me look affable. Yellow is a likable color.

"Lady Amadeus," says one maid. I nod and she leads me to my doom. We shuffle down the stairs. I try to walk as slow as possible. My feet touch the ground, but I don't feel the floor beneath me. The sun is shining through the castle windows, but the lights are going out in my heart as I see what the duke looks like.

He's twice my age, as expected, and has the most dreadful little mustache. His hair is thinning and an ugly shade of blond. It looks like he combed it with dirt. His sneering smile is chapped and saliva is building in the corners of his rat mouth. I scowl as I hold out my hand and he kisses it, ignoring my reaction.

"It's so nice to meet you, Princess," he says. My mother is giving me angry eyes. She looks like she is going to lunge across the room at me. To be polite, I curtsy and smile. This seems to please the disgusting duke who is staring at my breasts. I turn away to avoid his bulgy blue eyes. They are grossly wet, like some kind of fish.

"You are an enchanting creature," he says in a lilting voice and reaches for my face. I allow him to pull a curl. Keeping a grimace off my face is laborious, but I don't want to be a disappointment.

"What? Are you not going to say hello to me?" asks the duke in annoyance. Of course, Mother wouldn't tell him. She never does. People hear rumors about me, but Erving is too insignificant for gossip to reach it. It appears one of his men has been briefed on my affliction. He steps forward and whispers in the duke's ear.

"My lord, the eldest Sloane princess is mute," he says, and the duke's blue eyes become bulbous.

"What?" shouts the duke.

"I was just informed—" the man attempts to speak, but the duke isn't having it.

"I may be a man of little status, but I will not marry a dumb girl," growls the duke. He turns to my mother. "Shame on you for bringing me here under false pretenses."

The Duke of Erving storms off with his itchy looking robe dragging on the ground. The men follow like sheep. I think everyone in Erving must be a sheep since there isn't anything stimulating about it. I'm glad he was appalled by me. His fish eyes and repulsive lips are more terrible than the rolling hills and wool clothing.

Everyone keeps their gaze down as I walk past and up to my room. Mother has already vanished. She can't handle seeing another rejection. Adrian is wringing her dress with contempt. If I could, I'd stick my tongue out at her. She probably thinks the Duke of Erving was perfect for me.

Penelope has her pristine and royal face on, but I know she is thinking something outrageous. My sister who cares about me. She winks at me as I pass by. The servants and maids all go back to their chores to avoid my ruthless mother. As I make my way back to my room, I feel a hand on my wrist.

"I'm glad he didn't agree to marry you. He was awful," says my youngest sister. Margaux and I never speak. Why is she sneaking up behind me and grabbing at me? I can't ask. It's quick, but my baby sister embraces me. I'm not sure what to do, so I pat her back.

"I want you to marry someone great. Someone you love," she says. Before anyone can see us, she rushes past me, out of my sight. This has me standing in the hall, unable to move. Margaux may not be under my mother's control after all. I go into my room to think and absorb the blow of rejection. He was a grotesque man from an unfavorable kingdom, but I need to be wanted. I long to be loved.

The fire is low and has a soothing orange tone. I lay on my bed and put my pillow over my face. If only I could truly not exist the way I pretend to. I can't process my shame or what my baby sister said because my mother is tearing the pillow off me and leering over my bed.

"Amadeus," she says my name low and cold. I sit up to have her smack me so hard I fall back. My hand touches the side she struck. It's warm and tingles.

"What am I going to do with you?" she sighs and paces around in front of me. My mother folds her arms and heaves another violent sigh. She walks back towards me and stands with the fire behind her. She appears like a demon.

Grabbing my face, she inspects every feature. "I despise how you resemble him, but have no other trait of his," she says. It stings and I reach for my heart. Father, do you feel ashamed I am the one who is your spitting image? "Don't worry, dear. I'll find you somebody."

My mother lets go of my chin. It has two tiny cuts from her nails. She storms out of my room. I think she would make lightning strike if she could. On the unharmed side, I lay and wait for the next day. Hopefully, better than the last sixteen years.

***

A hushed voice wakes me. It's Penelope. "Amadeus," she whispers my name. I scoot closer to the edge of my bed. My sister takes my hand and squeezes it ever so slightly. "I'm sorry about yesterday. I'm sure

Mother was quite harsh."

I nod, but throw up my arms and roll my eyes. Penelope stands up and sits with me. The blankets rustle as she settles down. My sister has bony but serious wrists. She reaches for my face and I feel her pulse radiating from blue veins.

"Someday you won't have to live like this. One day, a great man will marry you," says Penelope with a wicked grin. "Adrian and Mother will eat their hearts out." My sister gestures like she is stabbing her chest and dragging the knife down. The corners of my mouth touch my ears. We are more than siblings. Penelope is also my friend. I touch my temple and point to her, "You really think so?" I'm saying. She can understand me.

"I do," she says. My sister readies herself to exit my room. She calls to me over her shoulder. "Adrian ought to marry a bull. An animal as stubborn as she is." Penelope sticks out her tongue and I wave goodbye to her. Getting out of bed, I change into my nightshade colored dress. I lace up my boots. Taking my tousled hair to the side, I braid it and secure the bottom with a matching lilac ribbon. I'm not pretty like Adrian, but I don't think I deserve to be married to a hideous creature like the Duke of Erving.

Are my younger sisters amusing themselves by toying with me? Do they truly believe I deserve to marry someone great? Perhaps even someone worthy of my love? Who would this man be? What would he be like? I've been introduced to countless suitors, but none of them ignited any sort of emotion beyond disdain or disappointment.

Margaux rarely speaks to me. What has her saying such ludicrous things? Perhaps I should try to be closer to my baby sister. Mother dotes on her too often and tries to keep her, so she is easy to control. Now she's shown me sisterly affection. I've hardly paid attention to her. It hits me in the ribs. I'm acting like our mother. Grimacing at the realization, I make a mental note to be kind to Margaux. I'll make a point to be a good big sister.

Adrian has never liked me. She humored herself by playing with me when we were children, but she thinks she was above everything and everyone. By the time she was twelve, she was ordering us all around, bossy and shrill. I pity the man who ends up my sister's husband.

I make my way to the garden. The one to the east with welcoming blooms. If I can be near the green, green grass and pick a red flower, I'll feel better. I recall holding a blossom to my chest and staring up at the sky after Father died. I told myself over and over again if I could hold a flower and let the sun highlight my hair, everything would be okay. At least for a little while.

"Let the breeze move over your face," I said to myself with my eyes closed. The wind tickled my nose. I let the wheat and grass dance around my legs. "Feel the warmth of the sun and the softness of the ground," was my mantra, with the bright poppy pressed against my breast with the palm of my hand. "Nothing can hurt you when you are here," was the lie I told myself every day. But it worked. It still works.

There is a squeak coming from underneath one of the rose bushes. Peering down, I see who is the source of the sound. A daring mink comes rushing out to greet me. He's a hickory brown with beady black eyes. His body is slinky, and he slithers like a snake. I'm not sure if he is even a true rodent.

The mink makes himself comfortable on my lap. This isn't ideal, but I suppose company, any company, is a treat. For a squirmy thing, he is kind of cute. I pet between his ears with my fingertip and he becomes fond of me instantaneously. Something startles my new friend, and he darts back under the rosebush.

I'm on my knees gathering the scarlet flowers. My hair is red but not pretty like this. It's a lighter shade with honey undertones. The petals are waxy and smooth. I run my thumb on the outside of the flower and twirl it around in my other hand. In my world, I am safe. This space can be mine. Except it's not. A knight is entering, not one of ours. His helmet is on, but I can tell he is staring at me. He keeps his face turned in my direction the whole way to the stables.

***

Adrian is storming about my room. She keeps throwing my clothes on the ground and knocking all my items off their proper shelves. My sister displaces everything in her wake. Her frustration sometimes leads her to act foolishly as she is now. I hate picking up after her but enjoy seeing her fuming mad. Sloane castle offers me little entertainment.

"Why can't you be normal, Amadeus?" she shrieks and hurls a container with my favorite vanilla and rose scented powder. The sparkly substance sticks to Adrian's face, arms, hair, and is spread to the multiple rugs as she stomps around.

"I bet you find this hilarious," she says. I watch her grab my wine colored dress and toss it out the window. This pleases her and she grabs my emerald green and sky blue one and throws them out as well. I don't try to stop her. Adrian whirls around like a rabid she-beast. She yanks out another long dress with frilly bows. This one goes out the window, too.

"I'm never going to get married, and it's all your fault." She runs at me and shoves me into the wall. The rough material of the castle digs into my back. Adrian is gripping my face with mean and skinny fingers. They tear into the freckles.

"You're not completely horrible to look at, but I wish we could do something about your awful complexion since we can't do anything about your affliction," she says, and bores into my soul with her demonic doe eyes. My sister drops me. She is taller than me and keeps her nose up.

"Mother is right. You look like you've been playing in the mud," she says and saunters off. Adrian constantly tries to hurt my feelings. I go to the window and see the maids are already gathering up my dresses. They shuffle this way and that rescuing the grass stained fabric. Their white bonnets cover their hair.

I pick up the container of vanilla and rose powder. My books, pens, jewelry, hair ribbons, and combs are scattered across the place. Putting everything back in its home soothes me. Taking the berry colored rug to the window, I shake out the remaining powder. I cough as plumes of dust escape the threads.

My hands and face are covered in grime, so I wash up. It's exhausting being the eldest sibling. So much is expected of me, but I'm unable to carry out the family affairs. If they allowed me to engage people through writing or another means of communication, perhaps I would be more accepted. I scoff at myself. No man seems to be incredibly thoughtful. What a silly wish.

Was Father considerate to me because I was his daughter? Would he have treated me poorly if I were another commoner? His hair wasn't as frizzy, and his roguishly handsome face seemed better equipped for the hundreds of freckles. Did my mother think he looked dirty? If she did, she never said it out loud. She speaks ill of my appearance, but I'm the one who resembles him.

He had a mustache, but it wasn't wispy and lopsided like the men Mother tries to marry me off to. I'm sure Father would recoil at some of my suitors. He wouldn't let me be the wife of an ogre with the personality of a catfish. How my mother can cast me to the wolves so easily since he isn't around brings up a sickness in my stomach.

Father told me listening was twice as important as speaking. He said it was okay to be the way I am because words held little meaning, especially if exaggerated. Many conversations are insincere. "There is truth in silence," he used to say. My father would hold me up to the sun and spin me around. We were inseparable.

After sorting through my room where Adrian rampaged through, I return to the window. Beyond the castle gates is the forest. Hemlocks and red alders line the path leading to the neighboring kingdoms. The forest gets denser and darker the further it goes. The pines look like they could consume human flesh. Their height and intimidating demeanor make me fearful of venturing outside of the castle. I loathe it here. Perhaps what waits in the shadows is better than what tortures me in this wretched place.

Then I see a glimpse of blond hair. It's my baby sister. Margaux is sneaking through the fence. She looks around and sees no one. But she doesn't look up. If she did, she would notice me spying on her. With a quickness I didn't know my sister possessed, she darts through the wheat and weeds. She runs parallel to the river. I scan for what it is she is aiming for.

At the tree line is a young man. Taller than any of the knights here. He's wearing a tattered red cloak. Squinting my eyes, I get a better look. What I thought were low branches are attached to his head. He is a beast boy, one of the human animal hybrids. This one has antlers. A deer boy.

Margaux throws her arms around him. They embrace for a long time. I feel awkward watching my sister, but I can't resist. She has never seemed like the type to rebel. Maybe my mother hasn't been able to keep her an empty pot. My baby sister kisses the deer boy, and he guides her into the cover of the hemlocks where I can no longer see her.

BLOSSOMS AFTER MIDNIGHT

3

The bath is too hot. I swear the maids seek to scald me, hoping to burn off the freckles that take over a majority of my body. I sit in the chair next to the tub but keep my feet in. To busy myself while I wait for it to cool, I open my book. This one is about a lowly knight who climbs the ranks so he can meet the most beautiful princess who also is a sorceress.

I enjoy the princess' character, but it's the unremarkable knight who has me most concerned. He may be fictional, but the emotions he invokes in me are real. The man longs to be good enough to meet someone he's only heard stories about. It's romantic and girlish, but also deep. In the end, the sorceress reveals through her time traveling magic she had spied on him once at a party and longed to speak to him for many years.

Sinking into the bath once, it is no longer hellishly hot. I sigh a soundless sigh. The full inhale and exhale are moody. I blow bubbles under the water. My hair fans out around me. The castle decor is mostly white, ivy green, and citrusy yellow: "easy colors," she calls them. The curls stick to my frame as I sit up; they are an untameable texture. My mother also refers to the color as "ghastly." I pick it up and hold a long lock of it in my hands. It's not so bad, is it? I'm a mute, but I'm unbearably flashy with speckled skin and coppery curls.

My reflection in the water stares back at me with catlike eyes. They are full of disapproval. I hit the surface and send ripples in every direction. I keep thinking about princesses, enchantresses, and sorceresses with tangle free honey hair and big doe eyes. It's disastrous to be born first. What a curse.

I wouldn't care if I went all my life without a husband. The truth is, people let me down. They aren't what they seem. Not my family, not any man. I trust no one. Aloneness is the dwelling, the house, and home I accept. The trouble is I have to get married to set the rest of my sisters free. Even though I dislike Adrian, I want her on some minor level to be content. Our mother isn't someone we should stay at the heels of.

Penelope has to marry someone fantastic. Not anyone will do. I picture a handsome man with kind eyes and a welcoming smile. Someone who enjoys looking at the stars as she does. I can't bear the idea of her marrying a brutish pig like the men our mother tries to pawn me off to. The man who marries Penelope has to be good, strong, and brave. My middle sister shines bright like a star. He needs to carry the weight of that.

The deer boy kissing my baby sister buzzes around my skull like a fly. It's been a fortnight since I saw them. She's been acting peculiar. Margaux is obedient to a fault in front of our mother. But then she stops to embrace me or sneaks me a piece of cake from the kitchen. One night, she surprised me with a beautiful bowl of fruit, an assortment of grapes, berries, and apples. She took an orange and told me she wanted us to be closer as she sunk her tiny crooked teeth into the flesh of the citrus.

Adrian has been dragging her around the castle. Margaux lets her, but seems depressed. Then there's our mother who must tell her what to do, where to sit, what to wear, and how to talk. It must be excruciatingly painful to deal with our mother and Adrian for such long periods of time. I don't know how I never noticed it before. Margaux might be our mother's favorite, but my baby sister isn't anything like her.

Margaux acts dimwitted and carefree but is calculated. How she feigns childlike sweetness to get her needs met. My sibling is far from stupid. She is simply better at putting up a front. I have taken notes on this. She can act casual and attentive, but the truth is my baby sister has been sneaking out of the castle to see a deer boy.

Our mother would never approve. Everyone acts like the animal human hybrids aren't truly people. They aren't violent, but humans and other beasts treat them with disdain. I've never left the castle, so I can't be sure, but I've heard stories of men and women being cast out from their villages for sleeping with the hybrids. Carrying a beast child isn't illegal, but it's not supported. No one can be arrested for it, but this doesn't prevent people from shunning those who choose to lie with a hybrid. The harsh treatment of the hybrids is perpetuated with no means of stopping it.

Their lips touched. I run my fingers across my mouth. What is it like to be kissed? In books, it seems worth living for, worth dying for, and worth fighting for. To the knights, mercenaries, and apprentices in the stories I like, a kiss is the highest honor. Something to be cherished. I don't want to waste something as wondrous as a kiss on one of the despicable men my mother chooses for me. I'm proud of my baby sister. She is willing to throw away everything to kiss this deer boy, the man she chose herself.

***

"Amadeus, come here," says my mother. She is standing by the door with a sinister facial expression I can't read. The obedient pet that I am, I rise from my chair by the window and make my way to her.

"The prince of another drab little farmland in the center of the continent is almost here. You are to put on the yellow dress I have picked out for you. Wash your face, you look filthy," she stops talking to lick a finger and to my horror she attempts to scrub out a freckle under my eye. "Oh, and please have mercy on me and do something about your hair," sighs my mother with despair. Picking up a handful of unruly curls, she frowns with her full bottom lip.

I wasn't expecting a suitor today. No day is better or worse than another. I nod and begin fixing myself. That's what I call it, fixing. Because there is something so wrong with me. My hair is unbearably tangled and hangs to my hips. The skin I'm forced to live in is soiled with tawny spots. I'm a skinny girl. A mute, a ridiculous little fool.

The dress is pretty. It has a decorative bodice with lots of ruffles and the fabric is soft. The sleeves stop at the elbows and are adorned with layers of lace. To make myself appealing, I decide on a long braid over my shoulder. The curls are harder to notice and manageable this way.

22

My bangs frame my face and frizz around my hairline and ears, but there's little I can do about that. I tie the bottom with a white ribbon with gold flecks in it.

Making my way to the room where I'll meet another man is as exciting as a chore. I wish I could switch places with one of the maids. I'd rather be doing chores like cleaning and cooking than meeting ugly men with sad, sparse mustaches. The castle's steps are many, and it takes an eternity to get there. I dig in my heels when I stop.

The prince is waiting for me. Shockingly, he isn't old or fat. He doesn't have any gross facial hair. In fact, he is about my age, tall, olive skin, with brown hair and brown eyes. Not hideous at all. This makes me more nervous. The kingdom he is from is minuscule, but maybe it's nice there. As I approach, he kneels.

"It's nice to meet you, Princess," he says. I smile a demure smile. His clothing isn't extravagant but not made of wool like the man with all the sheep. The coat is fitted, leafy green, with silver buttons. His smile is alluring. It doesn't dissipate as it becomes obvious I'm not going to say anything. I wait for his disgust.

"I know of your affliction and it doesn't bother me," he says. At first I'm flattered. He kisses my hand and rises. Stepping closer, he whispers in my ear, "I actually came here because I want a woman who doesn't talk back." He has a nasty smirk on his face. This man might be attractive, but he is a womanizing creep. I'd rather die alone in this castle with my cruel mother than be at the hands of this prince.

It must not be visible I'm displeased because he keeps talking. "I like the idea of a woman who can't say 'no' to me," whispers the prince. It's a shame such a handsome person could be so vile. His hair is shiny, it's probably soft, and it's touching his chiseled cheekbones. But I can't marry someone like this. I ruin everyone's life and mine by spitting on him. It lands on his top lip. There is a shrill gasp from the crowd. My mother looks furious. The prince takes a gloved hand and runs it across his face to remove my saliva.

"You should have been happy to have me as your husband, Princess. I doubt you'll find someone better than I," he says in an all too dignified way. Turning his back to me, he marches out of the castle and out of my life. He is all shoulders and possessiveness. Good riddance.

Not sure how to react after my haughty behavior, I run up the stairs. I push past maids and brush past a knight. He stops and puts his arm out like he's going to touch me, but I veer off to the side and avoid him. It takes so long to get to my room. The yellow dress is wasted on a silly girl like me. I knock over a vase, but don't bother to mess with it. The servants will clean it up. Normally I'd do it myself, but I can't be out here, exposed, for another minute.

In the safety of my room, I throw myself on the bed and cry. It shakes my body; it rattles my insides. I hope to be loved the way men love princesses in books. The characters aren't real but I'd like them to be. Who are they based on? I think about the kind of man who inspires people to write poetic novels about what it means to desire somebody.

***

The warmth of the fire wakes me. I must have fallen asleep. Opening my eyes, I see it's dark outside. I've been sleeping all day and into the night.

"Amadeus," a whisper says my name. It's Penelope. I sit up and face my sister. She is holding a bowl of soup and a roll of bread out to me. "I missed you at dinner. Adrian chews like a horse." My sister sticks out her tongue and makes a face. This causes me to smile even though I feel awful. I accept the food she's offered. She gets into bed with me. I cross my legs and take slow bites. I'm still wearing the yellow dress.

Penelope unties the ribbon and begins to gently unbraid my hair. The curls poof and pop like blooming flowers. I swear it is audible when they are released. My sister talks to me as I continue to nibble on the bread.

"He said something horrible to you, didn't he?" she asks. I nod. My hair is down and spilling over my shoulders. Penelope leans over so she can see my face. "I'm glad you did what you did. I don't want you to marry a man who speaks poorly to you."

I shrug and make a gesture like someone choking me out. My sister knows what I'm saying.

"I'm going to shove horse manure in her face. Perhaps I'll start putting it in her morning tea," she laughs. I cover my mouth in shock. Penelope is unusual, but I adore her sense of humor.

She takes my empty bowl and sets it down. When she turns back, she grabs my hands. Her fingers are short and her palm is warm. "We could run away, you and I. We could head west and live near the coast or on the beach. Or to the south, where there are rumors of unicorns and sea monsters. I crave an adventure," says my sister. I point to myself and agree. We have wild hearts yearning for something else.

"It's not your fault people don't appreciate you. They don't take the time to get to know you and your beautiful heart." Penelope pulls a curl and watches it bounce. "You're going to make a man fall to his knees," she says. I disagree and shake my head. My sister laughs, but I can't figure her out.

"Let's go look at the stars," she says and yanks me out of bed. We walk to the terrace and gaze up at the twinkling lights. The moon is close, waning, and grinning. A star shoots across the sky. The other stars bob in its wake. "Make a wish!" cries my sister. She closes her eyes and covers her heart. I decide to do the same. Mostly to entertain her, but also because I deeply want to be loved.

"Did you make a wish, Amadeus?" she asks. I nod. "Don't tell anybody or it won't come true. I know you're good at keeping secrets." She smirks at me. "I'm going to bed. Sweet dreams."

Penelope runs off into the dark. I hear her close the door. It gives a soft thud. I'm alone, staring up at the stars. They are so far away. Can they hear wishes? Who is in charge of such things? In the blackness, everything glows brighter.

Outside the fence is a knight. He rides a red horse. His armor shines in the moonlight. The cloak he is wearing is dark blue and being picked up by the wind. It sways in the breeze behind him. He seems to be checking the perimeter. The ghostly horse and the knight disappear from my sight as they round the corner.

I go back inside and lay on my bed. Bringing the blankets over my shoulders, I hide. It hurts to be rejected. The man was foul, yet I hate myself for not being good enough. I hate how I'm about ready to give in. Somehow I don't.

A disturbed person such as myself still deserves to be loved. Father never made me feel less for my affliction. I shouldn't let these men define me. Besides, my father would never approve of any of them. He was a great man and he would have wanted me to be happy.

Dreams bring me to wonderful places. I can go to the highest mountain and pick wildflowers. I can see the river and walk through the grassy hills. I can touch the cool stream and hear the babbling brooks. I can taste the salt in the air from the beach.

In my favorite dreams, I see him. He has no face, only the shape of a man, the hood of his cloak hiding his features. Evening primroses open as he dashes through the forest. A knight with gleaming armor riding a black horse. The man pushes my mother aside. He takes me away from this castle and we ride away on the stallion with the sun setting next to us.

PRETTY TEARS

4

My mother is yanking me out of bed by my hair. Wrinkled fingers tear at the tresses and she screams at me. "How dare you!"

She throws me on the ground. My shoulder and hip hit the hard floor. Her foot is kicking me in the side. I cover my face. She can't marry me off so easily if I'm broken, bruised, and mute. It doesn't stop her from abusing me, though.

Pinching my face, she has me by the chin. "He was your best bet. Handsome, maybe a bit poor, but better than those hideous old fools. I know how you feel about them. I see the look of disdain on your face when they kiss your hand. You should be so grateful any man approaches you at all."

Her footsteps hit the ground with a menacing click-click noise as she storms out of my room. I stay on the ground, holding my side, and cry. There will be a sickly mark on my left hip. I can feel the black and blue spilling out underneath creamy white skin. She took out a small chunk of my lengthy red curls. I'm bleeding a little.

I wait until the shadows shift in my room to get up. Then I take my time. Cleaning myself up, I can act like a dignified lady. It's deceitful. A most quiet lie. Sometimes I need those lies. They help me stay strong. If my favorite sister and father think I am worthy, then I am.

Today I chose a blue dress. It matches the bruise left on my body. The freckles are blocked out by the purple and yellow undertones. I braid my hair on each side. This way, nobody can see the small chunk of hair missing or the tiny scab. I hold the rainbow crystal in my hand and look at myself in the mirror. The wish I made. I wonder if somehow this mysterious rock could grant a wish. No, that's ridiculous. I read once about a man who got three wishes from an entity living in a gold lamp. I'm becoming too invested in these fictional stories.

With slow steps I wander the castle. A few servants in the halls, but no sign of my sisters or mother. I'm too tired and sad to be around anybody. The stairs go on and on. No one's footsteps are echoing in the large room. Dinner has already been served. I'm not hungry but need to eat, so I grab a roll of bread before heading outside.

Back in my happy place among the poppies, I nibble on my small dinner as I lean against one of the bars in the fence. The trees are tall and expansive. A misty forest full of dogwood, ferns, and lilacs. Fragrant purple flowers are carried to me by the wind.

I sit in the damp grass and hold my side. It aches and I hold my hand to it, hoping to pull out the hurt. My boots have mud and grass on them. I look into the dark woods and in the shadows I see two gold eyes. He steps into the light. It's the beast boy I saw with my sister. The one with antlers.

He holds eye contact with me. I lose my breath. Why is he staring at me like that? We watch each other. I'm not sure what we are looking for. I step back from the fence. He turns on his heel and walks back into the darkness of the forest, where I can't see him or his nocturnal eyes.

I could go back inside the castle, but don't want to. The sun is barely visible on the horizon. Night is taking hold. The pink and vanilla sky give way to black indigo. It starts to rain. I pace the garden in my corner of peace. Bright red flowers stand out and reflect the moonlight with charm. I start to cry. The rain washes away the hot tears and cools my feverish face. Sobbing in the evening with the rain to keep my company seems rather romantic, so I let myself cry.

Now the wind is tearing petals off the roses. The raindrops get bigger and come down with a vengeance. It's storming outside, but no one is looking for me. Good. I don't want to be found. I stay in the garden and let the weather brutalize me. It feels better than my mother's fists. The stars twinkle and look like the breeze might blow them out like a candle.

I lay in the grass. It is sodden and squishes beneath my weight. My dress clings to me. It is soaked all the way through. I lazily pick poppies and hold them to my chest. Each time I grab a stem, I look at a star and make a wish. I attempt to make my dream a reality.

"Are you okay, Princess?" asks a sharp male voice. I sit up to see a knight on the other side of the fence. He must be on guard duty. Standing up, I shiver. "You should go inside. You'll get sick out here in the rain," he says. I nod and back up. This is embarrassing.

The knight keeps talking, "You're pretty when you cry." He rides off on the red horse. I'm not sure what to make of his comment. Was he ridiculing me? Or was he giving me a compliment? Men make no sense.

***

The library smells of old books and has notes of amber. A waxy scent of candles mixes with the dusty old of the pages. Sunlight is streaming through the window. Yellow rays make their way in. I walk around the maze of bookshelves, picking up novels that call to me. There are the ones I read again and again. Then there are the new ones. Some days I want to be comforted and other times I hope to be surprised.

I need an exciting new story. Long novels, short stories, and hardcover spines stare at me. Which one should I choose? "Pick me, pick me," they seem to say. I grab a gray and brown book. It looks like it hasn't been touched in a while. The first chapter has me hooked. This one is about a peasant man who helps a slave girl. They adventure across the Vetra-Sio Ocean and make their way to a village in the mountains where they start a new life.

It quickly becomes one of my favorites. My beloved books keep me going. They allow me to see a beautiful side of life. One where brutality can be met with sincerity, hospitality, and love. This is why the story about the mercenary is my favorite. Redemption is a theme plaguing my days.

Stories also offer a sense of connection. A feeling of belonging. I haven't read any stories about mute girls meeting handsome princes, but it doesn't mean there aren't any. At least that's what I tell myself. I read a novel about a woman with a stutter. She felt like a burden until a duke from a faraway land saved her from her terrible stepfather.

Not quite the same, but it restored my faith a bit.

"I should kill you," hisses Adrian. She steps out from behind one of the many shelves. I stand tall and prepare to face her. Adrian is nose to nose with me. "He was good looking for someone from a dumpy farming community. Why did you spoil your chance?" she asks. I keep my eyes open and stare into her big brown doe eyes. On my littlest sister, they are endearing, innocent and cute. On Adrian, they are too deep for someone so shallow.

My sister starts ripping books off the shelf. She throws them on the ground and tosses them over the railing. They drop and plumes of dust leave them like spirits. Heavy hardcovers, skinny novels, leather books rain onto the floor. Adrian paws through at least four dozen books before she's satisfied.

"I can't wait until Mother gets rid of you," says my sister as she exits the library. I kneel to pick up my friends. A page is torn out of the middle of one of the hardcovers. I hold in my tears. No use in crying over Adrian's cruelty. She so badly wants to be married. I'm ruining her life as well as my own.

"Let me help you," says a low, masculine voice. I stand up to see a knight picking up several books. He is tall and daunting. His face is covered by his helmet and his hands are gloved. He wears a thick black cloak. The armor he wears has a different emblem on it. Not one of ours. I shake my head at him to let him know he doesn't have to subject himself to picking up after my sister.

"Here," he says as he hands me an armful of books. I begin placing them back in their respective places. Looking over my shoulder, I see the knight is still here. I expected him to leave me be. Men are constantly confusing me.

"I'm sorry about this one," he says and hands me a novel with four pages falling out. I take it and gingerly tuck the pages back in. My breath is heavy and I let out a deep sigh. His footsteps hit the ground, and the noise moves about the large room. "Goodbye, Princess," he says without facing me.

After I gather up all the fallen books and put them back, I sink into the cushy chair by one of the windows. The sky is clear. A dove flies by. It must be nice to be free. I look down and watch the wind move through the wheat. The knight who helped me earlier is riding down the path. The horse is fast and runs into the mist, veiling the forest.

Peering into the fog, I see something else. It's the deer boy. His yellow eyes glow in the blackness of the shadows. I don't notice her at first because her hair blends in with the wheat and dead grass, but my littlest sister is running through the field. Her green dress and blonde tresses camouflage her presence. The deer boy holds open his arms and Margaux crashes into him. He falls back but catches her.

They are grinning. The deer boy doesn't seem scary. Just because he isn't like us doesn't mean he is bad. My sister reaches for his antlers and gives him a kiss. I pull my gaze back into the library. I've seen too much. Spying on my baby sister is wrong, but I'm not sure what to do. I can't confront her. Adrian would surely lose her mind if she knew. I can't even think about our mother's reaction.

Penelope would know what to do. Maybe I should entrust this secret to her. On the other hand, I don't know who I can trust in this castle. We are all waiting for someone else to move so we may have their place. In this house, no one is content with what they have. We all envy what the other doesn't even possess. Jealous of nothing more than air.

***

Penelope calls my name. She stirs me from my thoughts. I'm holding a poppy and staring at the mist gathering around the forest. The place where my baby sister goes to meet her secret lover. A hand is on my shoulder. I flinch.

"Sorry, didn't mean to startle you. No need to be so skittish around me," teases Penelope. She holds my shoulders and looks at the forest ahead with me. She gives me a knowing glance. "You know about him, too." I turn to my sister. She keeps her blonde hair down, never in plaits or braids. It's glistening under the late afternoon sun. I nod but don't keep eye contact with her.

"We could spoil it. Tell our family. But why would we do that? Who cares about where somebody comes from as long as they are loyal and sweet?" Penelope glares up at the castle with a sternness I usually see in our mother. She is dignified. More so than I.

The two of us walk around the castle. The sun is shining, but the fog never lifts from certain parts of the pines. There are places where the light can't reach. I'm not sure who is in there and how far it goes. Ever since I saw Margaux run into the darkness without hesitation, I've been aching to know what lies beyond the shadows of the hemlocks.

Golden waves of wheat whistle with the rushing wind. It's soft on my face. The breeze is tinged with the scent of lilacs and river water. Penelope skips and twirls beside me. Her long hair matches the field, and it whips the air as she turns her head. She's wearing a crimson dress with silver accents. My sister is beautiful.

"I'm envious of her, Amadeus," she states. Her skipping and dancing comes to a halt. I tilt my head and show I'm confused.

She throws her head back and cackles. "You feel it, too. I see the books you read. You long to know what it is like to be in love," she says over the wind. There is no hiding it from her. She knows my heart. I cover my smile because I'm embarrassed.

I haven't paid enough attention to Penelope. How could someone so smart and pretty have these types of insecurities? She isn't angry with me the way Adrian is. Why? My sisters should all despise me, but here is Penelope, holding my hand and grinning into the breeze.

"I hope you marry a man like the ones in your stories," says my sister. She lets me go and runs in front of me. We pass by the part of the fence that is broken. From a glance, no one could tell. Upon further inspection, one can see the eroded bar. Ivy has grown in patches here. The rose briars are climbing up the surrounding bars, adding to the illusion there is no hole in the wall here.

We run across the back of the castle. It is shadowy here. There are knights tending to their horses and servants carrying water from the well. For once, I don't feel like trying to be invisible and we cut across the yard. We hold our dresses so we can run faster. It's not ladylike. The lace at the bottom of my dress has dirt on it.

A servant jumps out of our way. My sister and I are invigorated by the purple flowers in the air. Two of the knights stop and stare. They're holding their helmets. Both of them have sandy hair. It comes to their shoulders. I can see their faces. The men are put off by our strange behavior. They don't know what to make of us.

Our mother wouldn't approve of us acting this way. She would say we were being immature. I'll take all the blame. If I have to put up with her beatings and scoldings, then I deserve to have fun with my little sister. The one who shows up for me. Penelope, who is so crass but adorable and kind.

My arms sway at my sides. There are frills at the elbows of my sleeves. This dress isn't meant for racing, but right now there are no rules. At this moment, I need to be with my sibling. A haze of yellow sky and blue dark of the woods. I hold on to this so I can keep it in my memory. Luminescent white moths come out to play with us. The moths have enormous black eyes and wispy antennae. They leave trails of shimmery stardust behind them.

Penelope turns to me. I'm smiling at her as we race into the setting sun. The sun reflects off her hair. The halo appears. Suddenly, her eyes widen and her mouth contorts as she coughs. She begins having a hacking fit. I let her lean on me as she recovers. There's blood all over her hand. My mother slams her fist down onto the table.

"What do you mean?" she growls at the doctor.

"I'm afraid Penelope can't be cured. I've given her medicine to aid with the pain and cough, but ultimately the sickness will take her life. Maybe not this month or this year, but in the end there will be nothing we can do," says the white-haired doctor with a solemn expression.

"Get out of my sight," sighs my mother.

"I apologize, my lady," he says on his way out.

Margaux and I stand next to Penelope. She's asleep in her fluffy bed. I grimace at the bloodstained handkerchief in her right hand. The sickness will take her. No matter what.

"We'll get another doctor," hisses Adrian. My mother and her stand by the window with their arms crossed.

"He will tell you the same thing," he says over his shoulder without aggression.

He disappears into the outstretched hall. Penelope wheezes and turns to her side. Margaux kneels and takes her hand. My baby sister has such petite fingers.

"It'll be okay, Penny. Don't worry about a thing," says Margaux through her tears.

"You're all a bunch of crybabies," snaps Adrain.

She makes her way out of Penelope's room. Her dress is pink and red. It drags on the floor and slithers on the ground like a snake. It's my mother's turn to sink her teeth in.

"Not one afflicted daughter but two," she says on her way out. Her slender fingers linger on the door as she walks into the hallway.

"Don't listen to them, Penny," says Margaux.

As soon as my mother is gone, I close the door and get into bed with my sister. Margaux joins us. We don't care if we get sick and die as well. Nothing is worth living for if it's not worth dying for.

There is a storm building outside. First, the clouds cover the crescent moon. Stars are blocked out, and it is darker than usual. The wind howls and the rain starts. Soon it is pouring and the rumble of lightning is heard in the distance. It strikes by the window and I jump.

"I'm glad we have each other," says Margaux. Penelope coughs. Her forehead has beads of sweat on it. I reach for a damp washcloth to wipe them away.

"I know you and Penny will keep my secret," she says. I sit up and stare at her. She is admitting her rebellion to me. "I love him, Amadeus. Mother and Adrian would never approve. But you and Penny understand," she says and lays back down.

Margaux looks out the window at the storm. I watch her blink with her short, blonde eyelashes. She is a child yet so grown up. I lean over so I can put my hand on the crook of her arm. She gives me her full attention.

"I never expected to fall in love with someone like him. Love is such a baffling emotion. Almost intolerable," she giggles. I find myself smiling. "One day I'm going to run away with him."

Her announcement jolts me. I could have fallen out of Penelope's luxurious bed. Thankfully, I'm tangled up in her layers of blankets. My sister continues, "His name is Hannes. He and his family live close to the castle in the misty forest. They are gracious people. I don't know why everyone judges the beast people so harshly."

I shrug. Condemning others has never been a hobby of mine.

"I'll be a disgrace to the family, but he's worth it," whispers Margaux as she yawns.

She is falling asleep. Raindrops hit the window like ferocious fists. Penelope tosses and turns. Her face is flushed and hot to the touch. I wet the cloth and put it on her forehead. It seems to calm her.

Margaux smiles in her sleep. She must dream of her lover. The deer boy, his name is Hannes. How did they meet? He must have beckoned her into the woods one day. No, Margaux was already rebelling. She ran into the forest for fun and found him. My littlest sister isn't an empty flowerpot. She is no fragile vase. In fact, she is the bravest one of us all.

Can love make someone brave? Does it give courage to the weak? Margaux has a vigor to her I didn't think someone so young could possess. I admire her authority over her own life. She didn't ask or speak of begging for forgiveness.

If his people can accept her, then will someone accept me? Truly accept me. Not in a vile or perverse way. Could a man truly love me the way I am? I close my eyes and hear men talking about changing me. If only I weren't so skinny, if only my hair weren't so unruly, if only I wasn't a mute.

THE YOUNG KNIGHT

5

My sister is dying. She is back to her quick-witted and humorous self. But we know what is to become of her. One day, the cough will consume her. She won't be able to spit up the blood she's choking on. Drowning in herself, she'll expire. It's completely abhorrent.

Why are the gods so cruel as to take my sweet Penelope away? Haven't I suffered enough? She is still here with me. We are sitting in the garden. The red flowers are in our hair and up our sleeves. Two sisters being sisters. I suppose I should try to enjoy the time we have together. Treat every single day like it could be our last. It could be.

"Are you alright, Amadeus?"

I nod my head. The poppies in my hand aren't making me happy the way they used to. The sun is shining high in the sky. There is no wind. Grasshoppers fly back and forth in front of us. I hear a cricket to the left of me. It is beyond the fence. "Can I tell you something?"

I nod and smile. She beams at me. "Of course I can. I can tell you anything," she says and reaches for me. Penelope's touch is soft. Her skin is smooth, no unevenness or imperfections. My sister gives me a mischievous grin. " I kissed a beast boy in the forest."

My jaw drops. I can't speak, but this would leave any sibling speechless. Especially royal siblings. Penelope giggles. Her round cheeks and pointed nose with a wide bridge make her appear younger than she is. I playfully shake her shoulder to show I'm teasing, but I want to know the whole story.

"He was a coyote boy. His name was Demetri. I snuck out one night because everything seemed dull and pointless. I darted into the forest with no idea where I was going and ran into him. He guided me back and kept me safe. I gave him a kiss as a thank you," she whispers. This is one of the most romantic stories I've heard in person. Penelope has watery eyes. "I want to see him again," she cuts off. I grab my sister and hug her with a greater amount of force than necessary.

"I promise not to die until you marry someone great. I need to meet him," says my sister. It brings tears to my eyes. Somehow, she can find the strength to be brave, sweet, and clever at a time like this. I don't know how she does it. An invisible power accessible to those who are worthy. I'm glad Penelope wields such grace.

"Do you think it's wrong I want to see him again?" she asks. I shake my head. Of course not, I'm saying.

My sister blushes. "If I get caught, it doesn't even matter. What can our mother take away from me that hasn't already been stolen? My life is mine," she declares. Continuing with more confidence, she speaks with greater intensity, "I wonder if he'll want to kiss me again."

I smile to myself. Two of my sisters are pining over boys with antlers and coyote tails. They long to see yellow eyes amid the forest. When they lay down, they need to smell pine needles and feel the spongy moss up against their spine. What a turn of events.

Penelope sits by me and plays with my hair. She is giving me two braids down my shoulders. Unlike the maids and my mother, she doesn't tug at it or rip it out in an effort to make it manageable. "I like your hair," she says. Turning to her in surprise, she laughs. "Regardless of what Adrian and our mother say, you are rather beautiful, Amadeus."

Could it be true? My sister is trying to console me. In the mirror I see frizzy curls, a face full of dirty tawny spots. With a light touch, she reaches for my face. She has a finger on my temple.

"I know they fill your mind with lies, but I see the truth. The men see it, too. I watch the knights try to hide their eyes. Our sister and the maids are jealous," she says and strokes my cheek. "Mother sees our father every time she looks at you. She may say hurtful things, but it's because she misses him."

Is she right? No one ever said anything negative about the king's appearance. In fact, everyone spoke of him as not only a noble king and commander but women of all ages would stop to admire his good looks, highlighted by fierce red eyebrows, a flat nose, and stoic jawline. My mother held his face in her hands with such affection. Never did I hear her utter contempt for his freckles or messy hair.

Penelope helps me up and we make our way back to the castle. Holding me close, she whispers in my ear, "When you have your first kiss, try to cling to that moment. It's what I think about anytime I'm sad or feel alone. The thing I dream about. I relive it in my memory often. It gets me through the toughest times."

I nod my head but am unsure of what my sister is getting at. Do beast boy kisses have a certain effect on young girls? Or can a man make a woman feel that way as well? I can't say for myself. No one has embraced me in his arms. No man has been close enough to touch his lips to mine.

***

I'm in the kitchen having a midnight snack. Dinner is an unpleasant situation and I try to get through it as fast as possible. My ribs stick out under my breasts. There is a table full of food every night, but I'm too thin. Food is flavorful and prepared with care in the castle. I can't stomach it when I sit with my family, though.

First, I help myself to a piece of bread. It's fluffy and has an assortment of seeds and nuts in it. Then I pick at the soup, cooled, but still good. It has big chunks of potato and pieces of beef. I graze on the buttery greens and carrots. It's nice to have this time for myself. The ability to enjoy food has been abstract.

It's late. I should go back to my room. Feeling rebellious, I take two pieces of bread and hide a peach in the pocket of my dress. Then I decide to indulge and grab a plum. I don't always gorge myself in the night, but lately I've been bolder.

Margaux and Penelope have expressed sisterly devotion towards me. They don't have the same heart our mother and Adrian seem to share. After hearing them say they wanted me to be happy and how I deserved a great man, the stir of self-confidence has been rising within me.

I gnaw on the bread as I wander the castle. The maids can clean up my mess like they are supposed to. I rarely harbor such resentful thoughts, but I'm different now. Learning of Penelope's illness, knowing she will die soon, gives me the courage to act as a better sister.

Passing by a large window, I peek outside. The curtains swoosh from the cool evening breeze. There are torches lit and two knights surveying the perimeter. Sheer blue clouds swirl around the moon and play with the stars. They touch each other and run away. Outside is wondrous to me.

I've never been beyond the fence. They keep me from attending events. It is better to keep me and my affliction mysterious. It may be passable as when a man meets me, he is first quite forward but quick to turn to anger. Or perversion, like the last man. He had a handsome face but was an ugly person. Penelope said he smelled like low quality cloth and cattle.

If I get married, I could leave this place. The countries, men, and adventures in the novels leave me disappointed with the way my suitors behave in real life. A knight's honor is supposed to be his most precious possession. The dukes and princes I meet are spoiled, nasty, and have no integrity.

"What are you doing up this late, Amadeus?" growls Adrian from around the corner. I shudder at her face, both elegant and indignant. She looms over me. Looking down, she notices the plum in my hand. Adrian is quick to snatch it from me. "A little late for dinner, isn't it?"

To my dismay, she takes a big bite from the purple fruit and shoves it back into my palm with her saliva on it. She wipes her mouth with the back of her hand. The look on my face makes her laugh. She is a banshee with blond hair and cherry lips. I flinch as she passes me.

"A lady of the castle eating sullied fruit. How pathetic," Adrian hisses as she walks down the hall. The flames of the candles bend as she steps by. Is she truly a demon? It wouldn't surprise me.

I wait for her footsteps to be inaudible. There's no one down in the courtyard. I toss the scorned piece of fruit out the window. In a wasteful mood, I take out the peach from my pocket. I sink my teeth through the fuzzy skin and into the sweet orange flesh. After a few bites, I'm full and toss it out the window, too. I lick my lips and fingers in an unladylike fashion.

The rain is coming. I smell the change in the air. It's metallic and earthy. The sound of raindrops outside is soothing. It's darker without the stars, but sacrifices have to be made. The grass will be greener and my favorite red flowers will be able to bloom more.

In my room, I shove another piece of bread in my mouth and cry. I'm pathetic. It's so incredibly shameful. I want to be somebody else. The book about the mercenary with a brutal background but tender heart is hidden under my bed. I take it out and flip to my favorite parts. This man doesn't exist, but he comforts me.

***

"Put this on," says my mother in a harsh tone. She throws an ocean blue dress at me. It has gold accents and white butterflies on it. I touch the bodice made with expensive material. It's like being a little girl and I'm playing dress up. I put on the extravagant garment and my mother ties it in the back. In the mirror is a young girl trying to be somebody she isn't. My mother puts an assortment of jewelry on me. I look ridiculous.

She sighs as she stares at me, like she is proud of her work. "Don't do anything to upset the new suitor. I mean it." My mother has a way of using a sweet voice to say vicious things. She can be ten people at once. In a single evening, she can be kind, cruel, deceitful, funny, hopeful, and menacing.

I nod my head. She leaves me with my thoughts. They are unruly and all over the place like my hair. I braid around my crown and pin it on the back with a gold comb. My hair ribbons keep going missing. My reflection appears to me as beautiful, but I see what's inside. An ugly mute. My hips are bony, as are my wrists. The jewelry and extravagant clothes disguise me.

The servants are scurrying about the castle. Maids dust and sweep the stairs. The gardeners are pruning the dead leaves and raking up debris from the yard. Together, they make a harmonious symphony of anxiety. The sound which I take each step to. Bristles touch the decorative parts of the castle and make hushed scratching noises. Towels are wrung out and fan away the dirt.

Our home is fantastic in all its splendor. High ceilings, marble features, silver chandeliers, and lots of yellow flowers. My mother chooses the sunny dahlias and hyacinth because they remind her of my other sisters. Soft and easy to look at, and likable. Ivy with black veins grows up the castle walls and I envision climbing down them and running off into the misty woods.

Today I'm meeting the Duke of Seravi. This is a bigger state within the country. I don't know a lot about it other than it is to the northwest and is snowy half the year. Seravi produces steel weapons. They are rumored to be rowdy and brutish. My mother isn't gentle about disposing of me. Nowhereland or the icy tundra, it doesn't matter. I'm certain she throws darts at a map of the continent to pick who she will summon to meet me. There is no way it could be done with actual care.

One of the older maids approaches me. She grins with tight, dry lips as she places a white shawl over my shoulders. It has tiny gems stitched on it. The maid arranges my hair around my shoulders and adjusts my necklace. She gives me a slight bow and sends me down the stairs, where I grip on the ivory railing with red hands.

Everyone goes silent. I hear the steps I take as the beating of my heart. Clanging distracts me. I look over the railing to see a young boy, newly knighted, drop his sword. His cheekbones sit low. He has big blue eyes and auburn hair. My gaze makes him flinch and one of the older knights elbows him before picking up the young man's sword. The older knight shoves it at the boy, and the boy holds his weapon. His eyes are on his feet.

I take the last step and wait for the duke at the bottom. Everyone is quiet. Margaux and Penelope smile at me. Adrian is frowning with her arms crossed and my mother is by her side, looking annoyed. It is like she would rather be anywhere else. I can't help myself and glance at the corner where the knights are. Their helmets are in their arms.

The door opens and a burst of flowery air comes in. Sunshine makes everything smell fresh and like a new beginning. I gulp and try not to look offended. The duke is more than twice my age, with a pudgy belly and hardy knuckles. His hair is thinning. It was once dark brown but now has streaks of gray in it.

"Lovely to meet you, Princess!" he says in a boisterous voice. His demeanor is jolly. I smell the subtle scent of wine. This man is already drunk. The people of Seravi wear fur and long robes to thwart the cold. I pity the poor animal he has wrapped around his shoulders. He takes my hand and kisses it. The stubble on his chin is rubbing at the thin skin of my wrist. His face looks like it's carved out of clay.

He takes a step back to admire me. His eyes move from my face to my chest and down the length of the dress. The duke gives me a smirk and surprises me by stepping too close. "You might be afflicted, but you are prettier than I expected," he says and licks his cracked lips.

I stand still and try to act like a noble lady. The man keeps talking. He doesn't seem to know how to properly greet a woman. His voice booms and echoes off the banquet walls. The servants and maids watch as I am accosted by the duke. No one stops him. He takes my hand again. This time he kneels and covers my hand, wrist, and arm with kisses. The grit of his stubble is stinging my skin.

"See? This is great. We're going to get along just fine," he is saying as she keeps tugging at me. My vision is blurring and my heart is burning in my chest. This man can't tell I'm frightened or upset. He keeps shouting and smiling. His men join in and the banquet hall becomes too loud. Without meaning to, I start to cry. No one notices. It's like I don't exist.

"Don't worry, Princess. I'll take good care of you. You'll love Seravi. Everybody does. It has the best blacksmiths. And snow, you are going to enjoy it there. It might be cold but more of an excuse for you to be close to me, dear," he says, ignoring my tears and taking my stillness for compliance. I close my eyes to shut out what is happening to me. In my daze, I succumb to this awful man who is too rough with me.

"Stop!" says a voice. It isn't quite a man's but not a boy's either. The voice belongs to the young knight with auburn hair. He puts his arms around me and pulls me away from the duke. "Can't you see you're scaring her?" The young knight is being glared at by my mother and Adrian. I can't have him suffer punishment because of me. Why is he doing this?

"Oh, c'mon young lad. I'm only greeting the lady," laughs the duke. He has no tact. Unheard tears spill out and I stifle my sob. I must remain dignified. The young knight doesn't let me go, though. Instead, he pushes me behind him and stands up to the duke.

"Look at her. She's crying from your insolence. And her hand, you've bruised it," snarls the young knight. His bright blue eyes shine with defiance. No one has ever come to my aid before. The duke becomes serious and the sparkle in his eyes is gone.

"The people of Syrosa are too soft," growls the duke. He makes his way to the exit, but not without another blow to my ego. "No one will ever want that puny dumb girl for a wife."

The young knight clenches his fist. He is about to say something, but I don't know what it is because I'm running up the stairs. "My lady, wait!" he calls.

Why did he come to my defense? Surely my mother will do something terrible to the young man. All he wanted to do was stop the duke from making me cry. But what made him want to do that?

***

"I should kill you," says Adrian. I have no time to react. A moment ago, I was asleep in my bed. Now my sister is straddling me with her hands around my neck. Opening my eyes, I see the rage animate her face. She is beautiful, the way angels are beautiful. Clean, perfect features with enormous eyes. Too bad hers are full of fury. I kick my legs and squirm. It's no use. Adrian is five inches taller than me and much stronger.

"Why can't you be normal?" she asks like it's a real question. Her gaze is taking me in, drinking me up. It is unbearable how intense it is. I thrash under her weight. She moves to strike me and squeezes her thighs, crushing my hips. Her hands are heavy on my throat.

We are face to face. Her eyelashes are tickling my eyebrows. "I'm going to make sure the knight pays for interfering. What is a lowly soldier to a royal? Nothing." She leans back like a possessed demon. "Have you been toying with the boy's heart, Amadeus?" My sister's crooked smile is malicious. I shake my head profusely. This makes her laugh harder. Her shoulders are bobbing with her nefarious cackle.

"You're worse than a cowardly dog. I hate the way you act like everyone mistreats you," she hisses as she stands. Adrian saunters out of my room, slamming the door as a final goodbye. The sun is rising. It hasn't been a full day since my rejection, but feels like a hundred hours ago. Time goes by at an excruciating pace for someone who has no purpose other than to be married off for the benefit of others.

I watch as the thin line of gold becomes an entire sun. The sky's pink and orange gives way to blue and white. Life is cold. It's empty and, at times, gut wrenchingly miserable. Sometimes it's devastating. When it is, as it often is, I look for magical things like the sunrise. Watching a flower bloom on the first day of spring is a luxury I've had. Silence can be a good teacher. I notice tiny details and learn what others could never understand.

A butterfly emerging from its cocoon is like watching the merging of two worlds, the mystic and reality. First, the tiny thing is wet and looks like it can never open its wings. Then slowly it peels them back. They are rumpled and dull. It happens gradually. The butterfly's wings are dry, brilliant, and she flies against the wind over the fence.

Down in the garden, I wait for the day to begin. Servants are hauling water. The knights are leaving. It's too early for anyone else to be up. My legs are restless and I decide to walk around the grounds. I'm met with many eyes. The maids and servants are polite, but they have to be. They know my weird schedule and see the way my family loathes me. I'm an outcast more than any of them.

Three knights walk by me. I try to avoid their gaze. Out of the corner of my eye, I see they have angry faces. I'm certain they dislike my affliction, my status, and how the young knight treated the duke to protect me. I'm grateful, but my guilt overtakes my thankfulness. He should have let the duke bruise my arm and leave scratches on my hand from his stubble.

I hide in the castle's shadow by the willow tree. The drooping branches are in sync with my mood. On my knees, I press my palm into the base of the willow. My father loved sitting here with his spine against the bark. This is where he would tell me stories. He is the reason I love to read. Many nobles can read and write, but none of them devour books with the fervor I do.

The wind combs through the hanging leaves. Sunlight reaches a spot here and there. I feel safer in the dark. People can't see my bright hair or freckled face in the shade. Hidden from judgment, I close my eyes and clasp my hands. I pray to my father and hope he sends me someone to help me. When I open them, I see the young knight with auburn hair walking by. He has a black eye and a limp.

I rise and step out from my hiding place. This startles him, but I put up my hands to show I mean no harm. He stiffens and acts the way a knight should. In his bright blue eyes is a look I recognize in myself, embarrassment. He straightens up before he speaks. "I was punished for my outburst, but the queen has allowed me to stay."

It pains me to know he was hurt for aiding in my defense. He tries to offer me solace. "It was worth it, my lady. A man should never be so rough with a noblewoman such as yourself," he says. I don't know what has come over me, but I embrace the young man.

"It's alright, my lady. Don't worry about me," he says, and I let him go. His arms remain glued to his sides. In my awkwardness, I run back into the shadows of the willow tree. Can my father hear me?

BLOODSTAINED PETALS

6

The fires crackle in the hearths of the castle. Stars are scattered through the sky like it was painted by a renowned artist. I go to the library to visit my favorite friends. They greet me with open arms. I read the best chapters out of them until I can't stop yawning.

Penelope had another coughing fit today. She had to stay in her room. I wasn't allowed to see her, but saw a maid bring out her laundry. There were several handkerchiefs with red spots on them. I clutch the hem of my dress and pull out a loose thread. It's a bad nervous habit. Mother would thrash me if she saw what I was doing: sitting with my legs crossed in the chair, reading a book, and ripping out a silvery thread from my dress.

How long will I have left with my sweet sister? I don't want to think about it. Yet it sits on my chest. It clings to my shoulders. The devil walks around with me. We are hand in hand. He says "she's dying" over and over. I dart out of the library to get away from him.

They linger in my mind as well. Dukes with stubble, handsome men who say wretched things, their stares, and their contempt. I ruminate on it. Their voices bounce off my skull. I cover my face with the pillow so they can't see me.

I get the urge to go to the window. The moon shines down on the forest, illuminating the tops of the trees. White dogwood stands like otherworldly beings. A climbing vine frames my window. The ivy has heart-shaped leaves with black veins. They aren't sturdy enough to use for escape.

It appears someone has already freed themselves. Margaux's flaxen colored hair stands out against the evening blue. She looks both directions, inspecting the area for a knight. When she sees none are guarding the hole in the fence, she runs for it. I see the curtain of moss and ivy ripple as she slips out and onto the other side.

Beneath an oak tree, I make out yellow eyes. They are her guide and she heads straight for him. The deer boy takes her into the mist where I can't see anymore. Mysterious boys with antlers and coyote tails must be hypnotic. If I were to meet one, would he enchant me? Do beast boys always get a kiss?

I can't take it. Out of my room and into the hall I go. The candles soothe me with their light, but the shadows welcome me, too. Nighttime is a friendly encounter. I slink against the wall. There are tables with vases of sunflowers. I'm careful not to knock them over and sneak into Penelope's room.

She coughs and turns to her side. I can see in the low light of the fire her face and chest are sweaty. I grab the towel off her forehead and soak it in the cool water next to her bed. Gingerly, I place the cloth back on her burning face.

Penelope opens her eyes and grins. "Hello sister," she says, her voice strained. I kneel by her side and take her hand. My sister's palm is as cold as ice. I put my hands on hers to warm them. Bangs soaked in perspiration and lips with the fresh scent of blood on them. My sister is not her sunny self. Penelope wilts like a daisy during a heatwave. Then someone coughs blood onto the white petals.

"I was going to sneak out to see him, but I was too sick," she confesses with an impish smile. I open my mouth in mock surprise. "Margaux and I were going to go together. I told her to go without me." I nod. My little sisters and their unexpected lovers. The thought makes me giggle.

"Have you ever kissed a boy, Amadeus?" she asks. I shake my head. "Really? I thought you may have kissed the young knight who protected you." My sister raises an eyebrow at me. It moves the cloth and makes us both laugh. I shake my head again.

"I'm glad he was there for you. The duke had fewer manners than a pig." Penelope's big brown eyes have heavy lids and lengthy eyelashes. I watch them caress the pillow as she blinks.

"The boy with auburn hair and blue eyes suffered for you. It's tragic, but I find it strangely romantic. Don't you?" she asks. I get into bed with her. The blankets are plush and smell of lavender. I ponder her question. The knight stood up to the duke, and he did it for me. I guess I haven't thought about it, but my sister is right. It is romantic. I turn to my side and put my hand on the crook of her arm. A dove lands on her windowsill and spies on us. I squeeze my sister's elbow. She can read my thoughts.

"His bruised eye is sentimental," she whispers. I fall asleep thinking about what it was like for someone to truly see me.

***

My dress sways around my ankles as I peruse the castle halls. The long sleeves have white ribbons that tie off around my elbow and shoulder. My boots hit the dense floor and my ghostly appearance is disrupted by echoing footsteps.

"Come here, you incorrigible girl," says my mother with a tight mouth. She has snuck up on me. I can tell she is pleased by my surprise. I keep my head down and my hands together as I approach her. She leans down to get in my face. Adrian and she are both taller than I. Her big brown eyes betray her mean scowl. "What am I to do with you, Amadeus?"

I recoil as she reaches for my chin with her sharp nails. "Have you been tempting the poor boy? He is barely a man, newly sixteen. You must know the effect you have on him." She is digging into my cheek now. I shake my head slowly to not let her open up the skin below my eye with her claws.

"His name is Mason, but you probably already knew that," she accuses me again.

I shake my head, and tears spill out. It brings me shame, but my lip quivers and this gives my mother more of a reason to antagonize me.

"Don't lie, my daughter. You are a thorn in my side, but you are my thorn. I'll choose the man you marry and it's not him. Don't even think about it." Remaining steady in the wake of my mother's fury is impossible, but I keep it together enough for her to loosen her grasp on my face.

"Are you still pure, Amadeus?" she asks in a cruel, lilting voice. I nod my head and keep eye contact to show my sincerity. My mother lunges at me and picks me up by the shoulders. She is tall and thin, but much stronger than she looks. My back is to the wall and my mother hisses in my ear as she pins me, "Your virtue is the one thing you have of value. Don't make my duty of securing you a husband difficult. Do you hear me?"

I nod and cry with no sound. She drops me like a mangy animal. I'm on my knees and she hovers over me. "Never forget what you are," she whispers. Then she beats me. She kicks me in the side twice. My hair is being yanked, and she slaps me with her other hand, not holding a fistful of curly red hair. She rises and kicks me once again. I roll on to my side and hold myself.

"I'm sorry, but you have to learn your place," says my mother as she ambles away.

I wait until I hear no footsteps. And then I wait some more. Sitting up causes me horrible pain. I lean against the wall and hug myself. The slight pressure makes me nauseous and I spit up blood. No one comes down this hall. I watch the sun move in the sky. Margaux is singing to herself and finds me slumped over with blood on my lips.

"Amadeus, are you alright?" she shrieks.

My baby sister rushes to me and kneels by my side. I nod my head and try to reassure her, but it aches in my ribs. She helps me up and we walk to my room.

"This is Mother's work, isn't it?" she asks.

I nod.

My torso is filled with soreness. I hold myself with one arm and grip onto my sister with the other. She is patient with me. We are getting close to my room when we see Adrian. I stop dead in my tracks. Margaux glares at our sister with burning eyes. Adrian gives a hearty chuckle and bites her lip.

"Margaux, why are you wasting your precious time with our dishonorable Amadeus? Aren't you disgusted by her wickedness?" asks Adrian in a cheeky voice.

She doesn't know about Margaux's secret lover. Adrian would envy their relationship but act appalled by it.

"Leave her alone, Adrian. Can't you have a shred of decency towards our big sister?" asks Margaux in her most grown up voice.

My baby sister wasn't born until months after our father passed in battle. She recently turned seventeen but appears maturer. I'm proud of Margaux. She isn't an empty flower pot at all.

Adrian scowls and crosses her arms at us. "Not only is she afflicted, but she's a harlot. You shouldn't keep such distasteful company. Do you want to die here, alone, and unmarried because Amadeus can't speak or keep her legs closed?" Adrian's words rip me to pieces.

"No, don't say that about her. Amadeus is virtuous and kind. You are a slimy eel, Adrian. I saw you slip away with the prince of Arwin at the last ball. You two disappeared for quite some time," says Margaux.

She has a sly smile, and Adrian's face turns rosy pink. My baby sister has left her speechless. Adrian rushes past us and knocks over a vase full of yellow dahlias.

I grin at Margaux to show my thanks. She is laughing uncontrollably. Her crooked teeth make her look younger when she smiles. Somehow she appears ten, fifteen, and twenty. A face able to adjust to the task. Her dynamic demeanor alters her personality and age drastically. She flips her hair over her shoulder and laughs all the way to my room.

***

Now everyone suspects something between me and the young knight. I make sure to keep my distance. Not from him, but from all the men. I dart from my room to the library and spend most of the day hiding between bookcases. It's been warm with a hint of fluffy clouds, but I don't dare go outside. The garden is my safe place, my retreat from the harsh world, yet I have to deny myself its solace. At least for a little while.

I've been pretending to be ill. When the servants check on me, I act tired and writhe in misery. They've been bringing my meals to my room. I haven't sat with my mother or sisters in three days. It's better this way. I don't think I can face all of them at once. Their perceptions and imaginations terrify me.

The sun is setting. One of the maids must have started the fire while I was napping. Sometimes my pretending is too convincing and I fall asleep. There's a tray containing a small game hen, a peach, and a bowl of greens on the table. I don't think I ever want to go back to eating with my family. It's nicer to eat at my leisure and read a book by the fireplace.

I'm nibbling on the peach and turning the page of one of my favorite books. Adrian and my mother haven't bothered me at all in the last few days. Penelope has checked in on me twice. Margaux snuck me an extra piece of bread and left a note saying, "Feel better, dear sister." What is she up to? My curiosity entices me to go to the window.

I must be psychic.

The sun is lowering on the horizon, but it's not completely dark. The mist has dissipated this evening. The forest is clear black. Shadows of the trees stand like people with differing heights. In the amber colored field is an apparition wearing a leafy green cloak. It has honey colored hair sticking out from the hood. Margaux is running into the woods to meet her lover.

The deer boy's eyes are reflecting yellow against the deep indigo. I knew he would wait for her at the edge, but it still shocks me. I wonder if Hannes is handsome. The thought embarrasses me. I have only gotten a glimpse of him. He might be a beast boy, but he likely has an attractive face. I assume the coyote boy is also beautiful.

I finish my dinner and go back to my books. Feeling grimy, I decide to take a bath. The bruises down my side are shades of purple. There is a faint green hue outlining them. As I wash my back, I notice how tender other parts of my body are. My mother is a forceful woman.

The mirror points out the other injuries. Tiny spots on my shoulders from her fingers. My face looks dirty and has a red tint to it where my mother struck me. It's hot to the touch. Will my husband abuse me the way she does? Will I get married at all? Perhaps she'll kill me first.

What is it like to be in love? No matter what I read, I can't truly experience it. I doubt the man I marry will be someone I could fall in love with. With my mother's intentions, I'm certain he will be a brute. Adrian is probably egging her on and having her pick the most disastrous sorts of men.

I dream about benevolent princes and valiant mercenaries. Every day, I read about heroic knights who search the continent far and wide to find the right gift for noble ladies. Adrian screeches at me anytime she sees me reading. "Amadeus, you have that frizzy head of yours in the clouds."

I braid my hair by the window. The stars blink and line up to create masterpieces in the sky. My sister and I made a wish together. In another life, I'd run off into the woods with Margaux and Penelope. I'd tongue kiss a beast boy at twilight to see what it felt like. Being who I am, I retreat to my bed and hide under the covers.

Safe in my space, I'm lulled to sleep by twinkling stars. I wake up to the sound of thunder. Lightning strikes the forest. I get out of bed with the blanket wrapped around myself. For some reason, I want to witness the building storm. Wind gathers around the leaves and shakes them off the trees. The poppies droop from the weight of the rain.

Lightning strikes and this time I'm ready. It lights up the dark forest. For a few seconds, I can see the happenings of the mysterious woods. There are eyes reflecting red and green. A herd of deer run towards the river. On the trail leading north is a knight. He is riding a black horse. I can't see what else is happening because the lights go out. Nighttime and mist veil what happens beyond the hemlocks.

THE ADOPTED SON OF A KILLER

7

There is whispering throughout the castle walls. Constant chirping and rustling between the maids and servants. The knights nod at each other and speak with their eyes. Some of them give me a side glance as I pass by. I don't run into Mason, which is a blessing. The whispers would intensify and bring the castle down.

No one wants to include me in their conversation. I have little to offer, but it seems important. What is everyone talking about? My anxiety makes me suspicious. This must be about me. Who else could cause such a raucous in this hollow place? The silent princess, of course.

"Amadeus," my mother calls my name and gestures for me to come into the dining room with her.

My heartbeat can be heard in my ears. I can feel blood pump through the veins below the spotty skin. My mother sits down in her chair and sighs. A servant brings us tea smelling of strawberry leaves.

My mother and I haven't sat together in a long, long time. She can be ten people at once. My once vibrant and caring parent has become detached, hostile, and depressed. Every now and then, she is whimsical once again, but it doesn't last for more than a minute.

She raises the teacup to her lips without firm corners. "Another war has begun between the humans and the chimeras," she says.

I sit up straight in the wooden chair. Remembering how vicious these beasts are and how they are the reason my father is gone makes

57

my spine stiffen.

"Our people will be protected, dear daughter," she continues and blows the steam off her tea. I swear it turns to ice. Looking into the topaz colored liquid, I contemplate what will happen now. War has touched me deeply. The thought of it has me ready to hide in the rose bushes and poppies where it can't get me. I hold back the urge to dart out of the castle. The shadow of the willow tree would be another nice place to seek refuge.

"Kade Soloman of Tessafaye has agreed to fight our battle. I gave him your hand in marriage as payment," says my mother. I look at her and she stares into my eyes. Her face is smug as ever.

I have heard many rumors about the son of Seneca Soloman. It is said the great warlord was an aging man who had no wife. One day, a young boy broke into his castle and tried to steal a black stallion. Seneca caught the boy and, to everyone's surprise, he adopted him as his son and heir. If what I've been told is true, then Kade is as ruthless as his father. The warlord died valiantly in a battle during the Wyvern Wars seven years ago, and his son took over.

The people of Tessafaye are made up of mercenaries but also refugees. I read about their culture in a book. They don't live as nobles do. Instead, they train as mercenaries and become bounty hunters. They are swords for hire. It is a military lifestyle. The Tessafaye army has an impressive reputation. They say Kade Soloman has windswept black hair and eyes the color of desert sand.

My mother reaches for my hand. "He will be here in four days for your wedding. Then he'll be leaving with his army towards the central countries where the chimeras are."

I'm always nervous when I have to meet a suitor. This time I'm especially anxious. Most of the men my mother gives my hand to are country people with little noble blood or aging dukes who need someone to bear a child. This is an unexpected candidate. An adopted son of a warlord with no royal lineage. I'm guessing he isn't different from the other men. I'll prepare for rejection. Not an ordinary rejection. This one will leave Syrosa without an army to protect us.

"Please don't hate me, Amadeus. I'm trying to do what's best for you. What is best for all your sisters. Can't you see that?" she asks and reaches for the crook of my arm.

I flinch and knock over my tea. It breaks, fractured, the way I'm broken. My mother picks up the shattered pieces.

Holding them in her hands, she bares her teeth. "I know things have been difficult since your father died. It hasn't been easy for you. Do you know how bad it hurts to see these pitiful men scorn your presence in front of me? They should be so grateful I'd bother to invite them," she growls into the broken porcelain.

My mother is acting like a wild animal. She can be fifteen different people. A capricious predator, a concerned parent. I'm never sure what to expect.

"He may not be of royal blood, but I need you to do this with grace. Our lives are in your hands," she says and stands next to me. With neat precision, she sets down the destroyed tea cup. "You can be upset with me, but I have no choice, my eldest daughter. It has to be you." Her robe whips the back of the chair as she turns on her heel.

If Kade refuses me, we will be left undefended. It will bring Syrosa shame. I've stopped caring what the men my mother picks for me think. But this time, it does matter. Everyone is counting on me.

***

Penelope is sicker than before. She can barely open her eyes. Her forehead is hot to the touch. Blood stains the white handkerchiefs. The lacey cloth is eerie as it tries to appear composed. I kneel by her bed and look at the sky over my shoulder. Am I allowed to make another wish? I can't live without my sister.

"Amadeus," she whispers my name. Turning to her side, she faces me and opens an eye.

We laugh at the gesture together. "I heard you're going to get married in three days." I nod my head. Penelope is pleased by this.

"You two will be happy. I saw it in my dream," she says. My sister must be having delusions from the fever. I grab a cold cloth from the basin and put it on her burning forehead.

"I heard the warlord's adopted son is a handsome rogue who fights with no fear," she says in a hushed voice. The thing about being locked up in a castle is only hearing about the outside world. We don't get to be a part of it. I shake my head at her and cross my arms playfully.

"I'm serious. One of the maids met him when he came here ten years ago with Seneca. She said he has the shiniest black hair and doesn't smile. Apparently, he has a beautiful face," she giggles.

I ponder what is to become of me. What will happen to my sister? The one who tried to be there for me for as long as she could. What about my baby sister and her daring heart that is connected to the forest?

Penelope sits up, and the cloth falls to the ground. I pick it up to rewet it, and place it on her again. She pushes it away and points to the window. "I want to look outside, Amadeus," she says.

I give into her whim and help her out of bed. The sky is hazy blue with clouds shaped like sheep. When the wind herds them off, the sun comes out and makes the air smell mossy and fresh.

We sit at the window and look into the forest where the trail leads out into the world beyond. Many knights and carriages pass over the path and use the bridge crossing the river. Soon I'll be married. It may be my ticket out of Syrosa—if my husband doesn't die in battle. I don't know this man, yet I already am making myself grieve over him. I've lost my father and now I'm going to be married to a man who will leave the day after our wedding to fight a war our people refuse to fight.

"Don't fret, big sister. Soon, you will be free of this place. Our mother's burdens aren't for you to keep."

In her feverish state, Penelope is insightful.

The breeze moves around our hair. It dances on my curls and picks up my sister's smooth locks. Mason and the other knights are training. Nothing has happened between us, but I blush and look away. If I get caught so much as glancing at the young knight, I'll be in trouble. Now the man I'm supposed to marry is on his way. My mother may not risk abusing me. What man wants a mute woman with tawny freckles and bruises on her stomach?

The clanging of blades fills the air. Men swear and huff. They make grunting noises. Penelope eyes them with thirst. Some knights have taken off their shirts. It's terribly unladylike. I can't help but laugh. She notices me and gives me a mischievous grin.

"What? I'm allowed to look. Who is cruel enough to deny a dying girl a chance to see such a spectacle?" she says. I give her shoulder a shake, but not too hard. She swats me away. "They look at us all the time."

I raise an eyebrow. Really, now? I'm asking. Penelope sighs and throws up her hands. She turns and starts running her hands through my hair. My sister takes my face and turns me over with her elegant fingers.

"The color red is rare in this part of the continent. Father was from the Scorse Isles off the southern coast, where most people have copper hair and freckles like you. I know people treat you unfairly, but I think it is because you are the silent princess who stands out among the dull without ever saying a word."

Penelope's words hit me hard, and I start to cry. I take her hands in mine before I let the sobs pour out. Being seen is magnificent, but all-consuming. In this moment, her perception takes me in and makes me real. I am witnessed.

My hands are a bit smaller compared to my sister's. She has sun-kissed skin with no spots. Her knuckles are red from clutching the blanket. Looking down, I see how my spotty skin differentiates from hers. I'm unruly. She's uncomplicated.

"Don't cry," she says and we embrace.

I let my sister hold me until Adrian barges in and forces us apart. She can't stand the closeness I have with Penelope.

"The heartless warlord agreed to marry a scrawny thing like you," hisses Adrian, as she practically drags me down the hall. "I would think he'd want a sturdier wife!"

Adrian laughs at her own mean joke. I get a rotten feeling in my stomach. It's not from a bruise. What if my new husband is more abusive than my mother and sister?

***

I'm pulled from the story I'm reading. It takes a second for it to register. I hear yelling. It's my mother's voice. I set down my book. It was getting to the best part. No time now. Who is she arguing with? Then I hear the shrill shrieking of Margaux. Oh, no. I run down the stairs and nearly fall over my own feet. The stairs are numerous and encumbering. Adrian is standing in the doorway watching the mess. My mother is yanking Margaux around by the wrists. Margaux tries to fling her off, but my mother has a tight grasp on her.

"You think I wouldn't notice?" asks my mother. Margaux's eyelashes are drenched in tears. The sleeve of her dress is ripped. Mother and she must have been quarreling for a while. She tries to pull away, but my mother won't let her go. Adrian has a crooked smile growing on her annoyingly pleased face. How can someone look sweet and inviting, but be the total opposite?

"Please, Mother. Let me go. You're hurting me," says Margaux.

My mother shakes her. The lines in the middle of her forehead fold and her mouth is snarling.

"Not the way you have hurt me," hisses my mother.

"Stop, let me go!" shrieks my baby sister.

"You haven't bled in three months. Who is it?"

"I'm not telling you."

"Is it one of the knights? I'll line them all up after the child is born. Trust me, I'll be able to tell who it belongs to."

"It's not," says Margaux. My mother lets her go.

"Don't tell me it's one of the servants or stableboys," sighs my mother.

"No," says Margaux with defiance.

Adrian steps closer to watch the tragic story of my little sister spill over like a glass of milk. Margaux rises with pride and brushes herself off. I get a breath caught in my throat. My sister is able to be brave. Where did she learn to be courageous?

"Then who, dear daughter? Who is it you lay with at night like a harlot?"

"I love him. Why are you against that?"

"You are the youngest Sloane princess and you're pregnant with some man's child. What were you thinking?" asks our mother with menace. Her spit flies out with hatred.

"I want to be with him." Her answer is simple.

"Who is it, Margaux?"

"His name is Hannes. He's a beast boy," she admits. Our mother's jaw drops. Adrian puts both hands on her mouth to stifle her laughter. She is delighted by this turn of events. I don't know how to respond. I'm afraid my mother's rage will damage Margaux and possibly her baby. I want to run to her side. I want to aid in her defense. My feet remain on the same tile of marble.

"Get out," says my mother. Quiet at first.

"What?" starts my sister, but our mother interrupts with a voice booming with fury. It nearly knocks me off my feet.

"Get out!"

Margaux falls over for a moment but scrambles to pick herself up. She runs through the mahogany doors. Her fist knocks them open and they slam behind her. They are saying "get out" as well. Adrian has tears falling down her face from laughter. It takes an effort for her to stop herself. With no decency, she holds her stomach and laughs. She thinks this is hilarious. Wiping her eyes, she brushes off her smug grin as she approaches our mother. They start whispering, and I know Adrian is fueling the fire.

I sneak past them and through the mahogany doors. They are too preoccupied to notice me. A maid with pretty blonde hair keeps her eyes down as I rush by her. I think she was the one who tended to Margaux. She must have heard what the commotion was about. My mother's anger is justified. Her first-born daughter is a mute with rusty red hair foreign among the people of Syrosa who have flaxen colored hair. Then her middle child is sick. Now her youngest is unwed and pregnant with the baby of a beast boy. We aren't the easiest daughters.

A middle-aged knight and I walk far apart from each other. His face is red and his hair is damp with sweat. He must have seen Margaux run this way with tear-filled eyes. Did he feel anything when he saw her? It's simple logic: ignore the sad girl. We make brief eye contact, but he looks away first. His face is stubborn, but he can't meet my gaze. My reptilian eyes intimidate people. Mother says they are full of judgment. What she means is I have too many of my own ideas.

I get to the front door. It's wide open, and leaves are blowing in. I step out into the midafternoon light and see the last glimpse of golden hair disappearing into the dark woods. My life has changed overnight. In such a short amount of time, I found out Penelope was ill. Then about the war and my marriage to the warlord of Tessafaye. Now my mother has disgraced Margaux for being young and in love. Just like that, my baby sister was gone.

A DARK HORSE AND A WEDDING

8

Kade will be here tomorrow. The maids have been doting on my hair and rubbing lotions on my skin, pressing floral powders into my cleavage, and making sure everything about me is enticing. I have to get up and walk around. The anticipation is a killer like my husband to be.

I knew I'd have to marry a man I've never met. Why is it incredibly frightening this time? Perhaps it's because I've heard too many rumors about this one. My other suitors weren't interesting enough to warrant any kind of conversation about them.

The stories I've heard about the northeastern warlord come to my mind in fragmented pieces. They didn't seem valuable at the time, only stories. Today I'm racking my brain for everything I've ever heard about Kade Soloman. I go into the library and find a book about northeastern territories, the climate, their culture, and it includes a portion of history but mentions nothing about Seneca.

One time I heard a knight mention he fought alongside Seneca for a previous lord. He said they swung their weapons in well practiced but berserk motions. The army's fighting style earned them multiple victories. I'm not properly versed in the art of war. I can't even stand up for myself.

There was gossip about the warlord's son among the maids years ago. How he had an attractive face and showed no emotion. Not one to smile. At least we have that in common. I daydream about tousled black hair and dune colored eyes. He has visited Sloane castle, but I wasn't looking for him. Have we met and I don't remember?

In my frustration, I throw myself onto my bed and cry. What if he is worse than my mother and Adrian? If he wants to strike me, there's nothing I can do. As his wife, I'll be his property. Will we be happy like in Penelope's dream or will I be forced to endure him? I long to see her. My feet hit the floor in the hall and I'm met with Adrian. She doesn't say a word but leers at me. She wants me to suffer.

The castle smells of early summer rain and the sweet invigorating scent of hyacinth. The yellow flowers brighten up the monotonous white tones of the marble and stone. Ivy hangs on the windows outside. They cast heart shaped shadows on the jade and gold rugs. A vase full of dahlias is sitting on the shelf outside my sister's room. Someone must have replaced them. They were withering yesterday. I wonder if her illness is sucking the life out of the plants.

I go into Penelope's room. She's not here. It's sunny, but it has been raining off and on. I head for my safe place. The poppies cheer us both up. I wish she could hear the first one of the season bloom. Down in the garden is nothing but red flowers, green grass, and black stemmed rose bushes. Rounding the corner horrifies me. Penelope is lying on the grass with a new bloom. Her arms are sprawled, and she is on her back. Her eyes are closed.

On my knees in the wet grass, I try to wake my sister, who I already know is gone. I shake her anyway. Unable to call for her, I sob and grip her shoulders. Penelope, how could you leave me? Not now, not today. You haven't even met the man I'm supposed to marry yet...

I'm losing my family little by little. First, it was a tidal wave ripping through us, taking my father away. Then we went untouched for two decades. I should have been more appreciative. One can never guess when everything will be taken from them. In less than a week, I have lost both my sisters. Tomorrow I will gain a spouse. It's not a fair trade.

I get an image of our father. The beloved king of Syrosa. He came here as our mother's suitor. She could have chosen another, but she wanted him. His fiery hair and boisterous voice charmed her. Her daughters look exactly like her, except me. I'm his ghost. My father's apparition is beside me and I'm its spitting image.

Penelope is limp, and her dress is soaked through. The grass has left green stains on the eggshell cloth. I lift her up and hold her in my arms. Her smooth hair is tangled, and the rain keeps rolling down her face and off her chin as though she were crying. Please, I don't want to let you go.

An older servant spies us. He is running towards me. I can't let her go. He keeps trying to take her from me. I fight him for her. She's my sister! Don't touch her, I want to yell. His voice is hoarse and grandfatherly. "Amadeus, let me carry her. We need to get inside," he says.

He is trying to help me. I don't want his pity or for him to carry the weight of my dead sister's body. I want to stay right here in the rain and let the world fall apart around me. The servant reaches for me and says in a soothing voice, "Let's carry her together."

This makes me feel better. I get up and he helps disperse the heaviness of death and wet clothes. We walk through the sodden grass. My boots sink into the earth. Our feet make loud sloshing noises. It takes a thousand years, but we make it to the front door of the castle where my mother is waiting.

***

My sister has to have a funeral, and I have to have a wedding. A mockery to my marriage. What a travesty. I'm told to hold in my tears; a red face with puffy watery eyes will not be tolerated. The maids have me standing in front of a mirror. It distorts what I look like. I appear like a perfect bride.

The dress is sleeveless and swan white. It has pearls sewed into the bodice. There are sparkly gold threads accenting the hem. It touches the ground and drags behind me several feet. I don't like my shoulders exposed. More freckles are present and I worry about my new husband thinking I look dirty.

"Her hair," whispers one maid with a mousy demeanor and violet-blue eyes.

She is too pretty to be a servant girl. What if we could trade places? Kade would prefer her. She is two years older than me. Her name is Emily. I'd make a lousy maid, but I'd be better at that than being the warlord's wife.

Emily brushes my hair. She doesn't rip out chunks of it or tug at the tangled parts. The other maids are busying themselves, spraying my hair with rose scented water. They dust me with white powder, sweet like vanilla and spices. I try not to wince as they adjust my breasts and lace up my dress.

"There. What do you think, Princess?" asks Emily.

She is kind to me. I've never had her tend to me, but I'm glad she is here today. The other maids look displeased by me. They are fifteen years my senior. I think they are concerned Kade will reject me and we will be left defenseless. Emily tries to distract me. I keep staring at the sour faces of the older maids.

"Do you like it, Princess?" she asks again. I turn back to the mirror.

My lengthy hair has been braided and pinned up in an intricate updo. She takes a few pieces to frame my face and pushes my bangs to the side. I look attractive, albeit unusual. My copper hair and freckles can't be hidden, but Emily has made me look refined. Mother will be pacified.

Emily volunteers to walk me out. She seems to care about my nervous mood. Or perhaps it's to save her own skin. Making me appear a beguiling creature gets everybody what they want: security. The white shoes I'm wearing have a low heel and are decorated with pearls as well. I've never worn such fancy clothing. The silent princess has never been a fashionable person.

"You look beautiful, my lady," says Emily.

She gives me to my mother, who lingers in the door frame like a demonic shadow. She clutches my wrist with angst.

"Don't ruin this, Amadeus. I mean it," her tone is flat.

My mother has me take her elbow, and she walks me to my wedding ceremony. Kade will be waiting for me. I haven't met him yet.

The war is raging on and he's taken time out of his precious schedule of slaughtering beasts to marry me. Our wedding is expensive and grand. My mother had the servants prepare the best food and filled the banquet hall with an abundance of white roses, sunflowers, and buttery begonias.

Peering from the shadow of the door, I see Kade's back is to me, but I make out broad shoulders and tousled obsidian tresses. He is wearing a black tunic and belt. We step into the room and everyone rises for me. My mother walks me up to the altar. I hold my breath as he turns

68

around.

He has dusky tan skin. A handsome sculpted face: strong jaw and deep-set eyes. The rumors are true. They are the color of desert sand. I take a step. Then another. I'm walking deliberately and too slow. Once I am at his side, I realize he is taller than any man I've met. He has enormous hands and reaches for mine. They are warm and rough. He places the ring on my finger and I'm in a daze the whole time the priest is speaking.

I sign the papers, changing my name, making me his property. My mother no longer has to worry about me. Adrian is going to a ball to see the Prince of Arwin in ten days. No one has to wait for me anymore. The ceremony is over and everyone celebrates by drinking and dancing. Everyone but Kade and I. He stares down at me with heavy-lidded eyes. I hope he doesn't notice the slight trembling in my body.

My mother escorts me to the room where we are to consummate our marriage. She shoves me in and closes the door. I go to the vanity and unbraid the hair Emily worked so hard on. It has been tugging at my scalp. I need something to do with my hands.

Waiting is torturous. Finally, he comes in. I can't say "hello" and he doesn't greet me. He stands beside me for a moment, then kneels. The candlelight is hitting the hollows of his cheeks and jaw just right. My husband is handsome but a stranger. He runs his massive hand through my hair. I hold back the shudder in my spine.

"Do you want me to leave?" he asks.

If I deny him, then our marriage is invalid and leaves us with no army to fight for Syrosa. My mother may do more to me than beat me. I shake my head and put my hands on his shoulders.

"Are you sure?" he asks.

I nod my head. I've lost everything. My father, my sisters, my family as I knew it. I can't stand to lose my home, my people. I don't want our demise to be my fault. He kisses my neck, his hand moving up my thigh. Not wanting to be alone anymore, I put my arms around him. His lips taste like anise.

"Is this okay?" he asks.

I nod, even though I don't know what I'm doing. To make up for the silence, I run my hands through midnight black hair and let him take off my dress.

* * *

***

When I wake, I'm reminded of the ache in between my legs. There's blood on my thighs and the white sheets. Stubble has left a burning sensation on my neck. I'm raw and sore. He isn't here. His army had to leave today. I didn't expect it, but I wish he would have said goodbye.

This is ridiculous. I don't even know this man. Why am I already desperately clinging to him? We're supposed to be together forever, but I'm not sure he'll return from the war. My father didn't. I can't permit myself attachment. It will be too painful.

The sun shining through the window illuminates the dust in the air. They sparkle like they are greater than dirt and grime. I lay on my side, feeling sorry for myself: naked, bloody, and alone.

Penelope would have checked on me. She can't, though. The dead can't offer condolences or write a note and slip it under one's pillow. I check anyway because I miss her. My baby sister is in the woods somewhere beyond the mist with a beast boy. Did his family accept her? I hope they did.

My life has changed drastically but I remain a lowly mute girl. No longer the princess of Syrosa, but the warlord of Tessafaye's wife. Kade didn't treat me poorly, as the young prince from nowhere did. He didn't recoil at my affliction. He didn't say much, but he wasn't awful the way many of my suitors have been.

A dove lands on the windowsill. She coos and flaps her wings. I watch her dance with the dust specks. The sky is clear. Not a single cloud. Does Kade enjoy sunny days? Or does he prefer it to be overcast? I push the thought aside. My husband probably doesn't think about things like the weather. I've been a privileged woman. He has other things to worry about.

Smelling lavender and poppy on the pleasant summer breeze brings on a new anxiety. What kind of flowers grow in the northeast? What if there are no flowers? I chastise myself. Everywhere has its own kind of flora and fauna. There might not be any poppies, though. Where will I hide? I'll be far from the willow tree and red blossoms, holding my father's memory.

I sit up and pull the blanket around me. Red and white swirl together. It's morbidly poetic. I'm only a body used for fortune and security. Tears pour out and I grab my face. These are unexpected. I have a lot to cry about, but can't place what is making it happen at this moment. The door creaks and Kade walks in.

He is wearing his armor and black cloak. His boots and gloves are made of fine leather. I look at myself, a sad state of affairs. A skinny crying girl with a waist too small and hips that jut out. I cover myself with the blanket, but there is no point. He's already seen me. I flinch as he reaches for my hair. He pulls back and kneels. I shouldn't upset him. To apologize, I take his hand.

Windswept black hair sits above his shoulders. It falls into his eyes. My hands are taut, holding onto his. I've never met anyone with dusky tan skin. My freckles are sporadic across the tops of my knuckles. They are shades of tawny, umber, and rust. What does Kade see when he looks at me?

"Are you alright?" he asks.

I'm covered in salty tears and my own blood. His face remains slack. Kade is neutral in every sense of the word. I nod my head, but it's unconvincing. Tears fall down my face. The young warlord watches them but does not try to stop their course. He lets me cry and hold his hand. We sit for a while and listen to the call of the doves outside.

"I have to go now," he says.

Again, he reaches for my hair. This time I stay still as he runs his gloved fingers through a lock of red tresses.

"I'll come back for you. I promise," he says.

His voice is authoritative from commanding armies. No one tells him what to do. I envy him.

He gazes at me. I yearn to be invisible. It burns where his eyes fall and I feel myself shrinking from him. He won't approve of a wilting flower for a wife. I correct my posture and look at him. Pine green eyes wither in the desert heat.

"Will you be waiting for me?" he asks.

The question surprises me. I nod my head so as not to offend him. He kisses me, not for the first time, but now I'm paying attention. Last night was a blur. I know his lips were on mine, but I was somewhere else.

"Good," he says.

His boots hit the ground and thunder on his way out.

PICKED BY THE WIND

9

The months go by too slowly. I don't think they're changing at all. Sunny skies give way to gray clouds and colorful leaves. Winter had snow building on my balcony, but I didn't care to notice it. Blue birds left their footprints like an artist's signature. As it snowed, I dreaded the war more than ever.

My summer wasn't one of desire but lonely wonder. I thought about desert sand and the texture of its grit. The warmth of late August left me agitated. The knights would practice in the yard with their bare chest. Clanging metal and the smell of sweat ushered me into the castle. I paced around the library and tried to enjoy my meals since I didn't have to share them with Adrian. No matter what, I couldn't stop thinking about light brown skin.

Autumn was the season of my discontent. I resented my upbringing. How I could be used as nothing, merely a pawn in their game? I was angry with Kade. He's gotten to see the world. Somebody wanted him and believed in him. Seneca Soloman was not one to be trifled with and yet he took in a young boy who tried to steal a black horse from him. He didn't punish the young boy, but gave him a life.

Boys have it easy. They get whatever they want. It's not fair. If I were a boy, I wouldn't be property. I'd belong to myself. Men think the world revolves around them. I guess it sort of does. If I were a boy, I'd be arrogant, too. Imagine being a man able to use his words. I'd be unstoppable.

If he were here, I wouldn't wake up by myself. I wouldn't have to eat alone. He and I may have little in common, but I gave him a piece of me. I no longer belong to my mother. For that, I am grateful. My body may not withstand his beatings, but those have been put off until a later date. I eagerly await his return, but dread what may happen to me for the rest of my life.

The winter in my heart doesn't compare to the snowstorm outside. My youngest sister must have had her baby by now. It is a knife twisting in my stomach. A jab to the center of my core. Margaux and her child live out there in the cold. But she and her family are free. They may be wild, but our own people's way is barbaric. The beast people differ from us. They live as they want to, not by the expectations of society or the church. Being exiled may have been a blessing. I hope my baby sister has a happy life.

Battle isn't simple but the winter frost makes it unbearable. Swords are heavy and it takes limber muscles to draw a bow. Kade's army is strong, but I worry over the chill hindering their ability to fight back. I dream about black hair, snow in the desert, and spessartine eyes. In my nightmares, I hear screaming. I wake up with my stomach in knots.

It's been eight months since I've seen my husband, but I still smell him on me. Hints of musk and anise. The burn from his stubble is gone, but I reach for it, remembering the heat beneath my skin. How has he clung onto me?

In his absence, I've read at least two hundred books. I can't get my mind off the subject of war, bloodshed, and death. The stories about knights fighting for a kiss make me feel different. Kade probably wanted my family's money and our prestigious name. Our marriage has made Tessafaye a rich and royal nation instead of a land of mercenaries.

Adrian married the Prince of Arwin. Mother is relieved to have done her maternal duty. She is done with it now and lets me fend for myself. We don't speak or eat our meals together. The maids and servants treat me with respect out of fear of the warlord's temper. It's amazing, really. He's not here yet. He has all this power over them. I want to have his status. If only I were a boy.

My mother can be twenty different people. She has been over a thousand in the months since my husband went to war. In the beginning, she was aloof, distant. Then she would be angry and lash out at the cooks or the gardeners for not doing something right. After a while, she became cool and untouchable. I think she knew it would be unwise to damage the warlord's wife, and being aware of herself, has decided to stay away from me. It works out better for both of us. No need to make ourselves act like imbeciles.

Did my mother force him to marry me? She must have given him a substantial dowry. I suspect it was an offer he couldn't refuse. But why would the northeastern warlord take a mute girl for a wife? A princess is a princess, I suppose. Tessafaye isn't impoverished, but it isn't glamorous either. Our family's money could rebuild the whole kingdom.

Kade promised he'd come back for me. Why would he say that? He could have wanted to make me feel better. It was a rather pathetic sight, me bloody and crying. I would have said whatever to make it stop if I were him, too. Men do and say things that make little sense to me.

Snowflakes play with my hair. They hold on to the curls. I let the wind whip my face and turn my cheeks pink. The sepals of poppy plants will fall off soon, revealing the scarlet flower as it blooms. I stand in the garden and wait. To hear the sound of the first blossom is special. I don't want to miss a thing.

***

Dew drops on green leaves smell sweet. The sun is rising earlier and earlier. I heard it. The first flower opening. It's like a low pop but more beautiful. I can't describe it. The faint whisper of spring has an alluring voice.

I'm laying in bed with my books. They are my friends. I read the ones about love and war. The pile of novels telling stories about harrowing adventures grows. I devour pages describing what it's like to be the object of desire. Stories about thieves who steal hearts and jewels. Things I don't understand.

My mother passes by my room. The door is open. She stops like she is going to speak to me, but decides against it. I sit up for a moment. Blowing a curl out of my face, I lay back down. The aloneness didn't drive me mad this winter like I thought it would. I overcame it.

Now my sisters are gone, and she doesn't fill the castle with yellow hyacinth or sunflowers. The vases hold nothing but water. As I pass by Margaux's room, I see the purple vase holding a dead begonia. It must have been here for months. No one dares remove it. Like a superstition, we tiptoe around my mother's rage.

I skip down the hall since no one is watching. The sun dancing on the emerald green rugs has given me a burst of joy and I embrace it. I have a short list of things that make me smile: sunlight on the ground–snow or grass, flowers–all of them, and the rainbow crystal I carry in my pocket.

It's still my good luck charm. I hold it in my palm and hope it brings Kade luck as well. It's silly, but I like to think it does. I hope he's okay. The war has been going on for nearly nine months. War time travels at the rate of a snail. The battlefield moves with jagged movements, too fast and shaky.

"Princess?" says Emily.

She has snuck up on my girlish games and I feel embarrassed. I try to hide my face but turn to her.

She holds her apron and grins. "Your husband is here. The war is over, my lady. Kade and his army were victorious," says Emily with pride. The end of the war is a happy time. Chimeras and other beasts seek to destroy humanity, but we have prevailed once again.

Emily puts her elbow out for me. I hold on and she guides me towards the castle entrance. She pats my hand and attempts to ease my nervous fidgeting. I'm ashamed of myself but can't stop making jerky movements. The tha-thump, tha-thump, tha-thump of my heart is making me dizzy.

"Are you not feeling well, Princess?" she asks. I take a deep breath and wave it off. She stops and holds me in place. "My lady, I do not mean to offend you, but I would try to look glad to see Lord Kade. After all, he went through a lot of trouble for Syrosa. We are all indebted to him."

It hits me below the collarbone. The warlord kept his promise. I take another breath. My exhale is smooth. This is good enough for Emily and she keeps me steady as I stumble down the stairs. I can't focus my eyes. The young maid is patient with me and her kindness gives me the confidence necessary to face my husband.

He stands at the bottom of the stairs, holding his helmet. It has a knick across the front, but his face is as handsome as the day I first saw it. He has no discernable emotion displayed. Emily gives me a slight pinch. She lets me go and I smile at Kade as I ignore the chill making my spine stiffen.

We are reunited with no words. He is looking at me, but I think he may see through me. Seeing me for the worthless piece of property I am. The air around us steals time. It goes on forever. I hear the clang of metal and for some reason I can't recall the moment between this one and the one where Kade puts his big arms around me.

He's thrown down his helmet. I didn't think any knight or mercenary would do such a thing, no matter the state his armor was in. It's not quite as symbolic as throwing down their sword, which signifies their honor, but it is considered uncouth. I'm staring at the shadow beneath the helmet. It's like oil on the marble floor. He lets me go, but keeps me close to his side.

"Pack my wife's things and bring them out to the carriage," he says.

Emily scurries up the stairs. My mother sneaks up on us from the dim dining hall.

"Kade, what are you doing?" she asks in surprise. My mother analyzes his arm around me.

"I'm taking Amadeus back to Tessafaye," he answers.

I notice a lopsided grin spreading across her face. This happens when she's cross.

"Oh, I see," she says.

Kade makes a fist and his glove squeaks.

"You wouldn't deny me the right to bring my wife home. Especially after all I've done. Would you?" Kade eggs her on.

I have the need to hide in his cloak to avoid her sinister gaze.

"Of course not," she scowls.

I think knowing she has no power over me anymore hurts her. It must sting to see him have control.

"Good," he says.

My husband guides me out the doors of the castle. I look back at the place I've never left. The walls are high, ivy growing up around them. I say goodbye to the window of my room. Kade keeps his hand on the small of my back as he pushes me towards a carriage surrounded by his men. Their cloaks are tattered and frayed at the bottom. Blood has stained the bottom of their boots. Crimson tinged metal. Swords are tarnished with their victory.

He opens the door of the carriage and gestures for me to get in. I do as I'm told. My face is pressed up against the glass. The men get into formation. Kade is walking to the front. He stands taller than the other mercenaries.

"Nothing is to happen to her. Do you understand?" he says to his men.

"Yes Sir," they all reply in unison.

Kade takes his place at the front, and I fall back as the carriage moves. From the window, I watch as the castle gets smaller and smaller. We enter the misty woods. I put my arms around myself. The shade of the hemlocks takes over. This is an adventure. Not the one I anticipated, but at least I'm getting away from the place where I lost both my sisters.

I squint my eyes and peer beyond the dogwood and ferns. There are white butterflies, difficult to distinguish from falling flowers. It's a bright day, but the sun is hidden by the forest canopy. I sit back and try to relax. It's no use. I can't quell the buzzing tension.

The horses are mostly brown and red. They have black tails and manes. Hooves make the clopping noise on the well-traversed path. The mercenaries travel with stern faces. Some are wearing their helmets, but many are letting the springtime air touch their skin.

A lot of the men have the same features as Kade: tousled black hair, dusky tan skin, and deep-set eyes. Traits most people of the northeast carry. But then there are the others. Two of the men have fair skin, sunny blond hair, and icy blue eyes. They must be from the western part of the continent, like the Prince of Arwin.

The most interesting one is the female mercenary. She is slender and petite. Her hair comes to her chin. It's straight and has a glossy sheen. Upturned eyes with a unique appearance. One is blue, and the other is brown. She is a foreigner. I think she comes from across the sea. The far east continent is said to have the straightest blue black hair. She rides a gray dappled horse.

Evening is drawing closer. The sky is orange beyond the stretching branches. Smears of yellow and pink sew themselves into the sunset. Yellow eyes linger in the shadows of the pines. Are they beast people or something else? Is Margaux close by? The carriage wheels squeal as we come to a halt.

The men start their fires. I smell them cooking and hear them laughing. My focus remains on the yellow eyes moving in the darkness. They distract me from my urge to look at the female mercenary. She is drinking something out of a flask.

She lives like a boy. I'm not judging. In fact, I'm overwhelmingly jealous. The female mercenary rides a horse, fights in battle, and drinks with the men. That's what I should have wished for. I should have wished I was a boy. Then I'd be strong, and brave, and able to do whatever my heart desired. My girlish daydreams are interrupted. Kade comes to retrieve me.

I get out of the carriage and wobble. My legs are numb from sitting. Kade takes my hand, and we walk to one of the fires. The men don't acknowledge us. They continue cooking, drinking, and talking. I look around and take in the faces of all the men who fought on our behalf. One of Kade's men hands us each a bowl of food. I take an unsure bite. It's a potato-based stew with carrots and turnips. The seasonings are different from what I'm used to. It's good. Kade hands me a piece of bread and stirs me from my thoughts.

"Eat this. You'll need your strength," he says. I oblige, but feel my face flush. My scrawny figure is unappealing to him, and he's too polite to say so. Kade's men make quick glances in my direction but don't seem to dare anymore than a second.

The glow of the fire is flattering on the young warlord's face. A wolf howls, and he turns to examine the sound. Bats fly out from the trees and scream for the night. I have read about many animals but haven't been around them. I like their chaotic nature. A hundred things happening within the confines of the dark. Nocturnal creatures with yellow eyes shift in the treeline. Dusty black moths with green eyes flutter next to my ear.

The men begin lowering their voices and falling asleep. For such a fearsome group, they fall asleep like children, going out like a light wherever they are. I look over my shoulder to make eye contact with the female mercenary. Monolid eyes analyze me with a mysterious gaze.

I can't help giving her my attention. Turning forward, I keep my head down. Kade helps me to my feet. We walk back to the carriage and I try to glimpse the moon through the crisscrossing branches.

Kade opens the door to the carriage and motions for me to go in. I don't want to be alone and tug on his cloak.

"I'm going to keep watch. Get some rest. We have a long journey ahead," he says.

I nod and do as I'm told. He closes the door. I lean back and pull a blanket over myself. Staring up at the sky, I find an open space in the leaves to watch the stars until I fall asleep.

***

The wheels roll over pebbles and the carriage bounces a bit. Horse hooves make the clip clop noise. Birds chirp at us from the trees. A hawk flies above the hemlocks. His call is intimidating. The other birds go quiet. Once the hawk is gone, they sing again. I let the sounds wash over me.

We travel through the forest and cross the tree line. There are wheat and weeds everywhere. No more shadows blocking out the sun. I shield my eyes and let them adjust to the brightness. The men take sips off their flasks, wine or water, I'm not sure. I try not to, but I sneak a glance at the female mercenary. She has her eyes focused straight ahead. Her winged eyelashes are visible in the daylight.

The dogwood and ferns disappear behind us. I can't smell the fragrant scent of lilacs anymore. The wheat is rustled by the wind. Thistles are scattered throughout the golden field. Who would have thought weeds were pretty? I really am an odd girl.

Kade's men pull the carriage and lead me further from my birthplace. It doesn't belong to me anymore. I'm no longer Amadeus Sloane of Syrosa. My new name, my legal name, is Amadeus Soloman. The new lady of Tessafaye.

The path becomes rockier and the carriage teeters. Kade instructs the men to slow down. They pace themselves in order not to tip it over. I hate being such a bother. The men must find me a terrible burden.

I can't read. The carriage bounces around too much. I can't take a nap either. To entertain myself, I count the red alders at the bottom of the hill. I lose track and count them again. Kade is at the front, obscured from my view. We hit a bump and I fall over. Good thing no one can see me.

"The carriage!" shouts one man.

What is going on? I hear a gut punching yowl. The undeniable sound of a werecougar. I haven't seen one, or heard one until now, but I've read enough books to know exactly what it was.

"Protect the carriage!" yells another.

A high-pitched screech rings out in the air. The clanging of the men's swords blend together with their shouting and the call of the wildcat. As I try to get up, I fall to my knees. The carriage window has a werecougar's flat nose pressed to it. The creature has a growl in its throat. It's menacing yellow eyes smile at me.

The werecougar is a humanoid shapeshifter. There is a man in the beast. What it wants, I can't imagine. One of Kade's mercenaries brings his blade down on the cat. The wound gushes blood, and the creature yowls before pouncing on him. Red liquid streaks the window. The carriage teeters and then rolls. It rolls again and I'm watching the wheat field turn to blue sky and then dead grass.

My palm hits the window and the door flies open. I drop from the carriage that crashes in front of me. A yowling werecougar is to my right. Another behind me. More werecougars are headed my way. I scramble as my boots tear through the wheat and thistles. The men are fighting the beasts at the top of the hill. Out of the corner of my eye, I make out blood splattered on the golden field. It smells pungent and animalistic. The men are shouting all at once. I don't take the time to look for Kade. My only choice is to run as fast as I can.

The werecougars are growling as they come up on me. They are going to pounce on me and rip out my windpipe. I'm going to suffocate as they consume my flesh. The red alders are getting taller. I'm getting closer, but it's of no help. The werecougars are closing in. I'm yanked off my feet. I cover my face and wait for fangs in my throat.

Kade's sword makes an incision in the wind. With a wide sweep, he cuts off one of the werecougars' heads. Blood sprays out from the severed parts. The head rolls further down the hill towards the red alders. He has me in his left arm, pressed to his side, with my feet off the ground. He turns to insert his blade into a werecougar's chest. The beast goes limp and slides off his sword. Kade slashes through the last two werecougars. Their limbs writhe in the withering grass. The once amber field is painted crimson.

I get chilly looking at my husband's work. He carries me up the hill.

The men wait for his orders. Werecougars bleed out, and the red liquid runs down the thistle filled knoll. He walks through sodden earth wet with death. I have my arms around his neck. His eyes are staring straight forward. Is he angry with me? This is how he looks most of the time, but I sense he is upset.

The men have resurrected the carriage. Kade tries to place me inside, but I flail. I don't want to be by myself. He tries to set me down again, but I'm being stubborn. I won't let him go. He faces me. Stormy eyes are half hidden by his bangs.

"Do you want to ride with me?" he asks.

I nod, and he carries me up to the front. His horse is a black stallion with a lustrous coat. The mane and tail are a darker shade of black. He mounts the horse and brings me with him. Kade has me sit in front. He takes the reins and pushes me back.

"Lean into me so you don't fall," he says. I follow his command. The young warlord signals for us to keep going and his men obey him without hesitation.

TASTE OF FREEDOM

10

The moon is a waxing crescent. It's sitting on the mountain like a person. Their feet dangle off one of the hills. Kade and his men have been riding all day, no stops. The terrain changes from wheat fields and thistles to lush green grass with large boulders. Moss covers the rocks and the bark of the trees.

I've never ridden a horse. I haven't done a lot of things. Now I'm experiencing the world in a whole new way. I've gone through the misty forest I thought I couldn't see past. There are different flowers this far north. Orange and yellow marigolds are everywhere. Sycamores, cedars, and fig trees have unfamiliar shadows.

Kade keeps his hands on the reins, and his eyes remain focused forward. This is the most time I've spent with my husband. My anxiety is reawakened and my heart jumps out of my chest. I put my hand to my rib cage to ease the pressure.

The men ride behind us. I can't see them, but I hear their individual coughs. An occasional whisper to my right. The female mercenary is the last one in formation. I chide myself for indulging in these obsessive thoughts about her. Kade's shoulders are too broad and his arms hold me too securely for me to sneak a glance to the back.

Kade hasn't acted harshly towards me. Yet. As soon as he realizes how utterly useless I am, he'll throw me around like my mother did. I never left the castle until Kade came for me. My life is theories and things I read in books. I have poor life skills. Especially as the young warlord's new wife.

The grassy hills embellished with marigolds go by in a blur. Horse hooves beat the ground. The grating sound has been constant. I look up at him. Desert sand eyes are filled with determination and stare ahead.

I steady myself from the movement of the horse by holding onto Kade's elbow. His hands are twice the size of mine. If Kade decides to strike me, there's nothing I can do. Who knows if I'll survive? Kade's horse slows and I see a town at the base of the hill.

Yellow light from the windows is a cozy sight. I almost feel peaceful. But then I remember who I am. The silent princess will not be well received. The judgment of others isn't visible, but I can detect the disgust in their eyes. Words are pretty lies.

It's late, and there aren't many people out. Men are laughing outside of the pubs but stop as we near them. They look up at Kade. As soon as they spy me in his arms, their mouths open. I don't know them, but they know who we are.

We approach a large inn with lots of windows. There's a cherry tree in front of it. The men wait to be told what to do. How long until my husband starts bossing me around? What does the young warlord desire? Kade puts his arm around my waist, and, in one graceful motion, dismounts from the horse. He sets me down. The men drop from their horses and follow us inside.

"Lord Kade, it's good to see you," says an elderly man with long gray hair he wears pulled back at the nape of his neck.

"Roscoe, we've been traveling for two days. May we secure rooms for my men and please feed them? You know how they get when they're ravenous," says Kade, who is shockingly polite.

"Of course," says Roscoe. He is about to say something when he notices me tucked away at Kade's side. The elderly man fumbles but smiles a genuine grin. "This must be your wife."

"Yes. This is Amadeus Soloman," he introduces me. The blood rushes to my face. I'm sure this man is going to be repulsed by my affliction. I try my best to smile and act like the noble lady I was raised to be. Replacing a verbal hello with a wave I hope is enough.

The man examines me, his bushy eyebrows wiggling. Oh, how I want to run. I don't want to be an embarrassment. Kade taking me with him to Tessafaye astounds me. But what else was he to do? I'm his responsibility now.

"I was told the silent princess has radiant red hair and forest green eyes. No one mentioned her complexion. Her coloring is rare here. She's very beautiful," says Roscoe.

The elderly man's compliment warms me up. A spicy cinnamon burn but better. Kade's gigantic hand has found its way into my hair.

"She is," says Kade.

He's never told me I was beautiful, but he tries to touch my hair all the time. It's different from his and everyone else's. The mercenaries with curls don't have the same tight spirals I do. Roscoe waves us off.

"Enjoy your supper and have a good night's sleep," says the elderly innkeeper. Kade takes out a pouch of coins and holds it out to the man.

"Oh, no. You won the war. I could never take your money."

Kade puts the pouch back in his pocket. Money is no object. He has accumulated my family's wealth and been rewarded by the other kingdoms he fought for.

"Thank you," says Kade. He ushers me into the tavern where the men are drinking and telling stories loudly. We take our seats and a woman with a weather-beaten face brings us our food. I look around the room. The mercenaries have faces wet with sweat. They're smiling and grabbing each other's arms. Kade's men are enjoying themselves.

My mother wouldn't eat at the same time as the servants and maids. She didn't want to be in the dining room when the gardeners or musicians were having lunch, either. Kade treats his men as his equal. I hate myself for doing it, but I steal a glimpse of the female mercenary. What is her story?

***

I was exhausted to the point of delusion and can't remember going to bed. When I wake, Kade's arms are around me. His breaths are unhurried as he sleeps. Realizing where I am, who he is, and wondering what's going to happen to me has my heart pounding. I try to sit up but am met with resistance.

"You need to relax," he says into my ear. I'm ashamed of my cowardly heart. Kade puts his hand on my chest. "It's not good for you to be worried."

The massive palm is rough but somewhat soothing. I make an effort to calm my anxiety. At the forefront of my mind, I have no waking thought, but the nagging pressure is overwhelming. Kade can feel the erratic pounding in my rib cage.

"Ama, just breathe. You are holding your breath," he says.

I didn't notice the air dwindling in my lungs. Kade presses into my collarbone and waits for my heart to settle. His arms go slack and I slide out. It looks like he fell back asleep. My curiosity entices me and I lay back down and stare into the face of the warlord.

The daunting features are melted by his slumber. His stern jaw, the tension around the eyes, is gone. Disheveled raven black hair contrasts with the crisp white of the pillowcase. The man I'm married to is handsome, but what does his heart look like?

"You don't have to stay in here," he mumbles. I'm startled by his deep voice. I didn't think he was awake. "We'll leave tomorrow morning. I'm tired and need to rest. You are free to spend the day as you choose."

I'm not sure what to do. Is this a test? My mother would play with my head like this. Say one thing but mean another. It is best I try to gain his favor now. My hand reaches for his. I should look happy to see him.

He falls back asleep. I can tell because he loosens his grip on me. I can't stay in here all day and he said I was allowed to do whatever I wanted. What a peculiar man. I get up and stand by the door. My body is trapped, but my mind is outside where the marigolds are. Kade is sleeping soundly. I open the door and step out into the hall. It's quiet, unlike last night. Newfound freedom fills me with glee and I run down the stairs. I rush outside and stand under the cherry tree.

"Lady Amadeus," says one of the mercenaries.

He is tanned with dark wavy hair, about the same age as Kade. His cloak is blood red and there is a scar under his eye. The man stands over me. I'm afraid I failed the test and now I'm going to be punished.

He takes another step and I flinch. "My name is Finn. Lord Kade told me to chaperone you today," he says. I look at him, confused, and he sighs. "You must want to go somewhere."

There are shops nearby and people shuffling past the inn. I've never been able to go where I please. It can't hurt to go for a walk.

I pick a random direction and go. If I think about it for too long, I won't get anywhere. The mercenary follows too close, but I ignore it. We walk by women in plain shift dresses and men with scraggly mustaches. The people steal glances at us. I make a point of being respectful. A man sweeping his stoop drops his broom. There's a shop with pretty hats and coats in the window. I stop and take in all the different colors.

"Do you want to go in?" asks Finn.

I nod, and he ushers me inside. The woman working isn't much older than me. She looks me up and down. Then she peeks at the mercenary standing guard behind me. She is nervous but remains professional.

"Good day, Miss. Are you looking for anything in particular?" she asks. I shake my head. "I'll be over here if you need anything."

I think she is grateful to escape the intense stare of the mercenary. Pretending he's not there is impossible, but I weave through the shop, touching the fur lining of the jackets, and trying on hats. In the corner are velvet hair ribbons. Impulsively I grab a leafy green one, the texture kisses my hand.

"Do you like it?" asks Finn.

I nod, and he walks over to the storekeeper and hands her a few coins. We exit and I put up my hair with my new treasure. The decadent scent of sugar and cardamom fills the air. I search out the source of the delicious smell. There is a bakery around the corner. The mercenary gestures for me to go in. I hover over the case of pastries, cookies, and cake. The baker comes out and stutters when he sees my guard.

"H-hello Miss, what can I get you?" asks the baker. He is a plump man with a hook nose and a bald spot on the top of his head. I point to one of the braided pastries with some sort of glaze on it. The baker obliges and hands me the treat. "Anything else, Miss?" I shake my head and happily devour the pastry as we walk down the street.

There are children playing. They hold each other's hands and skip in a circle to the left, then to the right, and then they let go of each other and spin, reunite in their hand holding, then do it again. I watch them sing and run about. It's nice to see people being themselves. One child with blond hair and earthy brown eyes runs up to me. She tugs on my dress.

"Do you want to join us?" she asks. The little girl resembles

89

Penelope. I glance at the mercenary over my shoulder. His face is neutral. I'm not being told I can't, so I let her pull me into the circle with the other children. They take my hands and we skip. The little girl is missing her two front teeth.

I go another round with them. We dance like we hear music. The children jump up and down. They tug at my elbows and beg me to stay. The mercenary approaches and the children flee.

"We should head back to the inn soon," he says.

I agree and let him guide me back. We pass by the bakery again and the mercenary buys me another treat. This is the most fun I've had in years.

The sun is setting when we arrive at the inn. Windows with yellow candlelight welcome us. I am effervescent with joy over my day. No one has ever let me do whatever I want. I walked with commoners and played with children. The pastries from the bakery were better than anything at Sloane castle. I thought I had everything, but I realize I had nothing of true value.

Freedom makes everything better. The food is tastier, textures of clothing are more appealing, and being alive is more than tolerable— it's beautiful. I'm half skipping, half walking behind the mercenary. He turns around right as I'm spinning around and my face flushes. Finn makes no comment about my odd behavior. We go into the tavern where the other men are. Kade is looking refreshed but has tired eyes all the time. He notices me and waves me over.

"Ama, come here," he says. The men are staring at me and I get the awful thought he's going to scold me or worse, strike me, in front of everyone. I keep my eyes on the hem of my dress and boots as I approach him. He does neither and instead pulls me down next to him. The mercenaries go back to eating. The woman from last night brings me food. I wait for Kade to do something cruel, but he goes back to talking to the men about our journey.

What they're saying is important, but I'm not listening. I take notice of the female mercenary. She's drinking and being loud like the other men. Her hair looks silky to the touch and impossibly shiny. I pick at my food. It's good, but the anxiety churns my stomach. I take deliberate bites. Kade has his hand on my hip, holding me to his side.

Finn joins us. The men are sharing their concerns about tomorrow. I can't pay attention. My eyes land on the female mercenary. What is it like to be her? She must be fearless. I'm ripped from my thoughts by the men's loud laughing. Kade doesn't partake in their laughter, but smiles. I didn't think the warlord would have a charming smile, but he does.

The tension in my back and jaw eases. Kade's men seem genuinely happy. They're a family of sorts. I get a bruise on my heart thinking about my mother and sisters. Kade was adopted and raised to be a man with a formidable reputation. I was born of royal blood. Our veins do not pump the same liquid as everyone else. There's something cold in it.

I manage to finish my meal. The stars twinkle in between sycamore shadows. I gaze at them. My perspective is entirely changed. This time I'm not locked up in Sloane castle. The wrought-iron fence that once kept me in will soon be a distant memory. I yawn and lean into Kade. He stops the conversation to take me up to our room.

I lay down, and he covers me with the blanket. My eyelids are heavy. I'm not used to walking around for hours. Today was a lot of fun but now I'm exhausted. Kade wasn't angry. He didn't even seem to care. I yawn again and let my face sink into the cushy pillow.

"Sleep well," he says. The floor creaks under the weight of his boots. His deliberate strides echo through the wall. I fall asleep before he gets to the bottom of the stairs.

It doesn't last, though. I wake up with hair sticking to my neck. My breaths are shallow, which makes my heart beat like a hammer. Or is it the other way around? Kade isn't next to me. The men are singing and shouting in the tavern downstairs. I get out of bed and go to the window. The sky has endless stars splattered across the bluish black night.

I wash the sweat off my face and back of my neck. My hair is matted. I brush it with careful strokes. The motion is reassuring. The air is cool outside, but it's warm in the room. It looks like Kade stoked the fire not too long ago. It's cozy, but I can't sleep. I throw myself around the big bed, hoping to find a comfortable position. Right when I'm about to drift off, I hear his footsteps.

He opens the door and I'm frozen. I have my back to him. My eyes are locked on a star sitting on top of a cedar. Kade's steps are different. I think he's drunk. His smoky anise scent has a boozy smell to it. He slides into bed. The wind blows and the tops of the trees sway. Kade puts his arms around me and I betray myself by gasping.

When he holds me, I don't feel alone anymore, but I'm not sure what to do. He kisses my shoulder. His hand roams over my body. The lack of air in my lungs brings on my racing heart. Kade is nuzzling the back of my neck, but notices the quickness of my pulse. He rests his hand on my stomach and stops kissing me.

Worried he'll hurt me later for this, I turn around. The light from the fire is dim. His hair hides his eyes. I lean in and kiss him, but I'm not sure what I'm doing. We are husband and wife. But he and I are total strangers. Kade returns my kiss. He pulls back and touches my face. What is it called when I nod my head yes, but I'm not being sincere?

***

Sunlight claws its way in. I feel the warmth of it on my face. I don't want to open my eyes. I didn't get any sleep last night. There's a large palm on my shoulder.

"Ama, you need to wake up," says Kade. It takes all my strength to sit up. He is fully dressed and ready for our departure. I'm a rumpled mess, still lying in bed. "I let you rest as long as possible, but you have to get ready now," he says and hands me one of my dresses but also a coat not belonging to me. The lining of it has soft fur. It's pretty. I look at him, perplexed.

He brushes my bangs out of my face. "I'll explain when you come downstairs." I nod my head and he vanishes from my sight like an apparition. The warlord's gestures confuse me, but men in general are irritatingly aloof. I get out of bed and grit my teeth at my body's soreness.

Putting on the awful corset is unbearable, and Kade doesn't seem to care about these sorts of formalities. Deciding not to wear it and putting on the chemise under my dress empowers me once again. I throw on my boots. The coat fits me perfectly. I put my hair in two braids. Ignoring the ache low in my core, I grimace at each step. Kade and the men are waiting outside. The elderly innkeeper waves at me. I roll back the thick sleeve of the coat and wave to him as I was taught to do. He drops his pen. I hear it hit the floor as I walk out.

I weave through the men and step up to my husband, who towers over all of us. He scoops me up and mounts the horse. I catch a glimpse of the mercenaries behind us. Their determined faces terrify me. People who get paid to murder have a look in their eyes that's hard to describe.

"We'll be crossing the desert today. It freezes at night. The horses will be okay, but we'll have to keep moving. If we stop for more than a few minutes, we'll die. I can't let you sleep, so I'll be checking on you, but it's nothing to be afraid of. My men and I have traveled across the desert dozens of times," he informs me. The coat makes sense now. "Let's go!" he shouts and the men loyally follow him.

We leave the place where I first tasted freedom. The hints of spice and cardamom earn my memory. I'll never forget it. The air becomes drier as we head east. I watch the landscape change again. The lush grass becomes sparse. Wildflowers in shades of orange, white, and yellow pop up. Prickly plants are prominent. There is no forest as far as I can see, patches of spindly pines and the occasional palm tree. Their shadows are short. The sun is high in the crystal blue sky.

Kade signals for the men to stop. We take refuge in the shade of a boulder and two juniper trees. He orders the men to drink and they drink. I watch as the mercenaries adjust their cloaks and put on their helmets. Kade hands me a canteen and I drink without him telling me to. He pulls me up onto the black stallion. The men get into formation.

The warlord and his men ride across the sands with fervor. Sienna waves break beneath the hooves of the horses. In the beige and taupe landscape are sporadic splashes of color. Purple petals are silky against the grainy ground. It glints on the horizon. A hawk calls to my left and I peek over my shoulder. The bird flies into the sun where I can't see it. Kade doesn't bother to look at me or the hawk. His helmet shines and hurts my eyes.

Too soon, the warmth of the day is gone and the icy air reawakens the ache in my core. I clutch onto Kade's elbow. It startles me, but he nudges me closer to him. He pulls his cloak over me to shield me from the crushing chill. It isn't too bothersome at first. Then I realize what Kade was talking about. My body is hard to move. I'm drowsy and start losing consciousness. Kade pulls back his cloak to look at me. He is gently shaking me, but it's hard to resist the temptation to sleep.

"Ama, you have to stay awake," he says. The stars and his face are blocked from view. He's covered me again. I'm able to fight the tiredness, but only for a short amount of time. Kade's massive hand is shaking me. I wake up afraid of angering my husband. The warlord's wife is weak and fragile. How frustrating for him.

He calls my name. I cough from the dry desert air constricting in my lungs. Kade shields me, pulls me closer to him, and I shiver. It's cold, but something else consumes me. Fear is ravaging my body. Kade is probably going to punish me for being such a puny and pathetic thing. I rasp on the breaths that are hard to take. Remembering Penelope choking on the fluid in her lungs horrifies me. I think I might choke on my splintering lungs and die before reaching Tessafaye.

"We're almost there," he says.

A soft shake of my shoulder brings me back. I hold my palm to my chest to push in my shameful heart. It threatens to break my ribs. The bouncing of the horse lulls me back to a forbidden sleep. Kade is saying my name. I don't mean to disobey him, but I'm consumed by the blackness and unable to respond.

WELCOME HOME

11

The tips of my fingers graze satin sheets. They are the first sensation. I twitch my nose. It smells familiar but foreign here. Spicy and sultry. Where am I? There is the heat of a man's palm on my stomach. It jolts me awake. I open my eyes to the face of the warlord.

"It's okay," he says in a quiet voice, soft on the ears. "You're okay." Kade has his arms around me. I embrace him and peer over his shoulders. Stone pillars hold up the high ceiling. There's a chandelier lined with green and blue jewels. His room has multiple pelts from different animals. There are taxidermied heads of monsters and regular beasts like elk and bears. He has plush red rugs with gold accents. There is a fire burning in the grand fireplace.

I fell asleep when he told me not to. Kade wasn't scolding me as I assumed he would. His people must find me to be a burden already. The least I could do was try not to die.

"I want you to rest today. You'll meet everyone later," he says.

Kade takes my face with huge hands. The desert and I meet once again through his eyes. I'm holding my breath again. Hopefully Kade doesn't notice. He gets up and I wait until he exits the room to lie down. The muscles in my arms and legs are tight. I caress the silky blanket lined with fur. It smells like cloves and anise. I drift off to sleep for a short amount of time. The curiosity entices me and I can't hold back from my childish desire.

Getting out of bed feels criminal. I tiptoe around the place. It's like

I'm not supposed to be here. Kade has countless trophies. Dragon teeth, harpy talons, claws from at least twenty kinds of creatures. The warlord also possesses many precious stones and gems. Bronze bowls with diamonds and rubies in them.

My things have been moved into the room. Trunks full of dresses, my chemises, and stockings. Kade has given me a vanity in the corner by one of the windows. My powders, favorite book, hairbrush, and trinkets are placed rigidly on it. A breeze moves through the sheer curtains. Trembling fingers part them. Outside is a mix of sand, spring grass, and cypress trees. Behind them are the dunes and in the distance are purple mountain peaks. There is a river cutting through the valley.

"Can I come in?" says a high woman's voice.

I step back from the window. She is young, plump cheeks, pouty lips, and russet brown skin. I nod, but am not confident. Arms crossed and nervous is not a good look for the new warlord's wife. The young woman approaches me. She is smiling wide with small square teeth. I relax my shoulders a bit.

"I'm Marisol, your maid," she starts. The young woman goes about drawing the curtains and securing them with gold ropes. "There, that's better."

The sunshine and fresh breeze brighten the room. The maid turns to me and I want to hide in one of my trunks. Burying myself in sage and wine colored dresses sounds delightful.

"I was told about your affliction, so I made you this," says Marisol. She holds out a piece of paper to me. It has symbols representing things such as a bath, food, a walk, and medicine. There are some I'm unsure about, but overall they aren't bad drawings. "I thought you could point to the things you need. It will take some getting used to, but I think we can manage. Don't you?"

No one has ever made such an effort to communicate with me. Marisol is illiterate, but she has given me a precious gift. She has given me her time. I can't help but let myself cry. Marisol tries her best to stop the tears before they start.

"Don't cry, Lady Amadeus. I didn't mean to offend you. Do you not like it?" she asks.

I take her hand and shake my head. To show my gratitude, I hug the piece of paper to my chest.

"Oh, good. I shouldn't keep prattling on. Lord Kade said to get a bath ready for you. Come with me," she says and puts her arm out.

She walks me across the hall to where the bath is. Marisol gives me privacy and I let the hot water revive me. Candles flicker from a draft in the castle.

I massage my scalp and wring out my hair. Curls stick to my body. As I run my hands over my arms and legs, I hear my mother's voice saying I look dirty. The suitors and their mean comments run through my head like a herd of deer. How puny I am, my affliction disgusted them, and the lascivious grins certain ones would get upon learning about my inability to speak. I look at my reflection in the bathwater. Layers of red curls, narrow pine green eyes, creamy skin splattered with rust and mud. Smacking the surface blurs my image.

***

Marisol is helping me get ready for tonight. I don't know what to wear. The maid is patient with me and doesn't chide me on my jitteriness. She holds up a snowberry colored dress.

"How about this one, my lady?" I put it on over the restrictive corset. The sleeves come to my elbows and have lace ruffles. Marisol sits me at the vanity and we both look at my curls in the mirror.

"What would you like to do with your hair?" she asks. Marisol has a soothing voice. She seems nice. I throw my hands up and make a funny face, indicating I don't know. We share a laugh and she puts her hands on her curvy hips. "I think I know just the thing," she says with a sly grin.

Swift brown hands with warm undertones twist my hair in many pieces and coil them around my crown. Marisol doesn't rip out any of my hair the way the maids back at home would. Most of my hair is up in the twisty plaits but she pulls a few curls out of their places. She leaves my long bangs to cover my right eye.

"What do you think?" she asks.

I nod my head and smile at her. This makes the young girl perk up. She is proud of her work. Marisol helps me out of the chair and we venture through the halls and down the stairs. The castle is more extravagant than I thought it would be. Silly me, I assumed mercenaries and warlords wouldn't care for aesthetics. The hallway has fine rugs and additional animal heads mounted on the wall. They are masters of their craft for certain. Lanterns illuminating the rooms have blue and green jewels in them.

"Everyone is excited to meet you, Lady Amadeus. I'm honored to be at your service," says Marisol. Glee is syrupy on her tongue. She isn't like the other maids and servants I've met. If I'm not mistaken, Marisol seems to enjoy her work here. I hear people talking in the dining hall. Soon I'll be facing them all. I freeze and Marisol stares at me. "It's okay, my lady. Give me your hand," she holds hers out to mine. I take it with a timid grab of the fingertips.

She guides me to a large room with big oak tables. Everyone is chatting happily until I walk in. They stop and take me in, an outsider. Too many eyes are on me at once. Kade rises and steps up to my side. He puts his arm around me and pushes me forward as though he is showing me off.

"Some of you haven't had the pleasure of meeting my wife yet. This is Amadeus Soloman. I expect each and every one of you to show her the same respect you show me," he says.

His people bow to me and say in unison, "Welcome home, Lady Amadeus." It rings a bell in my heart. Kade brings me to his table. Finn and three other men are making crass jokes and laughing, but stop upon our arrival.

Marisol brings me my food and winks at me. It extinguishes my anxiety a bit. The food is delicious. Things I haven't tried. Most of my meals have consisted of chicken, bread, potatoes, and other root vegetables. Marisol has brought me a bowl of colorful fruit: pieces of melon, berries, and orange slices. There's a cup of lentil soup with pieces of tomato and cilantro. She has also given me a plate with a bed of greens topped with a leg of lamb. It's impossible for me to eat even a fraction of this.

Everyone is talking or laughing. Some are drinking and spilling their wine. Kade doesn't separate his meal times from the others. Is the dining hall always this lively? Sloane castle was dull in comparison. I nibble at the numerous dishes in front of me. Desperate to understand them, I watch Kade's people as they consume their evening meal. Finn's voice interrupts my thoughts.

"It's good to be home, Sir," he says.

The other men nod. Kade takes a thoughtful sip of wine and agrees.

"Yes. It's been a long time," says Kade.

"Almost a year," says Finn.

"Now we don't have to leave," says Kade.

He runs his knuckles down my face and toys with my bangs. The warlord has accumulated enough money from winning the war and marrying me. He and his mercenaries don't have to pick up any job. They can work at their leisure.

Kade holds onto me the entire time. Perhaps my running towards the red alders after I fell out of the carriage has made him suspicious of me. But how could I run off on him? He'd find me without fail. I don't desire to run away. Kade gave me a day of freedom. I was able to do anything I wanted for an entire afternoon. Besides, I don't have anywhere to go.

My husband keeps me at his side and fiddles with the loose curls. I look up to see two of his men watching his hands on me. It must be strange to see him with his new wife, the silent princess of Syrosa. We both have big reputations, though I think his is far more recognized than mine.

No one made nasty comments about my complexion. People tend to find the worst thing about a person and gossip about it relentlessly. I assumed from what my mother and Adrian said, my skin would be rumored to be hideous. Splotchy tawny spots tainting snowy skin.

Kade hasn't scowled at my appearance or been impatient with my affliction. Not yet anyway. His people have been kind. Welcome home, Lady Amadeus. It's too soon to tell, but maybe the fearsome warlord isn't the merciless man he's been made out to be.

***

I went to bed early. Kade stayed up to celebrate their return. I tried to contain my curiosity, but couldn't. The dim fire and moon shining through the sheer curtains gives me enough light to further inspect my surroundings.

Kade has an impressive collection of feathers. Some are the size of my arm. What kind of creature possesses these? The things he has killed for money are too scary to continue to contemplate. Taxidermied black moths and amber butterflies are tastefully displayed. He has shelves full of seashells. They have delicate swirls and spiky tips. Their shapes and designs are otherworldly. The ocean could be a portal to the spirit world.

I'm jealous. Kade has been everywhere, seen everything. Because he's a boy, he's gotten to do anything he's wanted all his life. I shouldn't be angry. It's not his fault. Still, it's not fair. If I were a boy, I would've had a thousand wonderful experiences. I was raised in luxury, but it didn't equal contentment.

Mother made it obvious she wanted a boy. Giving me a boy's name without the privilege of a man is to add insult to injury. Kade calls me "Ama." No one else has called me by that name. I'm actually fond of it. My name is clunky and awkward. Ama is short and feminine.

I slide back into bed. It's like I'm psychic because right as I am pulling the blanket over my shoulder, I hear Kade open the door. He's drunk again. I act like I'm asleep. A rough palm is on my chest, pulling me closer to him. This time he doesn't kiss my neck. He goes to sleep with his palm on my collarbone. It's nice to not be alone and I fall asleep peacefully.

A bird singing in the window jars me. It's morning already. Turning around, I see Kade is gone. He doesn't need to sleep like a normal person. I get up and look out the window. Tessafaye is gorgeous. To see different trees, exotic flowers, and a river that's not the one next to Sloane castle is refreshing. I breathe in a sunny inhale.

I decide on the lime green dress with short sleeves. It has tiny gold flowers sewed into the bodice. I need to unpack my trunk of clothes, but don't feel like doing it right now. It can wait since I'll be here forever now. I brush my hair and pin it up around my crown.

As I exit Kade's room, I hear an older man's voice. "Excuse me, my lady." Turning around, I am met with a man who is at least twice Kade's age. He has white hair. It curls out at his shoulders. His eyebrows are still black. He has dark eyes and deep olive skin. I stop and wait for the man to approach me. "My name is Francis. I'm the steward of the castle. Lord Kade wanted me to come get you," he says. I nod my head and follow him. He has lines around his eyes but has a smirking mouth.

"I was informed you can't speak. Is that correct?" he asks. I nod. Francis and I exit the castle and are greeted by the heat of the day. "I'm sorry to tell you I'm the only literate person in the castle except Mirai."

I look at him, confused, and he chuckles.

"Mirai is the female mercenary," he says. My eyes widen. I look at my boots and keep my nosiness to myself. Francis goes on without any prompting. "She is from across the Sayako Sea. The farthest continent east. Mirai is the runaway princess of Nakamio," he says. I stop in my tracks. Five years ago, I heard the maids whispering about a runaway princess from the far east. They said her father, the emperor, tried to marry her off to a brutish dictator. It is rumored she jumped on a ship and stowed away.

Francis tells me more as he guides me around the grounds. There are palm trees and orange petunias. "A lot of the people who work for Lord Kade are refugees, runaways, and people looking for a new way of life. Marisol is from Yeracho, the southeast lands where there is genocide. It has been going on for decades."

I wouldn't have guessed. Marisol seems too young and cheerful to have witnessed the horrors of death. My life at Sloane castle has left me an empty pot. My mother got her wish yet again. I have learned a lot from the books I read but lack real life knowledge. Francis stops me with a gentle hand and hands me a notebook and pencil.

"Lord Kade would like you to write down the things you want and give them to me. I'll inform him of your needs," he says in a grandfatherly manner. I'm incredibly baffled. Kade cares to know what I want? Francis clears his throat. "He is training with the men. Even though he doesn't anticipate fighting for monetary gain anytime soon, he is adamant the mercenaries don't lose their edge." Francis is effusively speaking about Kade. I hide my smile. He must be proud. We round the corner and the air is pierced with the screech of metal meeting metal.

They aren't wearing their full armor: leather shoulder guards and gloves. Kade is practicing with one of the blond westerners. I stand in awe as I watch Kade strike, guard, evade, and in the end knock the westerner to the ground.

"Again," says Kade. The blond man rises, a scowl on his face. It must have hurt when Kade hit him in the chest. The two of them fight for a while. Stepping aside and dodging each other. Kade attacks him and the blond man blocks his first blow, but misses the second. The westerner is unlucky. Kade hits him in the stomach and throws him to the ground. They are both covered in sweat and huffing.

"Get up," says Kade and helps the blond man to his feet. He notices me. "Take a break! We're not finished for the day," he shouts. The men grunt and make disappointed faces. Francis nudges me towards Kade. I remember to smile. The heat creates a haze on the horizon.

Kade stares out at his land. It's beautiful. He turns to me. "I hope you like your new home, Ama." I nod my head. His charming smile flashes. "Good," he says.

SQUALLS FROM THE WEST

12

While Kade is busy training the mercenaries and tending to his other responsibilities, I'm free to wander the castle. I assumed I would have a job to do, but since there hasn't been a Lady of Tessafaye, there's nothing I'm in charge of.

Nobody acts bothered by my presence, but my guilt is a hummingbird. Buzzing around, constantly reminding me of how purposeless I am. Everyone in the castle seems to have some place to be, somewhere to go, something to do. Except me, of course. I wish I could be of more help to them.

I go up and down winding staircases. There are open bridges leading to towers outside. I'm invisible, but not like I was before. A gust of wind blows my hair back. The sheer force of it makes me laugh to myself. I can't see it, but I can feel it.

"Are you alright, my lady?" asks the westerner Kade was sparring with yesterday. He has a well-defined face, it's carved out of stone, cold blue eyes, and white-blonde hair. I nod my head. Turning back, I gaze at the juniper and cypress trees in the valley. The sun is hitting the mountains and black shadows spill out from behind them. I stare at the border, where the desert meets the grass, and wonder how Kade felt as he arrived home with his unconscious wife.

"My name is Dax," he says. I thought he left. Now I feel rude. I face him again and smile to make up for my dismissiveness. The mercenary moves forward and his toes are nearly touching mine. "I'm glad you're here," he says. His voice is raspy. There's a tinge of ill will in it. A breeze covers up the real reason why I'm shivering. "I look forward to seeing more of you," he says as a crooked grin slithers across his face.

He stomps off. I can't see his teeth anymore, but they pierce me. There wasn't anything wrong with our interaction. Why am I put off by this man? It must be the nerves.

I've never set foot outside Sloane castle. Now I've traveled through the misty dark woods, stayed in a town, and rode across the desert. Everything has been making me jumpy. That man probably meant nothing by his comment. I'm thinking about it too much.

I go down to the garden to gather my thoughts. There are petunias and fragrant jasmine flowers. The scent of white floral is a delicate surprise. A palm tree offers me shade. It's not quite like my hiding place back home, but it will do. I can't hide from him. Not for long. He calls my name.

"Ama, come here," says Kade. He's looking rugged and handsome in a loose white shirt. No gloves or shoulder guard. I dust myself off and emerge from the cool darkness. "I want to show you something," he says and takes my hand. We pass two of his men and the female mercenary. She watches me with an enchanting stare. Monolid eyes with wispy eyelashes stop time when she looks at me.

He guides me to the stables. The brown and red horses are being brushed or fed hay. Some of them are sleeping. Kade's horse, the black stallion, waits for us to greet him. "Hey boy," says Kade as he strokes the creature's snout. It's a fantastic horse. Must be the one he tried to steal from Seneca.

"This is Fang," he says.

Kade takes my hand and puts it to the horse's side. Fang allows me to pet him. I feel the short fuzzy hair under my palm. The rough but smooth texture of it. He makes a soft neigh and leans down for me. Standing on tiptoes, I pet the top of his head. I think he likes me. Kade gently ushers me away from Fang and to another horse. This one is brown with a white spot on her left eye and on her back. "This is Ari," he says. She is a smaller horse, but still impressive. Her eyes have an air of mystery.

Kade takes my hand and places it on Ari. "She's your horse," he says. I stop petting her to look at Kade. He continues to stroke her mane and pat the top of her head. "Do you want to take her for a ride?" he asks. I'm nervous and shy away from the idea. Kade ignores this and brings her out of the stable and places me on her back.

My thighs are shaking. I'm managing to keep my composure, but inwardly I'm dying. Kade walks by my side and keeps his eyes focused ahead. Ari isn't a rowdy horse. She has a steadiness to her. I let Kade walk us around the garden. The sun is streaming through the trees and lands on the jasmine flowers, illuminating their beauty.

Ari doesn't mind my sweaty palms gripping her reins. I can't believe I have my own horse. Why did Kade give me one? I thought he was concerned I'd run off on him. If this was the case, then why would he give me something aiding in my escape? Men make no sense.

He walks back to the stables, and Ari obediently follows. Kade reaches for me and pulls me off the horse. Instead of putting me down, he carries me in his arms. We turn to see the sun slipping into the west. I shudder, thinking about the westerner earlier and Kade hugs me tighter.

***

I'm slacking off and moseying through the castle again. Each day, I explore a new section. I don't want to overstep my boundaries. Every day I test what I'm allowed to do. No one has berated me or told me what I was doing is against the rules. I have more freedom here than I did in my old home.

Sloane castle is no longer mine, but it's my place of birth. Where I lived for twenty-four years. Only when Kade put me in the carriage did I see any of the world. My old home was extravagant, a pristine palace. I didn't fit in there. The elegant hyacinth and sunflowers clashed with my unruly hair. My mother said I stood out, and she didn't mean it as a compliment.

The castle here is fancy but lived in. People go about their days freely here. Sloane castle was a stifling building where one had to walk on eggshells to not offend or upset anybody. The men don't change their tone when Kade is present. They stand a bit taller and straighter, but no one pretends. It's unnecessary. There's something remarkably real about Soloman castle.

I'm not watching where I'm going and bump into Mirai. She doesn't wear skirts or dresses. Her outfit consists of a loose tunic, belt, trousers, and boots. She dresses like a boy. Her shiny hair brushes against her cheek in a bewitching manner.

"Pardon me, my lady," she says and tucks a lock of blue black hair behind her ear. Mirai's voice is whispery but stern. She talks like a boy. I put my hands up and smile at her to assure her it's fine. The female mercenary and I part ways, but I catch her looking me up and down.

Have Kade and her slept together? I've been wondering how many of the young strays he's been with. My mother told me men get to use us. Play with us like toys. Men are opportunistic. I don't think they can help themselves.

I'm sort of proud of Mirai. Good for her for doing what she wanted. She saw a chance at freedom and she took it. Now she fights in the northeastern warlord's army. The runaway princess is now a deadly mercenary. She is useful to herself this way. What good could come to a dictator's wife?

Kade lets me do as I wish during the day. At night, his hand sneaks up my thigh and his lips are on my neck. I haven't said "no." If he is using me, then I'm also using him. Staying in his favor has unlocked many doors. I reach for my face. The sensitive skin underneath my chin is raw from his stubble.

I'm examining a ginormous snake head on the wall when Francis clears his throat behind me. "Excuse me, Lady Amadeus. May I have a moment?" he asks. I turn my attention away from the reptilian beast with horns and purple scales. "I hate to be a bother but..." the elderly man pauses and shifts his footing. "You haven't written down anything you want and Lord Kade may think I'm not doing my job if I don't provide you with the items you need."

Francis acts as a grandfather figure. He must have watched Seneca raise Kade. It warms my heart how this man is worried I'm not asking for enough. I take out the notebook from my pocket and write in my loopy script something I want: books.

"I should have guessed. With all your wandering, I'm surprised you haven't seen the library yet," he says and gestures for me to follow him. For an old man, he walks quickly. I take fast steps to keep up. Francis talks as we make our way through the vast castle. "The mercenaries are illiterate but bring back books from their raids and occasionally they receive them as gifts. We have an exceptional collection."

He takes me to a part of the castle I haven't explored yet. Francis throws open the creaky wooden door to a dreamy room filled with books. It smells heavenly. There are stained glass windows and pine shelves. I let my fingertips run across the spines of books. Historical literature, encyclopedias, and ones in languages I can't understand. Weaving through the maze, I find what I'm looking for.

Compilations of poems by various authors. Romantic stories, novels about adventure, and books compiled of lovers writing letters back and forth to each other. The stained glass windows let in purple and pink light. It makes the dust dance and sparkle.

Francis is playing hide and seek with me. "There you are, my lady. Did you find what you were looking for?" he asks. I nod my head with enthusiasm. Francis eyes the growing pile of books in my arm and rubs his chin to suppress his grin. "I'll see if anyone in town has books of similar style. Would you like that?" he asks. I nod and my frizzy curls bounce around me.

"I'll get started right away," he says and hurries off.

There is a cushy chair by the window. A short table accompanies it. I lay out my books and flip through them, trying to decide where to start. First, I read a short story about a young girl who escapes her impoverished life by becoming a knight. Then I read a hundred poems. They haunt me in a beautiful way. I find tears in my eyes from things that haven't happened to me, things that haven't happened at all.

I forget about time and who I am as I read a book about an orphaned girl who saves herself by being clever. She is about to meet the man she is going to fall in love with, but she doesn't know it's him. A massive hand is rustling my hair. The other is massaging my shoulder.

"I was looking for you," says Kade. I practically jump out of my seat. He helps me up and inspects my piles of books. "Are these good stories?" he asks. I nod and grab the books I didn't finish. Kade takes them from me and holds my hand on our way out. Peering over my shoulder, I say goodbye to my friends.

***

* * *

This morning is miserable. I'm sore and don't want to get out of bed. Since I have no schedule assigned to me, I cover my face with the pillow and try to fade into a healing slumber. It doesn't work because Marisol is removing my shield and fussing over me.

"Are you not feeling well, my lady?" she asks with a worried expression. I'm morbidly embarrassed and glad I can't speak and use it to my advantage. Her luscious bottom lip sticks out, enhancing the youthfulness of her face. I put the back of my hand to my head and gesture I'm unwell.

"I thought so. Come with me. I drew you a hot bath," says Marisol with her ever sunny attitude. How someone could endure such atrocities and be as light and airy as her is astounding. She hands me the robe Kade had made for me. It's black with several types of fur lining the inside and hood. I like it a lot. Marisol has me lean on her as we walk the short distance to the tub.

The bath has pink and white petals in it. I strip off my robe and eagerly settle in. Tension melts into the flowery water. Marisol sits in the chair next to me and hands me a cup with a black liquid in it. I frown at her and she laughs.

"I know it looks awful, but it will make you feel better," she says. I raise my eyebrow at her. This entertains her as well. "You're an expressive woman."

The drink has a bittersweet licorice flavor. It warms my stomach and eases the pain low in my core. I hand Marisol the cup and she sets it aside.

"I'll be back to check on you," she says as she leaves me in a cloud of floral water haze. I wash my hair carefully. Finger combing the tangles when wet is a grueling ordeal but gives me something to do with my hands.

I rub the burn on my neck from his stubble. The steamy water relaxes me and the drink has dulled the aches. I touch my ribs. They're not as visible beneath my breasts anymore. My hips aren't protruding like they did when I first got here. On my right side is a bruise. The place where Kade keeps his grip on me.

To silence my thoughts, I hold my nose and close my eyes. Sitting under the water calms me. I'm an odd girl. Breaking the surface flings water everywhere. I hold my side and wince. The pain has subsided but is present. I exhale slowly and regain my composure. Marisol could come in at any moment.

It's like I don't know who I am anymore. I'm the warlord's wife, Amadeus of Tessafaye, but I see a skinny, foolish girl. My reflection is the same, but my soul has changed. I haven't seen the world as Kade has, but he brought me somewhere beautiful. The journey was exciting, difficult, and as much as I hate to admit it, I had fun.

Penelope said Kade and I would be happy. She saw it in her dream. My precious sister, ravished by fever, claiming to be a clairvoyant and speaking of my future. I wouldn't say I'm unhappy. Kade has given me things no one has ever offered: adventure, freedom, a new life. The people here accept me, whereas the people of Syrosa sought to discard me.

I worry about Margaux. Is Hannes taking good care of her? I should have been looking for her as we rode through the dark and misty woods. My mind was fractured at the time. Too many things happening at once tends to shut me down. The constant stimulation renders me useless.

There are no poppies to hide in. The one thing I can complain about. It's childish but I keep thinking if I could disappear in the red flowers for a moment, I can get through this. In Kade's arms at night, I'm consoled, but they're not the same as the garden to the east of the castle back at my old home.

I ball up my fist, thinking about Adrian and how she is the one who got everything she wanted. What a tragedy. Penelope should have had it all. She was the one who deserved it the most. The middle sister who went unnoticed but was the worthiest of us.

Adrian accused me of opening my legs to the young knight with auburn hair. She was sneaking off with distant princes and the boy was brutalized by the men. His black eye is a pang of guilt in the middle of my gut. Mason didn't deserve to be treated like that.

I plug my nose and sink into the silence. It's peaceful here. Nothing can get me. Somewhere between Kade's big arms and my favorite red poppies. I wish I could stay here longer. There is no more breath in me. I emerge from my quiet place and find the warlord watching me.

"Marisol told me you weren't feeling well," he says and reaches for my face. I put my hand on his and nod. "I want you to stay in bed today. You need rest. The climate is different here and your body has been through a lot," he says. My ears turn pink. He's my husband, but

I still feel like we are strangers.

"I know you don't like me telling you what to do, but I'm only trying to help," he says with a laugh.

I smile without prompting. Kade isn't as oblivious as I thought he was.

THE RAIN

13

Francis brings me more books. Novels about love, overcoming conflict, and journeys to dreamy places. It's thoughtful he picked them out for me. Looking up, I'm met by the elderly man's smirking face.

"Are you a romantic, my lady?" he asks. The skin under my collarbone is turning bright red. Francis waves his arms and sits across from me. "I apologize, Lady Amadeus. I didn't mean to embarrass you. I thought because of the books..." he trails off. I want this topic to be over, so I nod my head. Picking through my pile of books, I realize romance is the main theme through them. Even the ones about women saving themselves. They always fall in love.

"You haven't written anything for a while. Lord Kade wanted me to make sure your needs are met," says Francis, changing the subject. I take out the notebook and graphite pencil. It marks the paper with a satisfying scribbling. Holding it up, Francis chuckles at my request: Poppies in the garden?

"Of course, my lady. I'll order them right away," he says and takes his leave. I skip through the library. No one comes here but me. My movements kick up the dust and the particles sparkle in the pink light of the stained glass window. There's a desk with a round window in front of it facing west. I startle myself and fall onto my back. The thought of the westerner looming over me has made me jittery. I brush myself off and stand. To face my fears, I look through the round window once again. I'm being silly. Nothing to be afraid of.

I gather six books for today's collection. To prove Francis wrong, I pick three history books, a book of poems from the far east, and two about other countries. I try to read the historical ones, but their factual nature is relentlessly boring. The books about other countries piqued my interest. I long to see more places. Tessafaye is brilliant. I should see if Kade would take me to see the town.

The poems are magnificent. They are written in short, precise lines. No word too many. They are perfect in their unfinished style. I enjoy them thoroughly. I go back to the beginning and reread them. Perhaps Francis will be able to procure similar books like this. It's unique from anything I've read.

I read until Kade comes to get me. He stares at the books I have stacked in neat piles on the table. I take his hand and let him lead me to the dining hall, where everyone acts like it's a celebration no matter the day of the week. The men roar with laughter and the women whisper or giggle. Everyone is enjoying themselves.

He pulls me to his side and holds onto me, where the bruise refuses to fade. Would he keep gripping onto me if he noticed? It doesn't hurt anymore but an injury, no matter how small, is felt all the time. Kade is talking with the men, but I'm not listening. Marisol has brought me a bowl of vegetables in a creamy sauce and a piece of thin bread. The food is good here. Kade insists I eat more, but I can't eat a fraction of what they put in front of me.

"I miss going into battle. Riding into the enemy's territory and slashing our way to victory!" shouts one of Kade's men. It's the other westerner. He shaves the sides of his head and keeps long bangs. His eyebrows are thin and fair like his hair. They give him a devilish appearance.

"Calm down, Kristopher," says Finn, who looks like he would prefer a relaxing evening meal. The westerner shoots him a glare across the table. He grabs a piece of meat and shreds it with his teeth.

"Remember when we fought the army of ogres? We left the woods in a bloody mess. Wolves must have feasted on their flesh for days," laughs a man with big ears and lots of facial hair.

"Kade is ruthless on the battlefield. He fights like he has something to lose," says a man at least ten years Kade's senior.

The men erupt into a fit of hysterics. Their laughter blends with the crackle of the fire and the clanging of dishes. The westerner and I make eye contact. His grin is eerie. Kade surprises me by toying with a lock of hair.

"I do," says Kade.

The men turn to each other and then to me. I think they are as shocked as I am.

"Yes, Sir. You must be pleased to have Kathryn Sloane's most cherished eldest daughter as your wife," says Finn. He is a civilized person.

"I am," says Kade and the men go back to eating their dinner. Their chewing shows their discomfort.

Marisol brings me more food. Cantaloupe and honeydew melon arranged with adorable heart shaped berries. I can hardly take another bite. Kade and the men lower their voices and talk about stuff I'm not interested in. I have no opinions about war strategies or training schedules. What does concern me is when they talk about the creatures they kill. The kinds of places they go. Rocky mountains, rolling hills of wheat and thistles, caves lined with crystals, and mysterious forests.

They relive their glory and talk about the treasures they've earned. Gold pieces, jewels, silver, and fine materials like the stone used to build the castle. The man that goes by Kristopher seems thirsty for blood. He wants to fight something. Maybe it is himself he is waging war against. Finn has to tell him to calm down multiple times. One of the younger men brings up a time when they explored an abandoned castle in ruins with ivy overgrowing the walls and rose briars taking over the landscape.

Kade kisses the top of my head and whispers in my ear. "Don't worry. I won't leave you again," he says, but all I hear is the ba-boom of my heart.

***

The song of rain wakes me out of a deep slumber. Kade is holding me. His breaths are slow, indicating he is asleep. I slide out of his grasp and cross the fancy rugs to stand in front of one of the windows. A gust of wind whistles through the trees. The rainwater smells sweet. I sneak out onto the balcony.

Kade keeps pots of brightly colored petunias. Clematis crawls up the railings. There is a story in the rain. I let it soak my chemise. My mother hated when I'd stand out in the rain until I was sopping wet. I love it though. Raindrops roll down my chest. I take out my lucky charm. The rainbow crystal has been from Syrosa to Tessafaye, like me.

I cup it in my hands and let the rain run through my fingers. My good luck charm makes me smile. I don't know why, but I'm happy I could hold on to it during my journey here. Another gust of wind blows and chills the side of my face. The moon is a sliver.

If the sun is full, then I decide it is a man. The moon is female. She has haunting phases of wholeness, but it is fleeting. Every night is a new experience. Being a woman is unpredictable. The sun lives for the day and is worshiped. Our lonely moon is unappreciated as she goes from too full until she's too thin.

What would I do if I were a boy? Maybe I'd have adventures and go on raids like Kade. Who would I be if I weren't a girl? I haven't had the pleasure of being more than a body to trade. If I were a boy, I would drink and be abrupt. I'd get away with everything. Instead of a withering crescent, I'd be a perfect circle.

Enormous hands are on my shoulders. "What are you doing out here?" Kade's sleepy eyes analyze my absurdity. He looks at the rainbow crystal in my hands and takes it. Is he going to throw it off the balcony? I'm sure he's irritated I'm out here drenched in rainwater.

"These are from the crystal caves in the southwest. They're found in the mountains near a dragon's lair. A rare stone," he says and gives me back my good luck charm. Kade wraps his arms around me.

"You like the rain," he states.

I nod and look at the moon. How lost she must feel on a dark night. Plumes of gray clouds swirl around her.

Kade is like the sun. Whole and authoritative. No one argues with a star. It can be brutal but also warm. In the daylight I'm vulnerable whereas at night I can take up less space and disappear. The warlord is respected. There isn't a person on earth who'd tell the sun to be smaller. Ocean waves are moved by the moon, but the power of her femininity is unacknowledged.

It's difficult not to be envious of Kade. He isn't afraid of anyone or anything. I paw through his trophies and ponder their story. Earlier today, I found a giant reptilian eye attached to a gold chain. It was twice the size of my fist. If I were a boy, I'd get into fights, but I'd never be hurt because I'd be stronger.

Kade pulls me towards the door. "I don't want you getting sick," he says and rubs his tired face. Once inside, I slip out of my soaking wet clothes and put on the robe. I sit on the rug in front of the fire where I left the book I was reading. Kade sits in the chair next to me. He seems exhausted. I thought he'd go back to bed.

This is a good story. I'm at the part where the female knight meets the man she is going to save from a witch. I brush my hair forward and let the heat of the fire dry it. Peering over my shoulder, I see Kade is resting his head in his hand, watching me.

"I like how you look when you read," he says.

There it is again. The pounding of my heart pressing the air out of my lungs. After I finish another chapter, I put my book down. My hair is dry, and the fire is low. We go back to bed. Kade holds me to his chest and falls asleep instantly. Thoughts loop, and my imagination runs wild. The characters in my books aren't real, but I feel close to them. I'm invested in their welfare.

Then the crazy ideas start popping up. I can't stop thinking about Mirai. She is courageous and prettier than I. The female mercenary is better suited for Kade. I get anxious when I think about Dax. He doesn't seem trustworthy. In Kade's arms, I'm safe and ignore further thoughts about the westerner.

***

If I were a boy, I wouldn't have to try. No one would call me out. Men can do whatever they want. We all turn a blind eye to them.

The one person I have to please in this castle is Kade. He doesn't care how I spend my time. My husband hardly cares what I'm up to most of the day. It doesn't hurt my feelings. In fact, it's a relief. I don't mind spending time with Kade, but he makes me nervous. What if I do something to make him angry? I really don't want to see that side of him.

I hear the way the men talk about his ruthlessness in battle. When we walk through the castle, I see how some men shrink as he passes them. Kade has a rather foreboding demeanor. He hasn't raised his voice or punished me yet, but I assume the day will come.

There's a horrendous booming noise coming from the training grounds. I slink around the castle and try to determine the source of the sound. The beasts mounted on the wall snarl at me. I try not to look at them for too long. A giant bear with red eyes and sharp fangs glares at me. I lose in our staring contest and scurry down the hall.

Stepping outside, I follow the awful sound. Francis is down in the garden instructing the workers on how to do something. Must be the poppies I requested. The steward takes me seriously and delivers with haste. He was both proud and frightened of Kade. When the steward speaks to me about my needs, he subtly implies Kade might be furious if I don't get all the things I want.

Rounding the corner, I recoil at the jagged edge in my ears. I cover them and close my eyes. It's louder up close. I peek at the men who have metal weapons they pour a white powder into. They aim it at a target and pull the trigger. The bullseye explodes across the field. I watch in amazement seeing the men as the ruffians they are. They train to kill. We didn't have these kinds of weapons in Syrosa.

Dax prepares his weapon. The smug grin on his face is unpleasant. He enjoys the kill, but I think he is into the hunt. I sensed this about him. Meeting men was my duty for years, since I was fourteen, but the westerner is the one man who has truly frightened me. It's in his eyes. They're full of hate and lust. A dangerous combination.

The westerner hits the bullseye. A hole in the middle where he landed his mark. Kristopher and Dax are cheering each other on, spit flying off their lips, mouths baring teeth. More sharp noises. The men load and reload their weapons and fire in succession. Boom, boom, boom. Like my heart.

"Do you want to try, Ama?" Kade's voice is in my ear and his hand is on my shoulder. It startles me and I chide myself for flinching. He doesn't seem offended. We pass Dax and Kristopher, who keep their eyes focused on the targets as Kade hands me his weapon. "It's a gun. The powder ignites a small fire inside, releasing a bullet. They are too slow and bulky to use in battle, but they are great for domestic defense," he says.

I hold the gun and attempt to quell the anxiety in my stomach. Kade positions the gun in my hands. I peek over at the men to see if I'm standing correctly. To my surprise, the gun doesn't shake. I hold it still. Like a boy. I aim at the target I know I can't hit.

"Keep your eyes open," instructs Kade.

I don't blink. For a fraction of a second, I have power. I pull the trigger and the gun kicks back into my shoulder. Kade steadies me and we watch as I miss the bullseye, but hit the target left of the center.

Kade's men turn to me. I'm not sure if this is a praisable thing. The men's eyes are on me, but I'm alone in my world. I missed the mark but landed a hit. This must be what strength feels like. Is this how men feel all the time?

A rough hand brushes my hair to the side. "Not bad," says Kade.

I don't think I've ever been proud of myself. For most of my life, I thought I wasn't anything but an item up for auction to the highest bidder. Today I see myself as capable.

Kade takes the gun and kisses me in front of all the men. They seem torn between cheering for me and pretending they didn't see anything. The mercenaries decide to mind their business. Kade is reloading the gun. The booming is exhilarating. Sensing sky-blue eyes on me, I turn to see the westerners leering in my direction.

I tug on Kade's shirt. He stops what he's doing to look at me. His expression is neutral. He takes me in and surveys the men behind me. I look over my shoulder to see Dax and Kristopher with their eyes forward. Icy blue stares intently focused on the targets.

"Do you want to try again?" he asks. I nod and drink in the power. If I were a boy, I'd never be afraid.

A HOUSE OF MANY VICTORIES

14

Today I am bouncing off sparkling force fields. Kade let me shoot a gun. I have my own horse. It didn't occur to me until this morning, but I'm no longer a Sloane. I'm Amadeus Soloman. I don't have to hide in my own house. With Kade's last name, I can do whatever I want. My mother would rip her heart out if she knew the privileges I had here.

The mercenaries are training with Kade. Most of the servants are still having breakfast. No one is in this part of the castle. I skip around and touch the blue and green jewels in the lanterns. Sheer curtains wave from the breeze. I dance in those as well.

I open a creaky metal door leading to a spacious room with cerulean rugs and white statues. They resemble demons and dragons. I lean on a marble pillar and crane my head up to look at the ceiling. Diamond encrusted chandeliers made of gold. Definitely one of the fanciest rooms in the castle. Then I see why.

A painting takes up a majority of the west wall. It's of Seneca Soloman. Kade may not be his biological son, but they have the same determined eyes. A stoic, handsome man. I walk closer, as if under a spell. The warlord beckons me. Standing in front of him, I could collapse. Seneca wouldn't have approved of me.

A man clears his throat behind me. "Seneca Soloman was a revered leader of Tessafaye," says Francis. He joins at my side to admire the deceased warlord. Hard to imagine him as my father-in-law. "He adopted Kade when he was twelve. The black stallion he has is indeed the one he tried to steal sixteen years ago."

This makes the elderly man's eyes twinkle. I clasp my hands and turn to him. Smiling sweetly, I hope he understands my meaning. I want him to tell me more.

Francis gestures for us to walk about. I look one of the white dragons in the eyes. They have emeralds in them.

"Kade was a wayward boy born to a prostitute in the slums. His mother died, leaving him to fend for himself. At first he stole from vendors and lived as a pickpocket. Then one day he got the extraordinary idea to steal the black stallion," laughs Francis.

I giggle, too. The Kade I know is unwavering to a fault.

"A willful young person, but Lord Seneca was patient and worked tirelessly to train Kade to be a valuable mercenary. Seneca was an aging man. It was lucky Kade became the heir of Tessafaye. It's a lot of responsibility but he pulled himself together," says Francis and he escorts me out of the room. I want to know more though, so I look at him with eagerness. He chuckles and continues.

"Lord Kade has worked hard to provide for the people of Tessafaye. He's been slaying beasts since he was seventeen. As you can see," Francis gestures to the wall of mounted heads, "the mercenaries take their jobs seriously."

This is the most I've heard about Kade. No one has bothered to tell me anything about my husband, including him. Perhaps he doesn't indulge me because it's not fair. I can't tell him who I am.

"You know, it was a bizarre turn of events. Kade was a skilled soldier, but not invested in the job. Around the time he turned eighteen, he changed into an entirely new person. He stopped slacking off and pledged to win every battle and vanquish every creature, reaping a respectable bounty," Francis says with a shrug.

This humors me. I can't picture Kade as an insubordinate young man. He gets up early and works until late in the day. I hardly know him but to hear he used to be negligent and careless is hilarious.

He walks me down to the garden. I'm shocked: poppies—hundreds of them. They surround the palms and line the paths. I clap my hands in delight and smile for Francis. The steward is proud of his work and seems pleased to make me happy.

"I apologize, my lady. The red poppies from your home won't grow here but I thought you'd enjoy these," he says. These poppies are a golden honey color. The filaments are midnight black. "Do you like them? I can try to arrange..." starts Francis, but I wave my hand at him to tell him to stop.

The palm trees have sparse shadows. I lay down in a patch of grass surrounded by the gold and black flowers. Red poppies can't compare to these. I rest my head in my hands and inhale the spicy citrus scent of the flowers. They're perfect.

***

It's raining again. I throw on my thin gray dress. This one has cap sleeves with white lace. I tie my unruly hair up with a ribbon. Time to go outside. My plans are interrupted by Marisol standing in the door.

"Sorry to intrude, my lady. I didn't see you at breakfast today or yesterday. Everything alright?" she asks. I nod my head.

They feed me too much here. At first I couldn't stop myself from trying everything, but I've been full for days. I've been skipping breakfast since Kade is already gone by the time I'm up. Lots of time to frolic about and do whatever I want. I nod my head and smile wide with my teeth.

"Are you sure? You can tell me, my lady," says Marisol, in all sincerity.

I take her hands in mine and nod again. She steps back, letting me out of the room. I walk slowly and reserved until I turn the corner. Then I run. Back at Sloane castle I wasn't allowed to run or breathe too loud. As Amadeus Soloman, I get to brush my fingertips across the wall as I race myself down the hall.

I look out the window and admire the growing storm. It's exciting. Water falls from the sky and tastes like heaven. I want to see the gold poppy petals covered in raindrops. There's the sound of thunder. A bird flies by the window at the same time. It startles me, but in a playful way. Being scared can be fun if the danger is imagined.

Almost downstairs. There are too many steps separating me from my freedom. I run faster to close the gap between me and the rain. Once my boot touches the rug at the bottom, I'm unstoppable.

Racing to the front door, I come to a halt. On the settee by the window are Mirai and Kade. No one else is around. She blinks at me with hypnotizing eyes. They stop whispering when they see me. It is one thing to assume and another to see. Not expecting the unconfined hurt beneath my rib where my heart is, I look away and rush outside.

My suspicions about Kade aren't unwarranted. There are quite a few pretty young strays working for him. Mirai and he have been fighting monsters together for years. He's the lord of the castle. A man gets to do what he wants, when he wants. Knowing this to be true doesn't make the pain in my chest subside, though.

The rain intensifies and a sound of thunder is rumbling close by. I run through the garden, past the courtyard, and to the training grounds. No one is out here. A gust of wind blows my hair around, tickling my face. Rain falls sideways and hits me from all directions.

I stand where Kade let me shoot the gun. In this spot, I had power for one minute. I felt the way a man feels all the time. The image of Mirai and Kade whispering to each other perturbs me. To discard the thought, I step out onto the field where the bullets fly.

My boots stick in the mud and hinder my steps. I stomp through weeds and dead grass. The storm clouds are purple and black. A wound in the sky. More water pours out from the heavens and saturates my dress. My bangs stick to my face. The wind picks up and when it hits the back of my neck and I shiver.

The target where I landed a shot is in front of me. I press my palm over the hole. It speaks to me. It says: I am capable. I turn to the castle. Clematis climbs up the walls. The ivy back home comes to mind and I cry. Tears mix with raindrops. They are indistinguishable.

I'm not homesick for a place, but a feeling. I miss Penelope. She made Sloane castle bearable. The sister who tried to be there for me. My sweet Penelope, who deserved everything. I can't stop thinking about her.

Not feeling hungry, I skip dinner as well. I spend the evenings with Kade, but tonight I'm using one of the abandoned towers as my safe haven. He probably won't notice my absence. It's still raining. I haven't changed out of my soaking wet dress. My hair is a dripping, frizzy mess.

I don't entertain myself in the library. If anyone did go looking for me, that's the first place they'd check. I should go inside. I'm not ready to be close to Kade and decide to stay hidden a bit longer.

End of the longest day has ruefully arrived. I stiffen my spine and hold myself steady. Going back into the castle is awkward. None of the men say anything, but they give me shifty glances as I leave tiny puddles where I step. Kade is going to be irritated. I've evaded him all day.

Walking up to the room awakens the fearful thumping of my heart. I brace myself for Kade to punish me. Opening the door, I cringe. The fire is lit, but he isn't here. I let myself in but feel like I'm breaking a rule. Next to the fire, I peel out of my sodden dress. I take my hair down. Holding my knees, I sulk as I bask in the warmth of the flames.

A firm hand is gripping my upper arm. "Ama, I've been looking for you," says Kade.

I didn't hear him come in. This time I refuse to smile. I'm not in the mood to try.

"I wanted to give you these," he says and hands me three large flowers. They are white with orange tinged centers and covered in tiny brown spots. Why is he giving me these? Is it because he knows I'm upset?

Kade doesn't keep eye contact like he usually does. "If you were a flower, you'd be a tiger lily," he says.

They're opulent blooms. I haven't seen anything like them. They are unique. The spots don't make them look dirty. I think they're pretty. This makes me cry and Kade seems uncomfortable.

"You don't like them," he states.

I shake my head and reach for his hand. They're beautiful, but I'm not sure what he means.

THE WARLORD'S WIFE

15

The call of a hawk wakes me. A breeze blows through the curtains. My body jerks in reaction to bad dreams and the piercing cry from a bird of prey. Muscular arms keep a firm hold on me.

"Ama, you need to relax," says Kade. He's usually gone by the time I'm up. I stop my squirming. There's no point in fighting him.

He loosens his grasp and strokes my hair. "You shouldn't worry so much," he says.

I'm embarrassed by my pounding heart. Kade can feel it through my chemise, under the skin, deep in the ribs. My dreams are off-putting. I can't remember them, but my body does. Sweat beads build on my chest and the back of my neck. I should take a bath. That's not an option, though. I try to sit up, but Kade tightens his grip on me again.

"I took the day off," he says and pulls me down. Kade sounds sleepy and not entirely here. My husband never takes a day off. I know this to be true. In the forty days I've been here, he hasn't slept in.

His breathing changes and his arms go slack. He's fallen back asleep. A surge of courage courses through me and I turn to face him. We are married, intimate in ways I don't fully comprehend, yet I haven't been brave enough to look at him for too long. Most of the time I see him through his shadow, the side of his face, out of the corner of my eye. This time I'm looking straight at him.

My curiosity overcomes my shyness. I sweep his bangs out of his face. Light brown skin contrasts with mine. Sculpted jaw and defined eyebrows. His eyes are the color of spessartine. They haunt me. I don't need them to be open for me to know exactly what they look like.

I somehow wriggle out of his grasp. Marisol draws me a bath and I settle in. She's put in a concoction of orange petals and scented oil. I like the warmth and spiciness of it. It's invigorating and opens up my lungs. I let my curls lay suspended in the water. The anxiety from the nightmares and Kade's arms wrapped around me dissipates.

Marisol comes in holding something white in her arms. "Lord Kade wants you to meet him by the stables," she says and sets down a dress. It isn't mine. My heart flutters at the sight. Marisol grins and waves off my apprehension. "He had this made for you."

I'm not ready, but I get out of the tub. Kade waiting for me makes me nervous. Marisol helps me dry my hair and brushes it for me. I put on the silky dress with beaded sleeves. It reminds me of one I had when I was fourteen.

"It's perfect," says Marisol as she fusses over my neckline. "You look beautiful, my lady." She sends me on my way.

As I walk through the castle, the sensation of men's eyes creeps up on me. I peer through my bangs to see Dax glaring at me in a lecherous way. Kade's other men make brief glances but don't stare the way he does. I approach the stables. Kade has saddles on Ari and Fang. He hands Ari's reins to me when I enter.

"I want to show you Tessafaye," he says. I nod and he helps me onto my horse. She's smaller in stature compared to Fang. We ride side by side. The black stallion is going at a steady pace and Ari mimics him. Kade guides us out of the castle grounds and down the path leading to the city.

There is no forest here. Jade green grass flourishes, but the cypress trees are sparse. The horses bring up sand with their hooves. Asters grow in patches. Their amethyst blossoms add a cool splash of color against the desert reds. Ari is a balanced horse and I feel confident this time. The beauty of Kade's land distracts me from my anxiety.

We get to town and people step out of our way. Kade acknowledges them and they wave with fervor. They are glad to see him. I grin inwardly. He is a beloved warlord. His people's gaze switches over to me.

Their eyes scan me, taking in my copper hair and forest green eyes.

Kade's people have tan skin, black hair, and dark eyes. My fair complexion covered in tawny spots is a rarity. At this point, I'm not sure if it's better to look different or blend in.

Kade and I ride through the narrow streets. He shows me the church. A brick building with arched entrances and lots of windows. Marigolds grow in varied size pots outside. Then he takes me to where the shops and craftspeople are. Blacksmiths hit metal with metal and a twang fills the air. A woman is selling coats made of fur. People carry their goods with weaved baskets.

I don't know what the city of Syrosa looks like. The realization leaves a sour taste in my mouth. I run my tongue over my teeth to get rid of it. Kade escorts us away from the crowded streets. We walk on a white rock path leading to the river. Palm trees offer some shade. A lizard pops his head out from a fern but retreats as Ari's hoof comes down.

Kade ties up the horses and takes my hand. We walk to the edge of the river. There are glassy stones in the water. The sun is a full circle high in the sky. Milky clouds melt over the mountains.

"The people of Tessafaye are happy you're here," he says. I stop staring at the crystals at the bottom of the river to look at him. Handsome face, neutral expression, perpetually ambiguous. He keeps walking. "They've heard rumors about the silent princess for years. Your hair and freckles are distinctive."

I look at my reflection in the clear water of the river. The tight ringlets of curls cascade past my shoulders. Almond-shaped green eyes, button nose, splotchy skin. What does Kade see?

The current goes further east. I step closer to the edge of the river. His reflection appears beside me. "I used to know a boy who broke into Sloane castle just to see you," he says.

How silly. To think anyone would go through the trouble to see an odd mute girl.

***

The gold and black poppies have enchanted me. I sit in the grass and run my fingers through the stems. Analyzing my stay here in Tessafaye causes me to fidget in the garden. I don't know what to make of Kade or how I feel about him. He hasn't hurt me like I thought he would, but I'm not sure if I can trust him.

He is cold and aloof–a man is a man. But in subtle ways, he shows me he cares. Being the warlord's wife isn't what I thought it would be. He's given me freedoms I couldn't imagine.

I can spend my day how I want to. Since Kade took me into the city, I assume I'm not confined to the castle. He let me use a weapon and gave me a horse. None of my sisters would believe the things I've been privileged to do.

Seeing him whispering with Mirai is a coiling snake at the back of my head. It pulls on my scalp and gives me a headache. There's nothing I can do. Why bother myself with it? I can't be certain they've been together. Even if they have, I'd be expected to tolerate it. My mother told me women are under the guardianship of their husbands. The will of one's husband is to be accepted with grace.

"Pardon me, Lady Amadeus. May I sit with you?" asks Francis. I nod and he joins me at my side. He eyes me, playing with the poppies. "Are you enjoying the garden?"

I nod my head and let my curls shake. The creases around Francis' eyes intensify with his wide grin. "I don't mean to be a bother, but Lord Kade is worried about you," he says in a more stern voice. My hand stops toying with the stems, but I avoid making eye contact.

"Marisol has brought it to my attention you've been skipping meals." Francis softens his tone towards me. "Will you write down what's bothering you? Please?" he asks.

I turn to him. He is a reserved man, but shows great empathy.

I take out the notebook from my pocket. The graphite pencil rests in between my fingers. I bite my lip, thinking about what to write. How can I simplify what I'm going through? Francis is patient, and it comes to me:

I'm lonely. Kade is busy most of the day.

He bobs his head as he reads my loopy script. I can't tell him I'm jealous of Mirai. Or I don't know how I feel about my husband. There's not enough paper to explain how much I miss my sister or the agony of worrying about Margaux and her baby. I figure he'll report back to Kade everything I write, so I should try to be a little bit flattering.

"I told him not to work as much. He doesn't have to anymore, but he insists on this strict schedule to stay sharp," sighs Francis. I feel bad. What I've written seems to have upset Francis. He continues,

"Why haven't you been eating?" I write down the truth.

They feed me too much here.

Francis claps with relief. "Oh, I'm so sorry, my lady. I'll tell them to scale back on their portions," he says in his professional voice. Brushing my bangs out of my eyes, I peek out at the valley. My eyes keep landing on the spot where the desert meets lush green grass. The place where Kade brought me from.

"Is there anything I can do for you?" he asks. I ponder his question carefully. It comes to me.

Will you tell me more about Kade?

The elderly man seems touched by my question. I sense he feels proud of Kade. He clears his throat and prepares to tell me stories about my husband.

"Kade started aiding his father during battle after becoming a trained mercenary at seventeen. I've mentioned before he was a skilled soldier, but his head was in the clouds. Then, after he turned eighteen, he began taking on jobs of his own. He got rid of a two-headed serpent wreaking havoc on a small village. That was his first lone kill."

Francis looks at me to see if I am listening. He has my full attention.

"He defeated a red basilisk. It was poisoning the crops and preying on children. It reaped a high reward. One of his most substantial earnings came from beheading a griffin near the southwest coast. It was working for a corrupt sorcerer. Kade took his life as well."

I scoot closer to Francis. Kade is dauntless. He must see me as a withering flower. Francis continues, "When he turned twenty, Seneca brought him into a grandiose battle. It was the war between the elves and the people of Disota. The elves were stealing their resources and abducting their women. The land of Disota has a small population. Not enough for an army. Gems were prevalent in the dirt hills of Disota and they used a heaping sum to pay for Lord Seneca's assistance. Kade took out half of the elvish army. An unstoppable force," he says. Francis' boasting is adorable.

"I'm sorry, my lady. I've taken up too much of your time."

Francis stands and I smile at him to show him my gratitude.

It's getting too hot. I head inside to wait out the heat of midday. Up in Kade's room, I go through my books until I find my favorite one. The one about the ruthless but romantic mercenary. I've read this one at least ten times. My fingers browse the crisp pages. I feel the need to reread it again.

OUT KILLING MONSTERS

16

Clouds break over the mountains carrying rain with them. The weather is warm in Tessafaye but there are random downpours. I'm standing on the balcony. My mother would be furious and say I'm ruining my clothes. Kade doesn't seem to mind my peculiar fascination with the rain.

Marisol calls for me from the doorway, "My lady, I know you love the rain, but Lord Kade wants you to come down for dinner," she says in her sugary tone. I release my grip on the railing and go inside. Marisol holds out a towel to me. I smile with my teeth because it's funny. The people of Tessafaye give into my whimsical habits. Back at Sloane castle the maids would clean the trail of tiny puddles and scold me to stop making a mess.

"I think you should wear this one," says Marisol.

She is handing me my burgundy dress with silver stitching. It has flowy sleeves and a low back. I'm not sure why she wants me to wear this one, but I don't care what I wear and I like Marisol and want to make her happy.

She has gentle hands style my hair with half of it up. It's damp, but I don't mind. My mother would say it's unladylike, but Kade hasn't told me I can't play out in the rain or I have to look a certain way.

"You are stunning, my lady," she says and fiddles with my bangs covering my eye. "I heard stories about the silent princess and her cascading curls the color of copper. It's such a delight to be able to serve you." Marisol gives me a big smile with full lips. She has a tiny gap in between her two front teeth. Her face is too pretty, aligned in a most pleasing fashion, and the tiny flaw makes me like it more.

I didn't know my hair would be such a topic of interest. Adrian made me feel like the color was either too bright or too dull. She said the texture was coarse, and it wasn't pleasurable to look at. Marisol holds my hands and rubs my knuckles with her thumbs.

"In the southeast lands there are white jaguars. They have paper white fur and sepia spots. When I was a little girl, someone told me the silent princess had freckly skin. I would watch the white jaguars, how divine and different they were, and I wondered if you would be as pretty. You're even prettier." Her cheeks flush. "I'm sorry for bothering you with my stories," she says, but I nod and smile to show I like them. It's nice to hear kind rumors instead of the ones I'm used to.

Marisol takes me to my husband. No one lowers their voice when I walk in. Everybody is having fun. I have sort of grown to like seeing the rowdy dining hall. It's kind of exciting. Kade places his hand where the bruise is on my hip and holds me to him as he speaks with the other men. Kade and Finn are discussing hunting and how long they'll be gone.

I drop my piece of bread. For whatever reason, the thought of Kade leaving me alone here terrifies me. He is a foreboding figure, but I have grown attached and don't want to be left. Kade catches my reaction and strokes my hair.

"We'll be gone for three days," he says. The other men watching Kade assure me makes me dizzy. My face is hot.

"Don't fret your pretty little head, my lady. We'll take good care of him," hisses Dax. He's drunk. His spittle flies across the table. Kade gives him an icy glare. Suddenly, Kristopher is sitting next to me. His face is too close to mine. He's also drunk.

"Why would she care? She disappears most of the day anyway," he slurs.

Kade shoves him back.

"Don't," says Kade.

"What? I'm being honest. If my wife wasn't at my side doing as I said, I'd give her a good thrashing," he says and some of the other men join in with his demented laughter. Kade's voice cuts through theirs. It's much harsher.

"I'm not you," says Kade.

The anxiety is unbearable. I stand up and attempt to scurry out of the room before any more embarrassing things can happen to me. Kade is distracted by confronting Kristopher and he lets me slip out of his grasp. There is a rumble of angry men in the dining hall. I run out into the rain.

The heat in my face evaporates. Cold water soaks my dress and hair. Dax and Kristopher pointed out what a horrible wife I was in front of everyone. I wish I had guidance. Kade doesn't tell me what he wants. Has he given me the illusion of freedom to embarrass me with it?

More often than not, I don't know what I'm doing. I don't know what it means to be a wife. All I was ever told was to obey my husband, don't upset him, and don't fight back. He doesn't give me orders. I'm at a loss for how to make him happy. Kade hasn't tried to brutalize me, so I don't fight him. I let him do whatever he wants to me at night.

"Ama," Kade's calling my name. I turn around to see him chasing after me. My crying is camouflaged by raindrops running down my face. I still feel ashamed of my weakness. "I don't want you to burden yourself with Dax and Kristopher's insolence. They're wrong," he says and kneels down to pull me into him. "I don't want to change you."

No one has ever said that to me.

***

After last night's mortifying events, I've been slinking around the castle, lurking in the shadows, hiding in the rooms no one occupies. In this room, there's nothing but weapons mounted on the walls. A fireplace not lit in ages. The window faces the field where the men are training.

Kristopher and Dax act like disciplined dogs with their tails between their legs. I think Kade fights them with excessive force on purpose. They wince as he brings his sword down on them. Neither of them wins.

Kade is sparring with them individually. They fall one by one. Then it is Mirai's turn. Does he go easy on her? I lean closer to watch them fight one another. Mirai positions herself, and like a strike of lightning is zigzagging around Kade. He blocks her but can't counterattack. She is faster than the male mercenaries. Somehow, she knocks Kade down and points her sword to his neck. She withdraws it and helps him up. Mirai is the one person I've seen beat Kade.

I hate myself for spying. They've been together for years. I'm the intruder. The female mercenary walks past the others and I watch Dax give her a lascivious grin laced with malice. She pretends he doesn't exist. This irritates both Dax and Kristopher. They spit on the ground in her direction.

Retreating from the window, I rush back to Kade's room. It's a clear day but I don't want to be outside. I don't want anyone to look at me. This is one of those days I want to be invisible. To not exist in front of anyone. The perception of people is harsher than the desert at night.

I draw the curtains and lie on his bed. Crying solves nothing, but it makes me feel better at this moment. I can't help my jealousy. He and I are strangers. It doesn't make sense to me. The fur lined blanket offers me solace. I've grown accustomed to the fragrant scent of anise and cloves. Its soothing aroma lulls me to sleep.

Big arms around my waist beckon me from my slumber. I look outside. It's dark. I must have slept through the day, including dinner. This isn't going to go over well. The lady of the castle is not at her husband's side every waking second, tsk tsk.

Kade has his ginormous hands on my stomach and collarbone. They could break me in half. Maybe he should strike me. I'm a pitiful wife.

"You've been avoiding me," he says. The hair on the back of my neck where he's breathing stands up on end. I turn to face him and shake my head. He doesn't seem convinced. "Have I done something to offend you? I punished Dax and Kristopher for disrespecting you. Anyone who crosses you, crosses me," he says.

I shake my head again. Kade is aggravated. I don't know what to do. Impulsively, I embrace him and give him a kiss.

His jaw goes slack, and he responds by taking off my clothes. I'm the shore and he is the waves under a full moon. I open my eyes to look at him. His eyes are closed. Kade might be using me, but I am also using him. Giving into him satisfies my needs as well. In my defense, I don't want to be alone.

I wake up, and he's gone, but at least I never sleep by myself. His boots and armor aren't here. He must have left to go hunting. I lay back down. His sweat is all over me. I sniff my hair. It smells like him.

The sun is barely above the horizon. A sliver of gold lighting up the sky. I toss and turn but can't go back to sleep. I've been in this bed for a day and a half while Kade gets up before the sun does. I need to bathe and do something other than sulk.

There's a burning sensation above my sternum. I look down to see a red mark from Kade's stubble. My fingertips graze it and a twinge takes hold. Tears spill out. I try to wipe them away as they pool in my lash line. What is happening to me?

Does Mirai have little marks on her neck? I haven't tried to catch a glimpse. Why am I worrying myself with things I have no control over? She doesn't have his last name. I do, but what does it mean?

Kade walks in and I sit up, too excitedly. He didn't leave without saying goodbye. "Will you be okay while I'm gone?" he asks. I nod and he sits with me. Kade is a killer king with a gaze that sees right through me. It's unexpected, but he brings me to his chest. We collide and I wrap my arms around his neck.

"I don't want to go."

It's the most childish thing I've heard him say. Its sweetness makes me giggle soundlessly.

Kade loosens his grasp and sighs. "The men are waiting for me." I can't help but wonder if Mirai is joining them in their expedition. I scold myself yet again for my obsession with the female mercenary.

He stands and my heart flutters in my chest. Instinctively, I reach for his cloak. This stops him. Turning around, he flashes me his charming grin. The warlord leans down and holds my face in his gloved hands. "Does this mean you'll miss me?" he asks. I nod and he kisses me.

"Good," he says. I listen to him leave, knowing I won't see him for three days.

INDEPENDENT

17

The castle is half full. A dozen mercenaries have been left behind to guard the place. Finn is here, but not Dax or Kristopher. Their absence is a relief. Mirai is gone though. The gnawing, shameful envy turns my ears pink.

Kade has been gone most of our marriage. I know how I feel about him through his absence. How it's a thorn that pierces me. Do I love him, though? That's another question. I can't trust him. Or is it that I can't trust myself? If I were to be honest, I don't trust anybody.

Hazy purple mountains have lush green patches on them. The peaks are jagged and look like they could make an incision in the sky. Kade and his men are headed towards the sycamores, where boar and deer are plentiful.

I sneak down to the stables. Ari is standing, looking alert, like she has been waiting for me. No one is around. I haven't mounted a horse on my own but decide on teaching myself. She is patient. I'm rather short, but Ari isn't as tall as the men's horses. My first attempts are unsuccessful, as I assumed they would be. No one is around to watch me fail, so I keep practicing.

It takes fifty times, but I learn to hold on to a piece of her mane towards the base of her neck, jump, and use the momentum to swing my leg over her back. I clap my hands with giddiness. I could do it without the help of a man.

We ride around the castle grounds. The men aren't using the field for target practice. I have her walk us through the grass. She's an even-tempered creature. I enjoy the sunny day with my horse. She and I soak up the sunshine and silent company.

Feeling braver, I try riding Ari at a faster pace. She trots for me and it scares me half to death. I squeeze my thighs and sit up as straight as I can to steady myself. Ari takes me back and forth across the field. I get used to her quicker trot and relax.

Ari turns around and I see Finn walking near the castle. He comes to a halt and stares at me. I don't think riding my horse on the field is against the rules. If it is, nobody told me. Kade is a man of few words and everyone leaves me be. I have Ari trot out of his sight. Finn's dark eyes don't frighten me, but I'm not in the mood to answer to anyone.

I take her back to the stable. Dismounting the horse causes a sting in my ankles. I need to work on my landing. Something to practice. It will keep me busy. I have a skill to learn. Ari seems hungry. I feed her. She chomps at the hay with big white teeth. I brush her and get her fresh water.

"Do you like the horse Kade gave you?" asks Finn. He snuck up on me. I nod and hope he's not here to reprimand me. Finn stands at my side and pets Ari. "He bought this one special for you."

I smile with sincerity. Kade anticipated my arrival. I'm not an afterthought. Finn steps back but doesn't exit the stable.

"You didn't need any help," he states.

I stop brushing Ari to examine his expression. I shake my head.

Finn has a severe demeanor, but doesn't make me cringe like Dax does. I appreciated him chaperoning me the day I tasted freedom for the first time. He seems dependable. During dinner, I notice he doesn't drink. He prefers to be sober.

"Be careful, my lady. Lord Kade won't be merciful if you get hurt on my watch," he says on his way out. Kade must have left Finn behind to keep an eye on me. Once he's gone, I give Ari a peck on the snout to let her know I care about her.

My back and legs ache from my audacious day. I have Marisol draw me a bath. She brings me an elixir of something citrusy with honey and cinnamon. I read the best parts from the books about adventures. Now I experience them in a whole new way. Before, I could only imagine. But my life in Tessafaye is increasingly similar to my favorite stories. I've been attacked by werecougars, perused a town, and crossed the desert. I wish Penelope was here so I could tell her about my horse I can ride anytime I want to.

Marisol brings me dinner in my room. I eat the grapes and pick at the wild game hen. By the fire I enjoy my food and read. It's nice to have the room to myself, but I find myself missing him. When Kade asked if I'd miss him, I didn't know if I would. Getting into bed with no arms holding my waist makes me melancholy.

Is he thinking about me? Or is he lying with Mirai? I drift into a fitful sleep, wondering what my husband is up to. It's been too long since I've slept alone. I wince as the realization crosses my mind. It causes me to sit up. I've been taking Kade for granted.

He's been good to me, regardless of whether he's sleeping with the maids or Mirai. I expected the warlord to be abusive, but he hasn't beaten or raised his voice to me. It's been fifty-eight days since he put me in the carriage. No incident thus far. Having my guard up has closed me off to the fact Kade hasn't treated me poorly. My mother made those insinuations to scare me.

If Kade chooses Mirai over me, I hope he doesn't send me back to Syrosa. I couldn't handle the humiliation or my mother's solid grip on my neck. Too many dreadful things happened in Sloane castle. I never want to see it again. Penelope isn't there. Neither is Margaux. My husband might be betraying me, but I don't think he's a monster like my mother.

***

I entertain myself by riding my horse, reading, and meandering the castle. Kade should be home today. I expect his return. This morning brought sunny weather but lots of wind. My hair is blowing in every direction. I use a velvet hair ribbon to tie it up. The tail whips my face. The breeze is constant, but it's refreshing.

Somehow I find my way into the room where Seneca's portrait hangs. I inspect each brushstroke. Capturing the warlord's face must have been expensive. He stares at me with cruel eyes I now see also have a glint of sympathy in them. Francis opens the creaky door.

"Have you come to admire Lord Seneca's portrait, my lady?" he asks. I nod and turn back to the warlord. Francis steps closer but doesn't invade my space.

"Are you curious to know more about him and Lord Kade?" he asks, and I nod enthusiastically.

I enjoy hearing about who Kade was. Perhaps I will someday understand who he is.

"Lord Kade took over as military commander after his father died. He was twenty-one and inexperienced but it didn't stop him from becoming the best soldier Tessafaye has seen," he starts and I listen carefully.

"Because of his background, he has accepted various refugees. He's the first lord to allow women to join his army. Before Mirai, we had another female mercenary named Esmé. She was from the southeast lands, trying to escape the war and genocide. She fought in the battle against the skinwalkers. Shortly after she got pregnant by a fellow mercenary and they went to live in the city," says Francis as he guides me out of the room. Over my shoulder, I say goodbye to my father-in-law.

Another female mercenary. Was she beautiful like Marisol? Youthful with full pouty lips and russet brown skin? Francis and I walk through the empty halls. The place is quiet, without all the rowdy men.

"Lord Kade has rebuilt the impoverished parts of the city. He didn't want it to be the slums he grew up in," he starts again. I nod and he escorts me to the garden. Gold and black poppies are my sanctuary. We both appreciate their radiance.

"I haven't seen that man slow down in a decade. One time I asked him why he was working so hard all of a sudden and you know what he said?" Francis eyes me and grins. I shake my head to humor him. "He said there was something he wanted, but he refused to elaborate," laughs Francis. This intrigues me. I turn my attention to the mountains and contemplate what Kade desired.

"He should be here soon," he says and goes back into the castle.

I stay in the garden. Kade could arrive anytime and I should be here when he gets back. A good wife would be eagerly anticipating her husband's return home. Sitting among the poppies, I'm set free of my anxiety. Their fragrance is to die for. I close my eyes and let the sun kiss my skin.

As though summoning him, I sense the ground vibrating beneath me. The tiny rocks and pebbles slide across the dirt. I open my eyes to see a line of men in formation approaching the castle. Kade is in front.

I stand up and smile. He signals for the men to go ahead and veers off to the side. Kade reaches for my hand. He pulls me onto his horse.

"I brought you something." He fishes a strawberry sized stone from his pocket. It's sea green and black with dark red spots on it. "It's a bloodstone," says Kade. It's not like anything I've seen before. I like how he thought of me.

This evening we feast more than we normally do. The men are knocking over their cups of wine and dancing. A few of them take a maid's hand and they join in on their fun. The fruitful hunt brings a jovial presence into the castle. Kade and his men are discussing this month's preparations. I'm busy watching everyone celebrating.

"Would you care to dance, my lady?" asks a young mercenary. He nods at Kade and smiles at me. I look at my husband to see what I'm supposed to do. Kade releases his iron hold on me and the boy escorts me to where the people are dancing.

I'm thankful to know this dance. I had to learn it to please one suitor or another. The young mercenary and I press palms and walk around in a circle, sliding our feet, and he spins me around. The young man gives me to another mercenary, one older than Kade, and we repeat the dance. I feel awkward that Kade isn't the one spinning me, but don't want to be rude.

To my dismay, I end up with Mirai. She and I touch our hands together and it ignites the envy I have inside. Her eyes are bewitching, flawless fair skin, and straight black hair. She has a serious face. It enchants me. The female mercenary spins me and gives me back to the young man who asked me to dance in the first place.

"You're really good at dancing," he says. The crowd is cheering and laughing around me. "We are happy to have you here with us, Lady Amadeus." He takes me back to Kade, who has his arm around me in an instant. I can tell by the way he's touching me he's drunk.

"Having fun?" he asks. I nod. "I didn't know you liked to dance."

His words are slow but not slurred. The other men are making crass comments. There is tons of noise in the dining hall. I'm having a difficult time collecting my thoughts.

Dax and Kristopher are dancing with Marisol and another maid. I don't like Kristopher's grimy hands on her. They spin the girls and their hair fans out. Kade notices me watching and his face changes.

"Stay away from them, Ama. I don't want you encouraging them in any way," he says, and I nod. This is the first time Kade has made what he wants from me clear.

CHERISHED

18

I was going through my things, and found the round mahogany box I keep Penelope's notes in. Opening the lid unleashes crumpled paper onto the ground. I pick one up. This one says: "Adrian always looks like she smells horse manure," in her bold and precise script. I start to cry, but don't stop myself. Another note on the floor reads: "One day you will meet a man like the ones in your stories." This one makes me cry even more.

The sun moves past the windows of Kade's room. I spent the entire afternoon reading every note my dear sister wrote to me. Most of them are funny, some of them cheer me up, and all of them are precious because she wrote them.

Tears fall onto the white pages. I wipe them away quickly so as not to destroy the fragment of Penelope I have left. Instead of defying my urge to cry, I let it happen. What do I have to hide? Kade already thinks I'm a fragile, wilting flower. If crying makes me weak, then allow me to be weak.

Penelope is sitting next to me, her ghost playing with my hair. I reach for her, but she waves and is gone. Rereading her notes, I hear her voice again. It heals and devastates me. Why do people I love keep getting taken away from me? A thousand pieces of myself obliterated. Perhaps I hesitate giving Kade my heart because I'll die without the rest of it.

"Ama, why are you crying?"

He's standing right next to me. I have my sister's notes in a half circle in front of me. They are black and white, but in the shape of a rainbow. Kade kneels down and looks at the writing he can't read. If he was literate, we could communicate better. I sigh and gather up the notes to put back into their resting place.

Kade hands me a piece of paper. "These are from your sister, aren't they?" he asks.

I nod, and it starts up the tears again. Kade grits his teeth in discomfort. I don't think he is used to women crying around him.

"You and Penelope were close," he states.

I nod because it's hard to explain. After my father died, I thought everyone in my family hated me. Then one day Penelope was at my side. But of course she died, too.

"I'm sorry. I learned about her death upon my arrival for our wedding. I didn't know what to say." Kade keeps his head down. This is the first time I've seen him show remorse. I wave it off to show it's okay.

"I'll be right back," he says, and I put the mahogany box on the vanity. I sit in my chair and look at the disheveled mess I am. To assuage my shame, I clean up my face and start brushing my hair. Kade returns with his hands behind his back.

"Here," he says and pulls out a small white dog with brown ears and little brown paws. The puppy has brown spots on their back. It wriggles in Kade's powerful hands, panting. Kade gives me the dog, who immediately gets cozy in my lap and nuzzles me. "You like dogs, don't you?" he asks. The puppy stands up to lick my chin. I nod and smile for Kade.

"He's yours. His name is Rupert," says Kade. I'm perplexed by his sweet gesture. The puppy curls up in my lap. Kade pets the puppy, who yawns and kicks his paws. "I wanted to surprise you later, but now seemed like a good time to give him to you."

My icy barrier is melted by Kade's thoughtful gift. I hold the sleeping puppy to my chest. Rupert has short, soft fur and the lovely puppy scent. I stand up and kiss Kade, longer than I usually do. The puppy is making cute noises from his dreams and I want to show Marisol.

I find her fixing a floral arrangement near the stairs. She gasps in delight when she sees what I'm holding. I hold the puppy out to her and she immediately starts rubbing his tummy and between his ears.

"What an adorable dog. Lord Kade got him for you, didn't he?" she asks. I nod and turn around. Kade didn't follow me. "I think he's the cutest thing I've ever seen." Marisol is giddy from the intoxicating innocence of the puppy.

Rupert and I spend the rest of the late afternoon in the garden. After he wakes from his nap, he runs around the poppies, barking at them when the wind shakes the stems. It makes me laugh. The puppy's tongue hangs out, off to the side, as he bounds after beetles and butterflies.

I snap my finger to prevent him from harming the smaller creatures. He is a good dog and responds by stopping his chomping, but continues to parade around the flowers. Rupert grows tired and comes back to my lap.

"It's nice to see you smiling, my lady." It's Francis. I show him the puppy and he chuckles. "Lord Kade wants to ensure your happiness. You mentioned you were lonely. Now if he would stop with that damn schedule of his," he grumbles, but recovers immediately. "My apologies. I shouldn't be speaking of your relationship casually."

I wave it off. Francis couldn't offend me. He is a pure person. I know he means well no matter what it is he's doing. The shade of the palm tree vanishes with the sunset. Kade appears next to me. Desert sand eyes stare down at me and my new friend.

***

The scratchiness at the back of my throat was where it started. Then it moved to my back and my muscles began to ache. Soon I was sweating with fever. The sickness found a way into the bottom of my lungs, making them constrict and wheeze.

No blood on the handkerchief when I cough. This is reassuring. Penelope's sleeves had rusty stains on them. This doesn't stop Kade, Francis, and Marisol from worrying about me. I assume they know of my sister's condition and are prepared for the worst.

I don't mind dying. Not that I want to kill myself, but sometimes I tire of waking up and having to be alive. It hurts to exist. My life isn't worthwhile. Kade has my family's wealth. I'm just a body for trade. A piece of property.

My hair is sodden from sweating in my sleep. I want to take a bath but my body is heavy. It's hard to sit up or focus. I'm too hot and in a daze. Cold chills keep me from sleeping soundly. Nightmares invade my psyche as soon as I cross over.

Someone is saying my name. I can't stop coughing. My face is drenched in perspiration, bangs sticking to my cheeks. I hear it again. A man is saying my name. I shouldn't disobey him, but a thick haze engulfs me and I can't do anything.

In my nightmares I see my father, but he has no eyes in their sockets. He's kneeling, opening his arms to me, but his mouth has sharp fangs. A demonic version of my father. I run down the hall, but Adrian trips me. She has antlers and claws. I try to evade her, but she shreds me apart.

"Ama." Kade's voice tears me out of the horrible place. I try to get up, but his palm pushes me down. "Your fever is gone. I think the worst is over," he says. I nod and take in a raspy breath. This bothers him. I can tell because when he's irritated or frustrated, he squints his eyes. "Try and get some more rest," he says and is gone in an instant.

Four days of lying in bed has me bored and listless. I want to read, but my eyes are too tired. They are bleary even after two days of sleep. But is it a real rest if it is plagued by nightmarish beings?

Rupert has been a faithful companion, staying at my side. He licks my face and wags his curly tail. Having a dog has curbed my loneliness. He makes me feel loved. I nap with Rupert in my arms and wake to the sound of Marisol tidying up.

"Feeling better, my lady?" she asks. I nod and Rupert jumps off the bed and scampers out of the room. "I prepared a bath for you. Come," she says and puts her arm out for me. My knees are weak, but my lungs are clear and I don't feel as ragged. Marisol helps me into the tub. She has adorned with lily petals and dried leaves. It's a revitalizing aroma.

"You gave the entire castle a scare," she jokes as she gingerly washes my curls. Marisol makes sure not to be too rough and doesn't rip any of it out. I stare at her, confused.

"I know you can keep a secret, so I'll tell you," she starts with a devious grin. "Lord Kade was worried about you. And when he's worried, he is a vicious man. Snarling at the doctors, getting into it with the men over trivial things. He even snapped at Francis and I but we knew he didn't mean it."

She continues to fret over me and rinse my hair. I didn't think anyone would care if I fell ill. If I died here, would everyone be sad? Dying in Sloane castle would be an isolating and depressing experience. It would be like nothing of importance happened.

"He'll be happy to see you up and about," says Marisol.

I splash water on my face. My fingertips trace my brow bone and nose. I hope Kade isn't upset with me for getting sick.

Hopefully, Francis isn't angry with me for Kade's aggressive behavior. Marisol is passive and doesn't let it bother her. There's a light mist outside. An innocuous drizzle. What if Kade doesn't let me play in the rain anymore? Would he impose such a rule now I've stressed him out with my fragility?

Kade's footsteps are distinguished. I can recognize them among the many men who walk the halls. He enters and Marisol makes a quick escape. Her long hair swaying in the doorway is all I see.

He hands me a glass of water with an assortment of tea leaves, ginger, and lemon wedges. It's refreshing considering how dehydrated I am. I drink it without any orders. He nods but doesn't say anything.

We sit in two worlds. Water sloshes out of the tub. Not totally quiet, but the steam captures the essence of it. Wind rustles the leaves of a begonia in the window. Teeny raindrops fall outside. The shape of silence is drawn as a sketch.

"I thought I might lose you," he says.

I reach for him. He doesn't seem agitated, but in his eyes I can see there's something dark lurking behind the dune colored iris.

PAPER AND POPPIES

19

The people of the castle have been polite to the point of excess. Everywhere I go it's "Oh, my lady, you look so beautiful." Or they say "My lady, don't go out without a coat, you might catch a chill." Marisol told me Kade becomes cruel when he's stressed out. Everyone must be on their best behavior.

I've been feeling better for over a week but still it's "You can't ride your horse yet," and worst of all, "No standing out in the rain."

Definitely a rule I'm going to break. I can't obey this one. I'm walking around the courtyard and garden with Rupert. He plays rough and runs like mad but falls over helpless and exhausted. I let him tire himself out and put him in his bed in Kade's room by the fireplace.

Not to sound distasteful, but I'm ecstatic to have a minute to myself. If the puppy isn't at my side needing affection and exercise, Kade is standing too close. Both of them have been at my heels for days.

Francis keeps asking if I need anything, if I have the books I want, and frets over the amount of food they give me. I have my appetite back, but I don't need four different dishes served to me each meal.

I read at least two books a day. There's not enough time to read more. It's okay, but I can't keep up with all the new material Francis buys from the shops in town. Then there's Marisol, who I adore, but everyday she touches my hair, my face, she laces up the back of my dresses. Hands are all over me. I used to get anxious at the idea of being alone and now I can't handle another hour of this nonsense.

Kade's phantom hand in my hair has me running for the door. I don't dislike his hands on me, but I'm not sure what to make of our marriage. He has been gone most of the time. Now he has me at his side or is right behind me as I peruse the library or wander the castle. I can't enjoy my exploration with him hovering over me, so I sit by the poppies or play with Rupert.

I manage to elude my husband and the others. Sneaking into the garden, I inhale the wonderful scent of poppies. A group of mercenaries are emerging from the stables. There's a brittle cypress tree with a large shadow. I step back into the dark and hope no one notices me.

Dax, Kristopher, and five other men are shouting at one another. They talk like they're mad at each other, but they're smiling.

"Might as well have a good time now that we're home," says Dax, who punches Kristopher and Kristopher retaliates by leading the pack.

"The girls at the brothel better be ready for us!" shouts one of the scruffy men.

"Doesn't matter if they're ready," jokes another.

They whoop and holler as they make their way down the path leading to the city. Does Kade talk like them when I'm not around? The men often make lewd remarks amongst themselves, but he doesn't participate. Who knows what he says in my absence.

This is my chance. I scurry from the garden to the courtyard. No one is out here and I skip around, reveling in my autonomy. Kade is probably looking for me, but I want to be by myself a little bit longer. Kristopher is right about me. I'm a rotten wife.

If I were a boy, I could be bad, and no one would blink an eye. They'd expect it from me. No one could tear me down because I'd be taller than all of them. If I were a boy, people would ignore me and it wouldn't bother me one bit.

I round the corner and am met with the seductive eyes of Mirai. "Pardon me, my lady," she says. Her shoulder guard is on and she's holding her sword. No one is on the field with her. She must be training on her own.

Mirai practices a few techniques in front of me. She is a skilled fighter. Agile and cunning, unlike the men. The runaway princess mesmerizes me with her prowess. She smiles at me over her shoulder.

"Do you want to try?" she asks.

Her accent is unfamiliar. I like how it makes her sound whispery. I step closer and decide I do. She hands me a sword. I mimic her footing, her posture. Mirai doesn't attempt to strike me. I initiate to see what will happen.

The female mercenary blocks me, of course, but she charges at me and I'm the one blocking her. My obsession gets the better of me. I look at her neck. No red marks. I chastise myself for being ridiculous. I'm fighting another girl with a sword and searching for signs of my husband's infidelity. Who am I anymore?

She digs into the grass with her heel and pushes into me. For a petite woman, she is strong. I step back and dodge her move. The breeze pulls her hair off to the side. She is a gorgeous assassin. Mirai wipes the sweat from her forehead. The glove on her hand is masculine compared to her beauty.

"You have spirit," she says and stomps off with a grin on her face.

What is the runaway princess so happy about? The sword in my hand makes me never want to put it down. It's like when I shot the gun. I feel powerful. Like a man.

***

Folding tiny red pieces of paper with care, I turn them into poppies. I use ink to make the filaments in the center. The crinkling of the paper has been a satisfying and singular sound. My fingers bend, fold, and crease. In the middle of my poppy field, I've made a horse. Kade is illiterate, but I wrote down our wedding vows on the piece of paper before creating a tiny replica of Fang.

It's our anniversary. The first year's theme is paper. It doesn't seem real. We've been married for three-hundred and sixty-five days. I've got to know him over the course of three months. He isn't a stranger to me anymore. Yet I can't figure out what he is. He's my husband, and I'm his wife, but what does that mean when one can't speak and the other doesn't?

I'm not angry with Kade. He hasn't been violent with me; he hasn't even scolded me. Most of the time, he is aloof, but we have moments of authenticity. I've been surprised by his acts of kindness. Kade might be the infamous warlord's son, but he isn't at all like what I imagined.

My mother convinced me I was ugly because my face reminds her of my father's. To her, his fiery hair and freckled skin were intriguing. On me, they were a bitter reminder. I glance at myself in the vanity mirror as I finish my present for Kade.

Since being here, I haven't been ignored or slept alone. There have been days where I was content. My reflection is me, but the way I see it has changed. I don't think I'm as pretty as my sisters, but I'm not hideous. In fact, I have grown to like my curious green eyes.

Kade keeps me at his side when we are together. It's nice to have someone even if it's one-sided. I'm not in love with Kade, but I've grown attached. It's silly to me. If he leaves for a few days, I miss him. I watch the way he acts around Mirai. The thought of them sleeping together lingers at the back of my skull. I hurt my own feelings. Sometimes I watch him training the men. Is this what wives do? Spy on their husbands and assume infidelity?

His people have been receptive. They are warm and welcoming. I never met my own people. Syrosa held me in contempt for being a burden to Queen Kathryn. No one was to mingle with the silent princess. Her affliction might rub off on someone. Kade hasn't allowed anyone to treat me poorly. No one teases me for being a mute. I haven't had anybody scoff at me since we've been together.

A strong hand grips my shoulder.

"Happy anniversary," says Kade. He leans down and kisses my cheek. His eyes move from me to my project. "Is that for me?" he asks. I pick up the poppy field with the horse in the middle and hand it to him. I smile really big. "Thank you."

Kade's charming grin consumes his face for a moment. I think he likes it. He helps me out of the chair. We make our way down the hall. Marisol and another maid are cleaning but stop to wave at us. Kade nods and I wave back. Marisol winks at me, which makes me giggle. She has this childish nature about her.

The sky is burnt orange. Summer air smells like fresh florals and sun soaked grass. Tessafaye gets cold at night but stays sunny all year. Back in Syrosa, we had snowy winters and dreadfully hot summers. There are occasional rains in Tessafaye but everyday feels like springtime.

My husband leads me outside and escorts me to the field. Everyone is waiting for us. I'm not sure what is happening. They are holding brightly colored paper lanterns. All of them are smiling at us, except Dax and Kristopher. They have bruised chins and bloody noses from Kade's unforgiving training sessions.

"Happy anniversary!" they say in unison. Kade kneels down and kisses me in front of everyone. The crowd cheers for us.

"Look," he says, and I open my eyes. Kade points to the sky and I see a rainbow of paper lanterns taking flight. His people light candles inside the lanterns and they are pulled towards the horizon.

His people are clapping and whistling. They seem excited for us. Tessafaye has started to feel more like home than Syrosa ever did. Kade lifts me off my feet and we watch the parade of paper lanterns cheek to cheek. The sun is setting, enhancing the glow of the flames inside. What a marvelous display.

"Do you like your gift?" he asks. I nod my head but can't rip my eyes away from the paper lanterns floating up into the sky and turning into stars. Kade holds my chin and has me face him. "Are you happy?" I smile and kiss him. "Good," he says.

A SECRET WHERE THE SUN FALLS

20

I'm running around the courtyard with Rupert. He is energetic. His vivacity rubs off on me and I skip around him as he barks and scampers. Our spirits bounce off one another. I can't stop smiling as I rush into the garden after him.

Rupert is barking at butterflies as he dashes past the gardener and two servants. They step aside and let us through. I wave to them as I run by. Francis is taking a walk and we interrupt his minute to himself with our racing. He seems taken aback by our wildness.

It's starting to feel like home. Everyone tries to make me comfortable. I don't think about my old life anymore. When I first got here, I compared everything to it. Now there is no need. Tessafaye's ruggedness is alluring. Syrosa was a refined kingdom, but lacked anything heartfelt. It was a soulless state. We didn't fight for ourselves after my father died and when he did, so did our integrity.

My dog jumps on me, and I scoop him up. His slobbery tongue is licking my face. Having a pet has eased my anxiety. Rupert's company offers me solace. Neither of us can talk to each other, but we have a connection on a deeper level.

The weight of silence can be heavy or as light as air. In Syrosa, I was a burden. My affliction was a substantial problem. At least that's what they made me think. The people of Tessafaye don't scorn me. Kade would never let them, anyway. He doesn't seem to mind my muteness. I assumed the young warlord would be reluctant to take on a dumb girl as his wife, but Kade hasn't treated me as though it is an issue.

He doesn't make rude remarks the way other men have. Kade doesn't imply my affliction is attractive or unappealing. He's the first person to not mention it all. Why waste his valuable time, I suppose. He knew what he was getting into. I wonder what Queen Kathryn said to him. Was a threat involved, or did he simply want the money and the fame?

Rupert jumps out of my arms and runs off towards the stables. I follow him. This time he isn't barking. He sniffs like he is on something's trail. His tail sticks straight and he looks up. What is it, Rupert? I ponder visiting the horses. Kade has let me ride Ari again. She seemed happy to see me. Kade tried to help me up, and I showed him I could do it myself. He looked confused, but maybe he was impressed. I hope it didn't annoy him to know his wife had been practicing mounting a horse on her own. A lot of husbands would forbid such an act.

I step in the direction of the door, and Rupert stops me. He won't let me pass him. Getting under my feet and herding me back. What is going on? I decide to walk behind the stables. Maybe there is a critter which interests him hiding in the ferns. As I near the stables, I hear loud men's voices. It's Dax and another man. I kneel by the window and listen.

"I can't wait to go hunting again. Ever since we stopped going into battle, I've been bored out of my skull!" shouts Dax.

"It's not all bad. We get to spend our days eating, sleeping, and screwing those whores down at the brothel," laughs the other man.

"I'd rather be waging war and having my way with the red-headed wench," says Dax. His throaty voice has grime in it. My cowardly heart creeps up on me.

"You shouldn't say that." The other man sounds unaffected, like he suggested it out of loyalty to Kade.

"Come on, Eli. Don't act like you haven't had those kinds of thoughts about our fine lady," spits Dax. I'm trembling, the swooshing of the grass against my boots gets louder, and my neck is on fire.

"Stop it."

"What? You worried Lord Kade might hear me?" Dax eggs on his comrade.

"You shouldn't be so brash, Dax. One of these days, Lord Kade might unleash the rage he has on the battlefield onto you," says Eli.

"He already goes harder on me than anybody else. I don't regret what I said. A woman needs to be put in her place once in a while."

"That's for him to decide. She's his wife." There's a pause. I hear them tending to the horses. The unbuckling of saddles and rustling of hay. This is my chance to leave. But Dax speaks again.

"Don't you think it's odd?" he asks.

"What?"

"Our feared and loathsome leader marrying a dumb girl. I've never seen him interested in a woman. Didn't think he'd end up with a royal from the demilitarized kingdom."

"What is your obsession with her, anyway? If you're smart, you'll put her out of your thoughts," warns Eli. The tingle down my spine is making me sweat. A gust of wind blows through my dress and I hold myself to keep out the cold.

"I've never met a woman who hid from her husband all day to read," says Dax.

"Lord Kade isn't offended by it. Let it go," warns Eli again.

The stable is quiet. A horse neighs, but the men's conversation is over. I pick up Rupert and make a run for the castle. If Dax or Eli know I heard what they said, who knows what they will do to me?

Marisol and Francis glance my way. I slow my pace to not seem panicked. Rupert squirms and I put him down. I wave to the two of them. Once they are behind me, I walk as fast as I can without running. I arrive at the garden. Peering side to side, I see no mercenaries or maids. I decide to have a seat among the poppies to quell the anxious stirring in my stomach.

Rupert rolls in the grass. He sniffs the poppies and nips at little flying bugs. All can be well if I'm close to the poppies. They are a sanctuary for silence. But the quiet is gone. Dax and Eli are walking past me. They're being obnoxious. Eli says something; Dax guffaws at it. I pay attention to the man Dax divulged his dark desire to.

Eli is older than Kade. He has dark hair and light brown skin, like most northeastern people. His hands are square and buff. He has a scruffy beard and neck. I would say he's not bad looking, but he's standing next to Dax, which makes him appear distasteful.

* * *

***

Sunshine trickles in and the stained glass windows paint the floor of the library. I'm holding Rupert in one arm and pawing through books with my free hand. He lets me carry him just about anywhere. Right now, he appears to be taking a snooze.

I build my piles of books and rearrange them according to what I want to read first. There's at least a dozen new ones from Francis. He says I don't ask for enough. It must concern him. He gives me enough books to bury me. I'm not complaining. Francis is subtle, but I can tell he is kind and eager to please.

Rupert snores in my arm and his nose twitches. I giggle at this tiny monstrosity's cuteness. Funny, Kade would give me a dog, but we've become great friends. Rupert makes this place feel like home. Kade pets him and indulges me by letting us run around the castle like wild animals. I'm not sure if he particularly likes dogs. Wouldn't he have one of his own if he did? It may be a betrayal to Fang, though. They've been through everything, seen everywhere.

I'm bouncing Rupert around in my arms like a baby when Kade surprises me as I emerge from the pine shelves. "Do you like your new books?" he asks. Large gloved hands turn over leather bound pages he can't decipher. I crane my neck to look at him and nod. He holds my chin in his threatening fingers.

"I have to meet with the Tsar. It's a formality I've been putting off since winning the war," he says. Rupert wriggles out of my arm and jumps on the floor. His toenails make a loud clack when his paws meet the ground. "I'll be gone for a week."

Kade's absence makes me nervous. It's bothersome to have him looming over me, but I feel insecure without him. Knowing no one will cross me in his presence has made me bold. If he's not around, no one cares about me. Their obligation is to the lord of the castle.

"I don't want to go," he says and drops his hand. I don't want him to go either. He senses my unease and kneels down. "You don't have to worry. I'll come back as soon as I can." Kade brushes my bangs out of my eyes. He sees right through me.

"I haven't wanted to leave Tessafaye. We've been apart so often," he says and takes me by the hand. We exit the library. He guides me out of the castle and towards the garden. Francis and the gardener are tending to the new editions. Kade must have ordered for them to put in rows of tiger lilies. They're fresh and add a unique flare. "Do you like them?" he asks. I nod.

We walk through the maze of white and orange flowers. They have black and brown spots on them, but they don't look dirty. They are divergent blossoms. I run my fingertips over the stamen part of the plant. Gold dust coats my nails.

Was he telling me he thought I was beautiful? He hasn't said so. What did he mean? Men make little sense to me. He puts his arm around me and we admire the new flowers. Does this mean Kade appreciates such things? My husband is ambiguous. He could adore or despise something and keep a straight face. Neutrality in all regards.

If I were a boy, I'd wear a straight face. No one would ask me to smile. I could go days without being seen and no one would judge me for it. Girls would compete for my affection even if I didn't say a word to them. They'd still pine for me. If I were a boy, I wouldn't have to follow the rules. Men would curse my name for reasons other than what I look like and the fact I can't speak.

He takes me back into the castle. Kade isn't one to announce where we are going or what we are doing. I don't mind being at his side. Then I'm not alone and despite his cool demeanor, I want to be close to him. We are greeted by Marisol, who is holding Rupert. He looks pleased with himself. Marisol winks at me and scratches behind Rupert's ear.

We make our way up the many stairs. Dax and Kristopher are heading down to the foyer. I peek through my bangs to see two sets of blue ice staring back at me. Kade stops and his sonorous voice is in my ear.

"I expect you two to be ready to leave at sunrise," says Kade.

The men grimace at his hand on my waist.

"Yes, sir," they say in unison. Kade waits for them to keep walking. He eyes them as they make their way to the bottom.

If I were a boy, no one could call me weak. I wouldn't have to take their rude remarks. They'd do as I say and people wouldn't talk back to me. I could command an army like Kade. There'd be nothing anyone could do to stop me.

Kade closes the door to his room and starts tearing off my dress. I kiss him back as he has his way with me. To be touched by someone powerful but feel no pain has me wondering what I am to him. Kade breathes into my ear and I hold him tighter. He and I fall asleep until the sun is about to set. The sky is my favorite shade of coral. I sit up to watch the day fade. The rich full sun is whole and the three-quarter moon is envious. Muscular arms wrap around me.

"I'll be gone in the morning," he says into the blanket. I run my fingers through his hair. He and I witness the stars come out one by one.

"Do you think about me when I'm not around?" he asks. I have a fistful of black hair in my hand. It's foreign against my freckled skin. I nod and Kade closes his eyes. "Good."

***

The castle feels barren. I'm relieved to see he took Dax and Kristopher with him. But I'm most melancholy, Mirai is also with them. He always takes her on these trips. I wave off my suspicions and let the sun warm my face.

I retrieve Ari from the stables. She exhales dramatically when she sees me. Luring her out with a carrot, she settles. I pet her and let her finish the treat before jumping next to her. It takes me a couple of tries to warm up. Once I'm confident, I jump and swing my leg over her while holding the base of her mane. I manage to mount my house on the first try. Ari neighs like she is proud of me.

There's no one out except us. It's sort of exciting to be alone since I spend a majority of my day with Kade. He still gets up before the sun to train, but since our anniversary, he's with me most of the time. I wouldn't take the warlord as a sentimental man, but his gift to me was beautiful.

Ari and I do two laps around the castle. She trots through the courtyard. Her hooves go clip clop and echo against the emptiness. No maid or servant walking about. Not even a single mercenary can be found. I have Ari run through the field. She trusts me and I trust her. I'm able to sustain faster speeds without my cowardly heart stopping me.

I hear Rupert barking by the garden. Ari and I make our way back at a leisurely pace. We run into Francis, who is admiring the new flowers.

"Good afternoon, Lady Amadeus," he says. No one has called me by my full name in weeks. Kade calls me Ama. I smile for him and Francis widens his eyes. "If you don't mind me saying so, you look absolutely stunning."

I put my hand to my heart to show I like his compliment.

"I mean it. You make Kade want to stay in Tessafaye," he says in a quiet voice and touches one of the tiger lilies. "Bringing you here has made the castle feel more like home." I dismount Ari and strokes her side. Francis is a bit flabbergasted by my intrepidation, but allows me room to be odd. Rupert is at my heels and panting.

"A kingdom ruled by a warlord meant there wasn't any thought put into things like art or beauty. Since you've been here, the library has grown two fold. The garden is immaculate. Before your arrival, Lord Kade insisted on planting the petunias and jasmine. I was delighted when you asked for poppies. Distinct, elegant, but formal," he says and sighs.

Ari sniffs the top of my head. It tickles. Francis clears his throat.

"We're all so very happy to have you here, my lady. Lord Kade especially. It's like he has what he wanted," he says and walks away.

I lead Ari back to the stables and give her fresh water. She's become a good friend. I think we get along well. Rupert is jealous of her.

I find it hard to believe a burden like me could be welcomed, let alone wanted. Why would someone powerful like him find interest in a scrawny thing like me? Kade told me a young man broke into the castle to see me. I wonder who it was. Are they here right now? Finn walks in to check on the other horses. He wears a tired but handsome face. Unlike the other men, he isn't boisterous.

"Hello, my lady," he says. I wave at him. Ari nudges me and I hug her neck. She doesn't want me to go. "Your horse is fond of you. That's good."

I grin as I leave the stables and let Finn have his space. He isn't rude to me, but I don't want to get in his way. Kade gave me freedom, but it was Finn who took me into the village where I walked wherever I pleased. I'll be forever grateful he was my chaperone.

Back in Kade's room, I hold Rupert as I go over the wondrous items and rewards my husband has been collecting for over a decade. I turn giant reptilian eyeballs in the palms of my hands. In my fist I hold jagged teeth from dragons, basilisk, and chimeras. Kade isn't afraid of anything. It must be exhilarating being a boy. To be a great warlord must have its own intoxicating sense of control.

My feelings for my husband are strange. I'm cautious around him. He can be daunting and aloof, but I miss him when he's gone. I think that's what he wants. Does he miss me? He said he didn't want to go. I've never been in love. Is this it?

The closest thing I can think of is how the stories about knights and mercenaries doing anything to have that certain girl affected me. Did Kade ever take part in competitions to win a kiss? I clench my fist around a shirt of his. He's good looking and brave. I know I'm not the only one he's been with.

THE GIANT

21

His absence makes me tense. Rupert is a fabulous friend, but it's not the same. My hair smells like cloves. I twist it in between my palms to tame my nervousness.

Marisol comes in with my dinner. She knows I'm too shy to eat in the dining hall without Kade. "Good evening, my lady," she says. Marisol sets the platter of vegetables, fruit, and lamb. It smells delicious, but I'm not hungry. I smile and touch my heart to say thank you.

"Would you like some company? You must be lonely with Lord Kade being away," she says and sits next to me. I nod. Marisol is an understanding person. I can relax around her.

She plays with my hair as I pick at the grapes and piece of meat. "Your hair is pretty, my lady. All the girls talk about how they wish they had lengthy red curls like you."

Marisol turns up the corners of her pouty mouth. The light of the fire dances on the bridge of her nose. Wispy eyelashes cast spidery shadows on the apples of her cheeks. I didn't think anyone would want my hair. The women I grew up with couldn't stand to touch it. Adrian told me it hurt her eyes to look at.

"No one cares for your hair more than Lord Kade, though. He instructed me sternly to not break a single strand," she laughs.

I look at her, mortified. Did he really berate Marisol to not damage my curls? She squeezes my shoulder in a sisterly fashion. "Don't be upset, my lady. Lord Kade wasn't harsh. But I could tell it was important to him."

Marisol twists the hair on the sides of my head and pins it to my crown. "Your father was from the Scorse Isles. I heard everyone there has coppery curls. In Yeracho, most people have reddish brown skin and dark hair. Travelers from the western and central parts of the continent pass through frequently, resulting in a small population of southeasterners with amber hair or blue eyes. I've met many people, but I've never seen anyone with forest green eyes like you," she says and stares at me with a warm expression.

I think she is happy to have met me. If I could, I'd tell her I feel the same. I surprise her and myself by embracing her. Marisol hugs me the way Penelope did. It brings back painful memories but also revitalizes the memory of my sister.

"It's good to have you home," she whispers. I finish my dinner and she gathers up my dishes. "Thank you for letting me keep you company. I'll see you in the morning."

Marisol leaves me and I make my way to the balcony. It's a starry night. The clouds are sheer cream that's spilled over the moon. She is complete and too bright to block out. A gust of wind chases away the clouds, swirling them, creating a ripple effect.

I hold on to the railing and look out past Tessafaye, beyond the lush green grass and sand, to the desert lined by mountains in the distance. The breeze moves through the juniper trees and picks up my hair. The fragrance is woody and clean. I imagine an invisible dragon weaving his way through the city to the castle.

There is no need to be creative when actual monsters exist. I shake my head, assuming it's my ridiculous thoughts, but it's not. From the desert I crossed to get here, a large shadow emerges. The ground quakes and a flower pot falls over.

A giant is approaching. They are dimwitted but crush everything in their path. He lumbers through the sand. Dirty feet touching the ground cause the earth to convulse. Sloppy beasts, they don't intend to destroy, but do so because of their lack of intelligence.

Kade left behind eight of his men. They stand dumbfounded in front of the castle. They're yelling at each other, unable to form a plan. The giant is coming straight for us. He is slow but ominous. There has to be a way to get him to turn around. We don't have the manpower to fight a creature like this.

I get an idea. It flies through my skull like a bullet. Before I know it, I'm rushing down the stairs. Francis has his mouth open to speak, but I push past him. The stairs go on forever. At the bottom is Finn.

"Lady Amadeus, stop! What are you doing?" shouts Finn as I evade his reach. "Grab her!" he yells, and another mercenary chases after me, but I dodge him as well.

Finn's bold voice reverberates in my ears. "Don't let her leave the castle!" I'm not strong like the men but because of my small stature I can outmaneuver them. They run into each other, trying to get a hold of me. Bulky bodies smash into one another and I make it out the door.

I stop by the field where the men train and open the shed. There's two bags of gunpowder. I take them both and put a flintstone and firesteel in my pocket. In the stable, Ari is cool and collected. The shaking earth does not perturb her like the other horses. I jump on her back and take off. This is the first time I've gone outside the castle walls by myself.

"My lady, wait!" Francis is calling for me, but I speed ahead. Over my shoulder, I see Finn and three other men notice me, but it's too late. They can't catch up to me.

Ari and I ride through the open valley. A mix of sand and feathery grass. The moon moves over me and the stars propel us forward. We get closer to the giant and I make out his idiotic daze. The eyes have no focus. The beast is drooling onto his chest. His feet move the earth with each step, but Ari isn't afraid.

I hope this works. In the bottom of the bags, I tear tiny holes with my desperate fingers. I hold them out and let the powder spill in a thin line at our side. I have Ari run back and forth across the meadow. The white lines shine under the full moon. I tie Ari to one of the lone cypress trees, away from the gunpowder.

The giant is leaving the desert. His feet meet the grass and my heart pounds. If this doesn't work, I'm not sure what will happen. I don't want anyone to get hurt. This has become my home. These people mean something to me. I can't let Tessafaye be destroyed while my husband is away. When the giant is close enough, I use the flint and firesteel to create a spark that lands on the piece of cloth.

Here it goes. I throw the burning cloth onto the white powder. It ignites for a moment, but the instantaneous flames frighten the giant.

He stumbles backwards, cowering. He is confused by what happened. Instead of inspecting further, he slinks back into the desert.

***

Finn is cross. I've never seen him like this before. "You could have gotten seriously injured. Do you know what Lord Kade would do to me if you were to hurt yourself?"

I put my head down and nod. Kade will be upset with me, too. Finn grips his hair like he wants to rip it out.

"I'm grateful to you, my lady. Your cleverness saved us. But it is also going to be the death of me," he says. I'm not sure, but I think Finn is praising me. "First, I was concerned you were going to break your neck riding your horse by yourself. Now I've got bigger things to worry about."

I shift my weight. My anxiety is making me fidget. I try to act noble and refined. It's hard to stand still. Finn steps closer to me. I recoil, expecting him to strike or scream. He does neither and kneels in front of me. Taking my hand, he says, "Thank you for protecting Tessafaye."

No man has spoken to me quite like this. He looks up at me and I realize he is truly appreciative. Finn isn't lecherous or obnoxious like most men. I understand why Kade chooses him to watch over me. This must be why he takes Dax and Kristopher with him. Better to keep the ones he doesn't trust close. I wince, thinking about why he takes Mirai.

Finn rises and sighs. "Please try to stay out of trouble."

He walks off towards his room, mumbling to himself. If Kade was stern with Marisol about brushing my hair, what does he say to Finn about keeping an eye on me? I let him be. Finn is stressed and doesn't need me reminding him of his nagging responsibilities.

My dog and I have a lovely time chasing each other around the tall tiger lilies and dashing through the poppies. He barks and wags his tail. We keep running around the flowers. I manage to lose him and hide in the shadow of a palm tree. Rupert's nose finds me and I jump out at him.

"Lady Amadeus," says Francis. I peek over my shoulder. The elderly man is standing next to a tiger lily. It sways in the warm and spicy breeze. He clears his throat in the most distinguished way. "Your astute ideas are unprecedented."

I lean down and pick up Rupert. He nuzzles me and immediately falls asleep. The snoring dog in my arms slows my pulse.

"We are in awe of you. Not only are you brilliant, but you displayed the kind of courage Lord Kade would have in that situation."

Really? I can't call myself courageous. The sad thumping of my heart won't allow it. I did what was necessary. I couldn't let a monster crush Kade's land.

"You kept us safe when we should have been watching over you," laughs Francis. He pets Rupert and speaks to me in a soft, grandfatherly way. "I hope this means you think of Tessafaye as your home."

I hold Rupert close to my chest and nod. This is my home. Kade gave it to me. I didn't know if anywhere could be home. Syrosa has faded because it lacked what it takes to earn my memory. I want to be here. Tessafaye has become a part of me.

"Glad to know you are happy," he says.

A maid and servant have questions for him, so he turns from me but waves over his shoulder. The maid and servant take me in with big eyes. They talk amongst themselves as they walk. The maid misses a step to get one last glance at me.

I wait until they're gone to collapse. This wakes Rupert, who licks my chin and yawns. My knees press into the blades of grass. Why can't I breathe? Am I falling ill? I choke on my sobs and hold Rupert next to my face. He licks away the tears.

The poppies whisper to one another. A gust of wind pulls out my hair ribbon. I concentrate on what the flowers are saying. The blossoms speak about loss, longing, and love. My hair is being tugged on by the breeze. I'm having a hard time catching my breath. Rupert whines, and I massage his petite body.

I've been called many things. A dumb girl, sickly, odd, dirty, and scrawny. My mother convinced me I was ugly, useless, and insufficient. The countless suitors I've been meeting with for the last decade have called me countless names. No one has ever said I was courageous.

ROUGH RECOVERY

22

The men have arrived. Kade isn't at the front like usual. I rush to meet them at the gate. There's a commotion among the mercenaries. Mirai is walking with Fang's reins in her hands. What's wrong with Kade? He's slumped over on the back of the horse. The booming of my heart threatens to explode.

Mirai senses my horrified plea for him. "Lord Kade is alright, he's just unconscious," she says. Fang pauses and the men go around us. I get closer and see Kade's right leg is bandaged. My hand reaches for him, but he can't feel me. "We were attacked by raptors. One of them got a hold of his leg. I sliced the creature's head off before it damaged him severely. Don't worry, it looks worse than it is," says Mirai in her boyish whisper.

Raptors are a hybrid creature. A combination of reptile and bird of prey. They stand on two feet, have a snake head and feathered wings. The pictures depicted of them in the books I read were terrifying. Their feet have ginormous talons and their mouths are full of rows of teeth.

I can't stop sobbing. It's unexpected. Kade has been my husband for a year, but I've only started to get to know him. He is aloof, meaning more to me than I mean to him. Still, it pains me to see him like this. I'm encumbered by my sorrow.

"My lady, please don't cry," says Mirai. She reaches for my face with her silky hand and wipes away my tears. I can't help it though. They keep pouring out of me. Dax and Kristopher cast dishonorable stares in my direction. Mirai glares at them and shields me from their view by stepping closer. "Save your tears. Lord Kade will be fine."

She leads Fang through the gate, and Francis is quick to call for Marisol. Finn and another mercenary lift Kade from his horse and carry him upstairs. Marisol has gathered water, towels, and clean bandages. She follows the men while I stand frozen in place.

I don't move until Marisol retrieves me. Her mouth is moving, but the words are indistinguishable. Clicking of tongue and breath moving through teeth. It's a language I can't understand. She's holding my elbow with a soft touch and guiding me to Kade's room.

Marisol takes a moment to stroke my hair and look me in the eye. "He'll heal quickly, my lady. It's a large wound, but the harm was minimal. You don't need to worry," she says.

This makes me cry relentlessly. Marisol looks remorseful, like she said something wrong. I shake my head and keep my eyes on the ground. She lets me have my moment of hysteria. I choke on sobs as we near Kade's room.

She ushers me in and closes the door. Kade is in his bed. The fire has been lit. It's cozy, but my thundering heartbeat is making me pace around anxiously. Every time I attempt to get near Kade, I lose my nerve and stay on the other side of the room.

In the light of the fire, Kade's trinkets glow. Precious metals and crystals. Eyeballs, claws, and teeth of beasts. I run my fingers through the feathers belonging to something huge. Kade's armor and sword sit off to the side of the chair. I fiddle with his helmet. It's heavier than I thought it would be. The armor has to weigh a ton.

The right greave is mangled. It looks like the raptor must have sunk its teeth into it. It's amazing it didn't permanently damage his leg. He has Mirai to thank for that. I'm his useless wife who is too weak and wilts like a flower in the desert heat.

Holding his disfigured greave, I ponder what it's like to be Kade. How taxing is being brave all the time? I push my heart back into the depths of my ribs and make my way to him. If he can fight monsters, I can face him.

There is tension around his eyes as he sleeps. Marisol gave him herbs to relieve the pain, but he groans as he shifts his body. Beads of sweat build at his hairline. I place my hands on his temples. They feel icy against his blazing skin. He coughs and opens his eyes.

"Hey," he says. For some reason, this starts up my sobbing again. I haven't heard his voice in a week. It confuses me, but I missed him like he wants me to.

Kade's voice is gruff. "We were almost home when we were ambushed by the raptors," he says and holds onto my wrists.

To be strong is a blessing and a curse. No one has great expectations for someone like me. For someone of Kade's status, this must be demeaning. I sort of like seeing him like this. A vulnerable side I didn't think existed. What a shameful thing to think. It makes me cry more.

Kade massages the inside of my wrist with his thumb. It pushes into the veins beneath the skin. He stares up at me with rueful eyes. The fire reflects in the dune colored iris. It catches me off guard, but Kade is smiling at me. He tugs on my arms to pull me closer.

"You're worried about me," he states. I nod, causing teardrops to fling from my chin. He sits up to kiss my lips. I taste salt and anise. "Good." He sinks into bed and falls back asleep, gripping onto me. I stare at the fire and stay by his side. Kade's charming smile remains on his face while he dreams.

***

My husband is calling for me. He has to walk on crutches for the time being. This slows him down, which irritates him. Since he can't follow me around constantly, he calls for me twice as often. I don't mind. It's better than being ignored.

"Ama, come here please," he says from the foyer. I rush down the stairs. If he's anything like the other men I've met, he won't enjoy being kept waiting. The thing is, I don't think Kade is like other men. I thought he'd be ruthless. He might have murdered for his money, but he's not the monster I thought the young warlord would be.

He calls my name again. I'm bounding down the last of the steps. Kade is leaning on his crutches, wearing an unnerved frown. I slow my pace and clasp my hands to keep them from fidgeting. His stern expression has me feeling nervous.

"Is it true?" he asks. I look at him, confused. He hobbles his way to the bottom of the stairs. "You spooked the giant back into the desert."

Will he be angry with me? I didn't mean to defy or disobey.

Tessafaye has become the place where I belong. I had to do something to protect it. He stands in front of me and I keep my head down but nod. I brace myself for him to strike me.

I time travel like when he returned home from the war, unable to distinguish one second from the next. His arms are around me. I open my eyes, realizing there is no danger. Kade hugs onto me long enough for the shadows on the windowsill to shift.

"Thank you," he says into my ear. I shudder from his breath on my neck. Kade pulls back and tries to decipher his cowering wife. "I hope this means you think of Tessafaye as your home."

We walk out to the garden. Kade scowls as we exit the castle, either from pain or from annoyance. Once we're in the middle of the tiger lilies and poppies, his stern expression fades. His eyes skim over the white flowers with orange tinged petals covered in spots.

"Do you want to go back to Syrosa?" he asks. Kade doesn't turn to me. His eyes remain on the rows of lilies. I hold on to his arm and shake my head. The thought of living in Sloane castle again is scarier than the precariousness of my new life. Kade tightens his jaw. "I saw your mother when I met with the Tsar."

My blood runs no more. It's frozen, dry ice sticking to blue veins. Is he going to give me back to her? I don't think I'll survive her next episode of rage.

"She said she missed you and made vague insinuations you may want to come home. I assured her you have everything you want."

Why would she do that? She was gauging Kade's reaction. My mother wanted to bait him into giving me back to her. She couldn't wait to get rid of me. Since Adrian has moved to Arwin and my other sisters are gone, my mother has no one to experience her wrath.

What nerve she has. My husband meets with the Tsar for winning the war against the chimeras and she has the audacity to imply she wants me back. She gave me to him and now she is seeking a return on her exchange. To ask at the Tsar's palace where Kade and his army were being honored astounds me.

Kade runs his muscular hand through my hair. "Kathryn Sloane is cold like winter." He lifts my chin so I'm looking right at him. "Everything about you reminds me of spring." I can't be certain, but I think the warlord might be a romantic as well.

The two of us stand next to tiger lilies taller than me. His hands are rough, but they are careful with me. We are surrounded by orange poppies where everything, including time and silence, come to a halt. The wind brings their peppery citrus scent to me.

Finn and Eli are headed towards the stables. They wave at us. I shy away because Eli makes me self-conscious. Their dark hair stands out against the light blue sky and the golden dunes. The breeze lifts their cloaks and makes whipping sounds.

"Do you want to stay with me?" he asks.

I grip onto the sleeve of his shirt and nod. Our marriage may have been forced, but I don't want to leave. I don't want to be with anyone else. Kade hasn't seemed bothered by my affliction. He lets me be myself.

"Your mother said someone was waiting for you back home. A young knight," he says. I shake my head. Unruly piles of curls bounce around my shoulders. My mother is trying to turn Kade against me by implying I wasn't pure.

"Her attempt at manipulating me wasn't successful. I knew she was trying to get a rise out of me."

I'm glad Kade can see through her royal facade. She is one to bark, but not foolhardy enough to bite. Kade isn't a man to be coerced.

"Kathryn Sloane thought I'd release you into her custody," he says and holds my shoulder, "But I'm not giving you up."

He hasn't been this forward with me. I figured he'd get rid of me if given the chance. It turns out Kade takes our marriage seriously.

NEVER THE SAME

23

Rupert gives me kisses while I peruse the library. The tremendous amount of books is intoxicating. There are lots of novels about beautiful princesses and brave knights. Francis made sure to include some adventurous stories involving intelligent young women who fight for themselves. I'm still a bit embarrassed about Francis asking if I was a romantic. He doesn't ask me about it anymore, but I see the subtle grin on the corners of his lips when he sees me reading a love story.

It's a possibility, but perhaps Kade doesn't find me to be an object, a plaything for when he is bored. What a silly idea: me, interesting to the warlord. He is an inscrutable person. Behind eyes the color of desert sand is a foreign universe.

What if I could speak? What would we talk about? Kade isn't a chatty man. It's fun to imagine the kinds of conversations we might have, though. We communicate in tenuous ways. I tug on his shirt or cloak to get him to pay attention to me. He puts his hand in my hair. Our marriage is wordless. No arguments or shouting. Kade raises his voice when training the mercenaries, but isn't one for yelling.

I hear a soft rustling noise. What was that? Rupert squirms in my arms and I put him down. He sniffs and lets a low growl grow in his throat. I set down the books I've been collecting and peer around the tall shelves. To my horror, I'm met with Dax and Kristopher.

"There's the sweet lady," says Dax with saliva coating his lips. I step back, but they lean forward.

"Look, she's frightened. I like the way she looks when she's scared," says Kristopher. I put up my hands to signal for them to stop. They don't.

"What kind of woman hides her nose in books all day?" snarls Dax. He lunges at me, but I dodge him and run into the maze of pine shelves.

"She wants to hide. Okay, Princess. Let's play a little game," says Kristopher. I sneak in between two shelves where it is most shadowy. The sun is in the middle of the sky.

"You treat Lord Kade worse than a dog. You should consider yourself lucky he'd take a wretched thing like you!" shouts Dax. His steps come closer. I hold my breath and he passes the shelf I'm hiding behind. Once he is far enough away, I slink through the dark parts of the library until I find a new hiding place. Rupert is looking for me, too. He's barking at the men.

"Piss off, you stupid mutt!" yells Kristopher.

Rupert keeps up his barking. He's following them, growling, and alerting someone to the library.

"Shut that thing up," Dax's voice is gravelly, filled to the brim with fury.

Then the most sickening sound. Rupert's small body being kicked into the wall. His barking ceases and I hear him whimper. I cover my mouth to stifle my uneven breathing. Poor Rupert, I want to check on him, but am worried about Dax and Kristopher's intentions.

"Come out, come out, wherever you are," sings Dax.

Manly footsteps draw near. They pass to my left and I scurry back towards where my dog is.

"Come here, Princess," Kristopher joins in on Dax's singing.

"Your little trick with the giant was real clever, but that's another thing wrong with you. You got too many ideas. A girl like you should focus on making her husband happy," says Dax.

"Yeah, why are you always veiling yourself in mystery? You think you're too good for us?" asks Kristopher.

I'm inching towards Rupert. He's lying limp on the ground. His stomach is moving. He's alive. Hold on, Rupert, I'm coming. As I tiptoe into the light to grab him, I feel a ginormous hand wrap around my upper arm.

"Gotcha," says Dax. His eyes are narrow and glazed over. I pull, but he's buff from fighting monsters. Kristopher is laughing, a hysterical fit. His eyes roll in the back of his head. I yank my arm, but it's of no help. Dax drags me over to the desk. I thrash in his grasp, knocking books off their proper shelves. There is a trail of them in my wake.

"Hold still," he growls and bends me over the oak desk. I flail, but he leans into me and Kristopher grabs my wrists.

"Do you think she fights him like this?" laughs Kristopher. Dax's bulge is pressed up against me. Big hands not belonging to Kade grip my breasts and hips.

Dax's lips graze my earlobe. "If only you could scream for me," he says. Kristopher's wild laughter makes me dizzy. His mouth is wide, unhinged like a snake. I thrash again, as hard as I can, but can't buck Dax or Kristopher off of me. "You and the runaway princess think you're better than me," Dax whispers into my ear. His lips are on my neck and his hand is pushing up my dress.

He's thrusting himself inside me, but I feel nothing. I go somewhere else. The day Kade gave me, Rupert comes to mind. It's what I think of as Dax defiles me and Kristopher watches. I endure his abuse for a moment and it's over. Kristopher loosens his grasp and lets me go. I look up to see his eyes wide, lip trembling. Over my shoulder is Kade with his dagger in Dax's chest.

Kade pulls out the blade and the westerner's blood exits the wound with force. It sprays onto the floor. Droplets land on my cheek. It's warm from his beating heart. Dax collapses and his body makes a hollow thud as it connects with the ground.

"Lord Kade! Please, no. It's not what it looks like," says Kristopher. He attempts to flee, but Kade grabs him.

"You either thought because of my injury I wouldn't notice my wife's absence or I wouldn't make it in time," says Kade.

My hands are palm down on the desk. I hold myself up but can't move.

"No, sir. It was all Dax's idea. He thought she was disrespecting you, thereby disrespecting Tessafaye," starts Kristopher, but Kade throws him onto the floor and begins wailing on him.

"Don't put the blame on her," says Kade as he smashes Kristopher's face into the cool floor.

Kristopher's blond hair is soaked with blood. It seeps out of his nose and mouth. In the sea of red are his icy blue eyes. They tear through me.

Kade turns to me but recenters his focus on the westerner. "Ama, don't look," he says. I cover my eyes but hear the disgusting sound of a blade entering flesh. There's a symphony of violent noises. I keep my eyes closed until Kade guides me out of the library.

Marisol draws us a bath. She was startled by the blood on us but asked no questions. Nothing seems real. I've started to shiver. My body isn't cold. It isn't anything. I can't feel my hands or my face. All I notice is the shaking originating in my spine. My body has begun to register what happened to me.

I get into the tub first. The warmth helps soothe my trembling arms and legs. I can't bear to face Kade. What does he see now he's witnessed me be violated by Dax? Kade has blood splattered across his cheekbones, the bridge of his nose, it's down the front of his shirt. He takes it off and tosses it on the ground like rubbish.

The water splashes over the sides as he gets in. We've done much more together, but I feel vulnerable like this. Kade's seen me naked. It's more than that, though; I'm stripped. I cross my arms to cover myself. He brings up a palmful of water and wipes the westerner's blood off his handsome face.

Kade reaches for me and I flinch. I make myself relax and try to ignore my apprehension. He moves closer and tries again. Sitting like a statue, I let him clean the dried blood from under my eye. He washes my hair with care. I'm lost inside and remain still.

Marisol returns with a cup of herbal tea. It has a sticky herbal aroma. I stare at it. She looks like she wants to say something, but Kade takes the cup from her and she sees her way out.

"Drink," he says and pushes it into my hands. I hold it with unsteady fingers. Kade watches me. I can't seem to bring it to my lips. "Please," he says in a softer tone. "It will prevent you from getting pregnant." It sounds abrupt in his mouth.

I drink it in one gulp. It tastes of bitter green herbs and smoky spices. It stings as it hits my stomach. I wince and hold myself. Kade takes the cup. I have the stirring in my heart. It happens when I know I'm about to burst into tears. I throw my arms around Kade's neck. My sobbing solves nothing, but it can't be helped.

The warlord is a murderer–I knew that. I saw him strike down the werecougars. There are hundreds of trophies scattered throughout the castle. It never occurred to me my husband would kill someone right in front of me. Especially a man determined to ruin me.

I'm not good enough. Mirai is prettier, cleverer, and stronger than I could ever be. This would've never happened to her. Kade gets looked at by women of all ages. Now he's seen me be used as Dax's plaything. I'm sure he finds me revolting.

I can't recall him penetrating me, but I know he did. Kristopher's grotesque smirk and an unfamiliar hand roaming over the parts of me only Kade has touched replays in my mind. Then it stops and blood is strewn across the library floor.

"I heard Rupert barking," he says into my hair. "I'm sorry, Ama. I should have gotten there sooner."

Kade holds me and I sense the rhythm of his heart in his neck. His normally steady pulse is replaced by a harsh, rapid beating.

"Actually, I should have gotten rid of them as soon as they disrespected you. They were my responsibility. I hope you can forgive me," he says.

This is not what I was expecting. I lean back to take in Kade's assertion. The tired eyes are full of mourning. He shields them with his bangs.

I'm not upset with Kade at all. This isn't his doing. I don't want him to feel as though he is responsible for the westerner's foul actions. I kiss him to say it's not his fault.

"I knew I'd kill for you, but I didn't think it would be my own men," he states.

Kade expected something like this happening to me? I suppose he did say people told stories about the silent princess and her radiant red hair and forest green eyes. My unique coloring sets me apart. Kade must have assumed a lustful man would find my freckles and curls too alluring to resist.

"When I was attacked by the raptor, I was suspicious of Dax. I think he let the beast latch onto my leg so my mobility would be compromised. The conniving bastard," growls Kade.

We take our dinner in his room. He doesn't want to be around anyone and neither do I.

Marisol is brief but caring. She has to clean the bloodstains out of Kade's shirt. I wonder who took care of the bodies. Did Finn drag them out of the castle? Another anxiety inducing thought: what will Francis make of this? Him knowing I've been tainted by the westerner mortifies me.

Kade and I finish our meals, but I barely remember what I ate. He scoops me up, taking me with him to his chair by the fireplace. The lids of his eyes are heavy. He reaches for one of my books on the end table and hands it to me. It's the one about the mercenary.

I turn to my favorite part. Kade is falling asleep. I read about beauty and brutality. He holds me close to his chest. While in the fire's light, I revisit a story that hasn't changed, but I have.

***

A small snout is nudging my chin. It's Rupert! I sit up and hold him to my chest. His leg is bandaged, but he seems okay. I lay back down and let my dog nuzzle me. He decides to nest in my hair by my neck. Sleepy puppy noises fill my right ear.

I put my hand over him protectively. No one is going to try to hurt him, but it eases my anxiety. Rupert's barking is what alerted Kade. I was worried Dax may have killed the poor thing when he kicked him into the wall.

Perverse men with vile intentions. Kade's guilt is misplaced. He isn't the one who assaulted me. I close my eyes and remember our first night together. How I said yes but didn't know what I meant. Even then, it was nothing like what Dax did.

Marisol brings me breakfast. "Good morning, my lady," she greets me in her cheerful voice. With elegant motions, she opens the curtains to let in the light. She picks up our dirty clothes for washing and puts them in a basket near the door. I watch her scurry about the room tidying things.

"Are you feeling alright?" she asks.

Marisol sits next to me and I pull up the covers, feeling ashamed of my naked body. She's seen me many times, but today is different. "I'm sorry, my lady. I should have asked if I could sit with you," she says and begins to rise. I reach for her hand to show I don't mind her next to me.

"Lord Kade's leg is better. He doesn't need the crutches anymore," she tells me as she begins to brush my hair. I cringe as her hands move around me. It's not her fault. I hold still and focus on my breathing.

"It is not my place, but I want you to know I'm here for you. I'm sorry about what happened," she whispers. I nod and giant tears pool down my face. Marisol lets me sob and continues to brush my hair. "They got what they deserved. Lord Kade interrogated every mercenary this morning."

She brings me my sage green dress. The one Dax ruined me in is the color of heliotrope. Marisol probably chose this shade because it is tranquil, light, and sophisticated. The ostentatious purple is a violent hue. It doesn't appeal to me.

Her flowy hair and buttery brown skin are a reminder I'm an outsider. Did Dax find me so abhorrent he sought to ravage me? I'll try to be a better wife from now on. The westerners thought I needed to be taught a lesson. A man is not to be ignored. Being a wife means not disappearing half the day.

Marisol guides me to the courtyard where she sits me in the sunniest spot. The rays of light cause the sand to twinkle like stars. It's a lovely open space with a towering juniper tree in the middle of the grounds. "I'll be back to check on you soon. Enjoy the fresh new day," she says.

I let blades of grass peek through my fingers. They stab my palm, soft and unnoticeable. The more I try to forget, the more I remember. I sigh and hold my knees to my chest.

"Lady Amadeus," says a low female voice. Mirai sits next to me, swift and quiet. "Can I have a moment?" she asks.

I nod and try to keep my composure. Mirai tucks a lock of perfect black hair behind her ear. The different colored eyes are shocking, mesmerizing in their own way. She takes out a small notebook and graphite pencil.

"Lord Kade asked me to do this because he feels it would be improper to ask Francis. He would like for you to write what is ruling your thoughts and for me to translate them. Would that be okay, my lady?"

I don't like this idea. I'm not unwilling to tell Kade my innermost personal thoughts, but I feel betrayed he would ask Mirai to be the one to deliver my message. I suppose it makes sense. This would be awkward for Francis or any man. I take the paper and start to scribble in my loose cursive.

Thank you for saving me. My apologies for the grief I must have caused you. I never thought I'd see such an act of beautiful violence.

I give the notebook back to Mirai. She reads it and her eyebrows furrow. "Do you see yourself as his burden?" she asks.

It's a bullet to the chest. I reach for my heart and nod. Mirai gazes at me with mismatched eyes, searching for my secrets.

"Lord Kade cares for you deeply. You should write more," she says and hands the notebook back to me. What should I say? He's my husband, but I haven't been tested in this way. I've gotten by with a nod or shake of my head. It's easier being mute. In the depths of silence is a simplicity others don't understand.

I don't blame you. You have given me everything I want. The westerner doesn't earn my memory. It's you who is on my mind, always.

It irks me to have Mirai scan such private thoughts. She is pleased with what I've given her. The female mercenary stands with the sun behind her.

"Thank you, my lady. Lord Kade will appreciate what you have written," says Mirai.

Her grin is unreadable. Is it smug? Does it delight her to know she gets to have him, too? I wait for her to vanish from the courtyard before I let myself cry. She doesn't need to know how much he means to me.

GRAINS OF TIME

24

Since the library contains the gruesome event, Francis has made a point of switching out my books and ordering additional novels, so I don't have to go in there. He has been gentle. I can tell by his mannerisms he doesn't want to do or say anything to upset me.

"The woman who had the series about an orphan who grew up to be king said you may like these," he says. Francis holds three hardcover novels. They look worn, but that usually means they're good because lots of people have read them. I offer him a big smile as I accept his gracious gifts.

Francis shifts his weight from one foot to another. He clears his throat. "I don't want to disturb you, my lady, but I want to say I'm very sorry about what happened. If there is anything you need, please don't hesitate to tell me. Lord Kade is concerned. You aren't making frequent requests," he says.

I look around the whimsical garden and at the pile of books next to me I haven't finished. Rupert is in my lap. I brushed Ari off and gave her an apple earlier. Not sure what to ask for, I shrug. Kade's given me many precious things already.

Francis sighs and sits beside me. Rupert yawns and gets comfortable in Francis' lap. I take out the notebook and pencil he gave me and write to him.

Will you tell me more about Kade?

This makes him chuckle and Rupert joins in by panting. The two of them are adorable.

"Lord Kade won a fighting competition in Raesa when he was twenty. He was given the finely made sword he wields now as his prize. They also offered him a kiss from their princess, but he refused it. The princess was distressed by his decision," laughs Francis. He pets Rupert's short fur. His olive tan hands are weathered but graceful.

"I watched him grow up. Such an insubordinate young man. I worried he would get himself into trouble because of his reckless behavior. I'm glad he's home," he says. A bird chirps to my left. It distracts me for a second. I concentrate on Francis telling me about my husband. "You're the reason he's home, my lady. If it were not for you, he'd still be out there waging wars and fighting beasts. Thank you. I can't thank you enough."

Francis' story has me wondering even more about Kade. How is it I can learn additional facts about him but feel like I'm further from the truth? What do I mean to him? I'm not sure who he is to me. We are something else.

Rupert leaps up and starts bouncing around. He runs off to chase a grasshopper. Francis continues, "If only Lord Seneca were alive to see him now. He was a good father and a fine teacher. I think it would have melted his cold heart to watch Lord Kade earn a respectable title and marry such a beautiful young woman."

I blush at his words. Would the fearsome warlord have approved of a tiny thing like me? I'm not strong or brave. To him, I wouldn't be anything but a mute girl. I don't realize I'm clenching my fist until Francis pats my hand as it fidgets, ripping up grass.

"You don't think you're beautiful," he states. I hide in the pile of curls on my head. At least I can make use of them for concealment. "It's not my intention to pry or embarrass you. It's just that, well, oh never mind," he cuts himself off. I push my bangs out of my eyes so I can take a peek at him. A sly smile starts in the middle of my face. Francis continues, "You must not notice all the longing glances."

I shake my head at his words. No, I don't.

"Pure scarlet is rare in nature. There are roses, poppies, and begonias. Not many creatures have red fur besides foxes. The mainland of this continent consists of mostly blond and dark hair. Red is considered the color of passion, war, violence, and love."

The word love has me shook. If it were possible to speak, I don't think I would dare utter the syllable. Francis keeps speaking as I sink into the grass.

"Deep green eyes are also uncommon. A majority of people have blue or brown eyes in this part of the world."

It's hard to hear such kind things. My entire life, I thought my hair was a dreadful tangled mess nobody would want to put their hands on. I thought my eyes were ugly and lizard-like. Francis kills me slowly. "I know your affliction has caused you problems, but I think it's endearing. Everything about you is striking. You're the most interesting woman I've ever met."

My knuckles ache from holding onto the grass.

"Lord Kade hardly takes his eyes off you," he says, a surge of seriousness in his tone. I think he is advising me to pay attention.

"I'll leave you be. Sorry if I was too informal." Francis waves goodbye and is on his way to the garden.

***

The mercenaries put their heads down as I walk by. Finn acknowledges me, but Eli and the others are sheepish in my presence. I make them tense. Kade wasn't merciful when he killed Dax and Kristopher. His men know his ruthless nature. Marisol said he interrogated them. What did they know? Did the westerners tell them of their evil plans?

Kade's arm sneaks around my waist. I'm staring out the window trying to see into myself. I feel terrible. I've been distant. My head is in the clouds, cold and misty skies. It's hard to stay here. I retreat into the veil, keeping me from connecting with the rest of the world. Kade doesn't antagonize me about it.

"Can I do anything for you?" he asks. I've been keeping my hair down so I can disappear into it. I shake my head. There is nothing I want. No item or experience can undo what happened to me or bring my sister back. Kade kneels and brushes the tousled curls out of my face. "I would turn back time for you if I could."

His rough hands are warm, but I can't register him touching me. I put my hands on his. Wistful eyes look me up and down. I started my

192

monthly bleeding. It's a relief, but brings on a fresh wave of anxiety. I don't want to have a child.

I've been careless, not even thinking about the consequences of my actions. Kade and I have been sleeping together for six months. A baby is inevitable. I'll be no good at that either. At least it won't be the westerner's. Still, I'm a useless dumb girl. What would Kade want with a child, anyway? There is no need for a blood heir in Tessafaye.

Perhaps my affliction has taken not just my voice, but my fertility. Has Kade been wondering about this the whole time while I've been oblivious? I don't even know how my husband feels about me, let alone children. The young warlord isn't who I thought he'd be. I'm not sure who I am anymore.

He takes my hand, and we wander around the castle. I admire his collection of trophies. Kade tells me about the wyvern's eyes. How the creatures stay near the coasts because they fly out to rock formations to breed. The feathers came from a siren, a female creature with a fish tail and bird wings. They sing breathtaking songs to lure men into their traps, where they feed on their beating hearts.

We end up in the room with Lord Seneca's portrait. I focus on the eyes, the brooding face, and the stoic expression. Kade picks me up and walks closer to the painting. "I remember seeing his furious eyes for the first time. I thought he was going to beat me to death. The day I tried to steal Fang changed my fate," he says.

Kade walks around the room with me in his arms. Not a man of many words, I look up at him to see if he will tell me more.

"My father was strict, but he was a good man, despite being an infamous soldier. It astounded everyone when he adopted me. Especially after the ridiculous stunt I pulled," he laughs. The charming smile shows for a second, a shooting star across his face.

"I would steal to survive. After my mother died, I scavenged and resorted to pick-pocketing," says Kade. The two of us stand before the portrait again. "I used to pray for all the things I have now." This is the most he's shared with me. We are close, but he is rarely this personal. Kade tightens his hold on me and gives me a kiss. "I have everything," he says.

He sets me down. Twilight is here. The mystic time where it is hard to distinguish where one ends and the other begins. When does day become night? At what moment do things start to change? The sky turns from light blue to burnt orange, and in the shades of indigo, initiates us into the evening.

It's time for dinner. This is the first time I've sat in the dining hall with everyone else in over a week. It's been too awkward to be around anyone. Kade keeps me at his side. Finn is waiting for us at one of the tables. He doesn't look up from his food.

"How is your leg, Sir?" he asks.

"Fine. I've suffered worse," says Kade.

There are three other men at the table. One of them is Eli. He takes notice of me but concentrates on his conversation with one of the mercenaries.

"It's nice to see you, Lady Amadeus," says Finn. I feel shy and lean into Kade. My bangs cover my eyes. Finn takes no offense and goes back to focusing on his meal. The dining hall is noisy. Usually I like the festive atmosphere, but right now it's making me nervous. Marisol brings us our food. She hovers over me. I think she wants to make sure I eat. To appease her, I pick up the roll of bread and take a bite.

"Is there anything I can get you, my lady?" she asks.

Marisol can sense my cowardice. I sit up straighter and shake my head. To make it believable, I smile and take another bite. Out of the corner of my eye, I see Kade watching me. He is aware most of my actions are a performance.

***

Everything is gray: the sky, the sand, and the river flowing through the valley. The tiger lilies and poppies add a splash of color to the otherwise dreary ambiance. The clanging of metal echoes on the field. Kade is training the mercenaries. He brings them down one by one. I notice he fights Eli with vehemence. It's subtle, but the mistrust is palpable.

I normally don't view their lessons. Back at Sloane castle it was against the rules. Women weren't supposed to witness the knights preparing for battle. I've been cautious around Kade, but today I want to witness it again, the beautiful violence he is capable of.

Kade sneaked up on Dax and Kristopher, stealthier than all the men. Maybe his years in the slums taught him lessons no one else could withstand. When he stuck his dagger into Dax's chest, there wasn't a sound, none. It happened too fast to elicit an accurate response.

When he told me not to look, I covered my eyes in my chilly hands. Not until days after the incident did I realize I how badly I wanted to witness Kade murder a man for hurting me. The atrocious thought sickens me. I let it fester in my core, prickly and acidic.

Eli blocks Kade but isn't fast enough to strike. He backs up to put distance between him and Kade, but Kade doesn't take his eyes off his opponent. Eli attempts to counterattack but ends up getting knocked off his feet. His forehead creases and he sits up. Kade puts out his hand to help him, but Eli refuses it. He grunts as he rises and walks into the crowd of men. There's blood on his neck. The satisfaction I get seeing the damage perturbs me.

My ears and cheeks turn pink with embarrassment at my thoughts. I run off towards the garden in search of Rupert. He is the only one I don't feel awkward around. I upset the crickets and they cease to chirp. Rupert is pawing at a bug. He jumps on my legs. Picking him up, I hold him close to my face. Soft white fur with brown spots makes me feel safe.

"Hello, my lady. Do you have a moment?"

Mirai is standing behind. The maze of tiger lilies sways around us. They sing a song no one can hear but me. I nod and face the girl I'm sure my husband is cheating on me with.

She takes out her notebook and pencil. "I think you should write something for Lord Kade," she says and holds her items out to me.

I set my dog down. He whines, but I can't deny my wifely duties. I should try harder to communicate with Kade.

I'm sorry about my odd behavior. I'm struggling with myself. It's difficult for me to navigate our relationship. Please don't take it personally. You did nothing wrong.

Mirai scans my note. The smug smile aggravates me. I hold in my sigh and try to be a dignified lady like my mother taught me. She said men use us, but we shouldn't act like animals about it.

"This is sweet. I think you should write more. Lord Kade yearns for you to be honest with him," she says.

I grit my teeth, making my smile crooked. My acting skills are limited. Good thing nobody expects me to talk.

I heard stories about the young warlord with windswept hair and eyes the color of desert sand. The rumors never mentioned what was in your heart.

The female mercenary scrunches up her delicate face. Her grin is ear to ear. What is so funny to her? Mirai bows to me and says, "Thank you, my lady. Lord Kade will be pleased."

Tiger lily stocks rustle as she sees her way out. Rupert barks at me. I decide to sit with him and he curls up in my lap. Does she do this to humiliate me? I shouldn't let it vex me. My life as a princess taught me to endure. Turn the other cheek, play pretend, and act like it doesn't hurt.

I lay down and take in the fresh citrusy scent of the poppies. Rupert naps on my stomach. He bobs up and down with my breaths. I put my hands over him protectively. He's healing rapidly, but it bothers me to know his tiny body was limp on the hard library floor.

Piles of red hair makes for a comfy pillow. The exhaustion of being on edge lulls me to sleep in the center of the garden. A butterfly flutters mere inches from my face, but I can't enjoy it because I'm already gone.

My dreams turn to nightmares. Big hands not belonging to Kade are all over me. The pressure on my stomach repulses me. Men's hands touching me, the kick of something inside me, a baby I don't want. I miss my father. He is nowhere to be found, but I hear his voice in the forest moving further and further away. No matter how far I run, I don't reach Penelope in time. She's dead in my arms. Margaux has grown antlers and fangs. Blood pours down her blonde hair and out of her gums.

"Ama."

I jolt and startle Rupert. He runs off. I thrash in strong arms restraining me. Kade says my name again, but the dream state I was in has its grip on me. He lets me fight him until I come to my senses.

"Hey, hey, it's okay. You were having a nightmare," he whispers, and I stop my squirming. "It's me."

Kade is sweaty from training. His shoulder guard is still on, and I'm digging into the leather with desperate fingers.

THE KISS

25

He treats me like glass: breakable, fragile- shatter into a thousand pieces in an instant. His people walk on eggshells around me. They tiptoe and whisper. It's reminding me of Sloane castle. Marisol is touching my elbow. I snatch my arm back and regret it immediately.

"I apologize, my lady," she starts. I take her hand to tell her it's okay. "I didn't mean to frighten you. Are you hungry? Or perhaps you'd like some tea?" Marisol's eyelashes flutter as she talks. I shake my head but pat her wrist to say I'm fine.

"Let me know if you need me. I'm here for you. Please don't feel as though you can't ask me for things," she says and takes off down the stairs. One of my boots takes a step in the library's direction and the other follows. I haven't gone in there since the day of the horrible incident.

Three weeks have passed. Time flows upriver. It's foggy in my memory, like a dream. I can hardly remember it. But now and then I feel the phantom hand that isn't Kade on my breasts and holding my hip where only one other person has touched me. It causes me sleepless nights. I get nauseated when the ghost of Dax thrusts into me.

The door creaks as I open it. It's forbidden and chilly inside the library. The books knocked off the shelves are put back in their places. I venture further into the back of the room where the desk is.

For unexplainable reasons, I'm drawn to it. I put my hand to it to verify it's real. The haze of my violation has me under the impression it might not have happened. I know it did, but my mind refuses to accept this fact and distorts it. Perhaps I am glass: fractured and fragmented.

The blood stains on the floor aren't visible until I kneel down. They are faint, but they are present. Kade isn't afraid to kill. I wonder if he fears dying. My fingertips graze the remnants of my rapist.

I knew Dax didn't approve of me, but I didn't think he'd go so far as to assault me. I should have guessed. Men like Dax and Kristopher are everywhere. They spit on the ground at women who are more skilled than them. Dax thought I needed to learn my place.

I go over to the wall where Rupert was kicked into. Nothing is amiss. There isn't a dent in the wall or blood on the ground. My dog didn't sustain too great an injury, but it pains me to know he felt the wrath of the westerner's boot.

The ghost threatens to take a hold of me. I rush out of the library. Darting out, I run into Finn, who is surprised to see me exit the room. I stumble and he tries to catch me, but I dodge him. Embarrassed and overwhelmed, I take off down the hall as fast as possible. Finn is calling for me. I don't mean to be disrespectful, but I can't stop running.

I turn corners and weave through the castle. With no particular room in mind, I keep moving. Motion eases the anxiety. I don't care if I look like a lunatic. Everyone thinks I'm crazy, anyway. I grip my ears to drown out the noise. It's loud in my brain. I can't stand it.

I'm not paying attention when I run into someone. It knocks me back. I catch myself, but wince at the weight on my elbow. Eli is looming over me.

"Are you alright, my lady?" he asks as he extends his hand out. I refuse it and start to crawl back. This riles him up. "What? I'm trying to help you." The back of his palm is covered in dark hair. I don't want him to touch me. "Stop cowering. I'm trying to help you." Eli scoffs and tries to get closer.

I'm up against the wall. I cover my face with my hands. "What's your problem? I didn't do anything to you." The statement is true but flat. I have the lingering suspicion he knew what Dax was going to do all along. I start to cry, which isn't helpful and angers Eli.

"Get away from her," says Kade. He blocks Eli from nearing. Eli's eyes grow wide.

"She fell down. I was—" says Eli, but Kade cuts him off.

"Go," says Kade.

"But sir, I swear I—"

"If you don't get out of my sight, I'll banish you to the desert. Or would you prefer for me to kill you?"

Eli is alarmed by Kade's harsh words. He is smart and chooses not to argue. Kade picks me up. My face is hot. Strands of curly red hair stick to my cheeks. Salty tears spill down my neck. Kade is carrying his wife, who is a pathetic sniveling mess. We go into his room and he sets me down on the bed.

"Did Eli do something?" he asks. I shake my head. Kade squints and his voice tightens. A dead giveaway he's getting irritated.

Kade raises his voice. "Did he push you?"

I shake my head again. Today I felt a little braver and chose to wear my hair up. The tail of it tickles in between my shoulder blades.

"Has Eli been bothering you?" he asks.

Now I'm the one being interrogated. I shake my head again. Kade kneels down and grabs my hands.

"Are you sure?" he presses for answers. I nod, but I can't smile for Kade. It hurts too much. I can't handle his intense focus on me. No one has seen through me the way he does. Kade sighs and relaxes his grip. He lowers his voice. "We're going to be together for the rest of our lives. I need you to come to me about these things. If anyone makes you nervous or uncomfortable, I want to know," he says.

This is the first time we've talked about forever.

***

Lips on my neck and a large palm on my stomach bring on my cowardly heart. Ba-boom, ba-boom, I'm sure Kade can hear it too because he stops kissing me.

"Are you okay?"

I peek at him over my shoulder and nod my head. Kade studies my face, his intense gaze burning through me. When I first arrived in Tessafaye, I expected my new husband to be abusive. In all this time, he hasn't struck or scolded me.

What are we? He gave me his last name and the freedom that comes with it. I no longer have to put up the facade of the perfect lady. Kade doesn't care what I wear or how I do my hair. He doesn't boss me around or tell me how to act. Being a royal was never this exhilarating.

"Do you not like me touching you?" he asks.

I put my arms around his neck and shake my head. Lately I've been craving him too much. Bad dreams have not so gentle reminders. To block out the horrific thoughts I've been clinging to Kade.

We kiss, then we collide. I run my fingers through tousled black hair. He whispers my name in my ear and the hair on the back of my neck stands up. It's taken me this long to figure out it's not Kade who scares me. It's me.

If I let myself love him, then I'm a fool. He could die in battle. What would I do then? Then there's the awful suspicion when he's not with me, he's with Mirai or someone else. Kade might not treat me poorly, but I don't trust him. In my world, it's unsafe to trust anybody. I fall asleep. Kade pressed up against me, breathing into my sternum.

He's up before dawn. I don't know how he isn't fatigued from his strenuous schedule. I yawn and stretch my arms. The sun is hazy on the horizon. I've become more comfortable in the castle and take my time with my morning routine.

I run my hands over my dresses. My ring finger catches on the purple one—the heliotrope. I grimace and shove it aside. Today I want to wear the aqua blue one. I pin up half of my hair and braid around the crown. It would be impolite to keep letting it hang down my back in a frizzy mess three days in a row.

As I exit Kade's chambers, I bump into her. I take a deep breath. "Good morning, my lady. Did you sleep well?" asks Mirai. I nod and have a tight smile on my face. It's not genuine, but I shouldn't scowl at her.

"Good, I'm glad you're getting rest. I know it's early, but can I talk to you about something?"

Oh, no. What does she have to say? I don't think I'm ready for a conversation like this before any tea or time to wake up. I nod and pretend it doesn't bother me.

"Kade…" she starts with his name. Why do I detest it in her pretty mouth? I feel my eye twitch and hope Mirai doesn't notice how nervous I am. "...is worried he isn't doing enough for you. Please, tell him what you're thinking."

Mirai hands me the notebook and pencil. I attempt to quell the shake in my hand. Where do I begin? I don't like my personal thoughts being passed on through her lips. Putting pride aside, I begin to write the truth.

I like it here, but I miss my sister. She died too young and too suddenly. I try to ignore what happened in the library and most days I can, but I still have bad dreams. My apologies for bringing it up. Such an ugly subject. I'm adjusting to my new life. Don't worry, I want to stay with you.

Looking at my feet, I hand her my loosely scribbly handwriting. It's sloppy compared to usual, but I can't think straight. Mirai frowns, but nods as she reads my note. Why can't she wait until she is out of my sight?

"Lord Kade doesn't forgive himself for what happened to you," she states. This stings, a cut to the chest. I shake my head and put my hand up. "I know. It's not his fault. He still takes the blame, though."

I teeter awkwardly on my feet and fiddle with the sash of my dress. Mirai doesn't walk off. She steps up to me. The female mercenary is confident. The way she holds herself is strong, like a boy.

"Do you not understand how much you mean to him?" she asks. Her question is bold. The assumption is abrupt. I'm not sure how to respond. No, I don't. In fact, I thought I was a prize for winning a war. Nothing more than a body traded for services. Kade has proven not to be a merciless military commander or power hungry bounty hunter. He has been my husband for one year, yet I don't know his heart.

The female mercenary's multicolored eyes scan me. My hair, my face, my frail stature, she takes me in with an enlightened expression. "He puts you first. But you don't think you're worthy," she says.

I stand there dumbfounded. How can she say this to me? While frozen in slow motion, Mirai closes the gap between us and puts her satin lips to mine. Her eyes are closed. Thick black eyelashes stick straight out. She pulls back and smiles at my confusion, amused.

"In my country, people said the silent princess had an intoxicating kiss powerful enough to take the words right out of a man's mouth," she laughs as she steps back. I clutch onto the sash of my dress, trying to decipher Mirai's intentions. When she turns her back to me, I touch the middle of my bottom lip.

PRETTY, DECEITFUL

26

Rupert snuggles me in the garden. It hasn't rained in a while. The poppies dance in the wind and clouds pass over the sun. My dog's company doesn't leave me distressed or mortified. I sigh into his short fur as I hold him close to my chest. He wriggles out of my arms and runs off to greet Francis and the groundskeepers. They like his exuberant personality.

I decide to visit Ari. Perhaps taking her out will relax me. She looks happy when I enter the stable. I give her a carrot and pet her snout. She makes the soft neigh sound. I let her out and guide her into the sunny day. It takes me three tries, but I'm able to get on her back without the assistance of a man.

Ari walks in a brisk fashion around the castle. We meander the courtyard. Rupert keeps at her heels and barks at low-flying butterflies. Eli is patrolling around with two other men who have disheveled hair and sharp noses. I think their names are Darius and Jibril. They're older than Kade, but I see the way they pull in their chins as he walks by. The horse bolts out of the shadow of the juniper tree and startles the three men. I know I shouldn't, but I look at Eli. He narrows his eyes and grits his teeth. Does seeing me cause him agony?

Leaves are cut down by the severe breeze. They fall to the ground, twirling. Ari slows her trot as we approach the side of the castle where the field is. The mercenaries are training. I stop for a moment to take in the beautiful violence. Kade knocks a man as tall as him to the ground. He motions for the next man to step up. This young mercenary is skilled and fast, but unable to win against the warlord.

Kade notices me watching. The men turn to see what he is looking at. They cast their gazes to the grass. All of them except Mirai. Her lips with perfect edges are parted. She giggles and covers her mouth. Is she laughing at me? Feeling unwanted, I wave at Kade and give Ari a small kick to get her to trot. I don't want to be here anymore.

I put Ari back in the stable. She seems pleased to have spent time with me. I give her some hay and fresh water. Rupert is mad with jealousy, so I scoop him up. He licks my chin and wags his tail. The heat is harsh today. I make my way back to the courtyard where the juniper tree is. We retreat into the darkest part where there are no patches of light.

Leaning against the trunk, I remember the willow back at my old home. It's not the same. Not better or worse, just different. My duty as a princess was to accept all things. Endure anything someone put me through, if it meant maintaining my family's status. Nothing is as I thought it would be. I have grown to love Tessafaye but fear one day it will reject me like everywhere else.

Francis finds me. We haven't spoken in quite some time. I think I make him nervous. Knowing I was violated in the library injures him more than me. After all, Francis and everyone else think I am some noble lady: a valuable high society princess. But really, I'm no one. A silly little fool.

"Glad you found some shade, my lady," says Francis. He smiles but stands far apart from me like I have a disease. I nod and rub Rupert's belly. He kicks his leg and twitches his ears. This helps me get through the tough parts of the day.

"Are the books I've been ordering to your liking?" he asks. I nod and continue stroking Rupert's short fur. His spots match my spots. "Do you desire anything else? More dresses? Boots or perhaps a new necklace. I know a fine jeweler in town."

Francis attempts to list everything a woman could want, but I wish for nothing. I have my dog, my horse, and my husband. These are the things holding my attention. I shake my head as a polite lady would. Francis seems frazzled.

"Please, my lady. I'm not trying to be difficult, but Lord Kade is under the impression you might think Tessafaye's clothing and jewelry isn't good enough for you."

I open my mouth in shock. That's preposterous. Here I am, being coerced into Francis and Kade's game of giving me too much stuff. I take out my notebook and lazily write a list:

I'd like three dresses: emerald green, brick red, and whatever color Kade likes best
  A new chemise
  Hair ribbons—any textile

As childish as it might seem, I want Kade to put in the effort to pick out my items. If he wants to hound me about not asking for enough, then he has to show me who he is as well. I rip out the page and hand it to Francis.

"Very well, my lady. I'll get on it straight away," he says. I appreciate the sweet grandfatherly tone he speaks to me in.

***

Today I'm restless and paranoid. I wander the castle like a listless apparition. No room is interesting enough to stay. I can't stop walking. My feet take me wherever they feel like. I'm on edge. It's aggravating me. The shadow, I can't shake it off.

What's been vexing me today is I sense someone following me. I enter a room, hearing my faint footsteps, then the discreet thud of another's. Who's there? I pick up the pace and fast walk up and down stairs. The castle has a hundred doors. I open and close them as I please.

Everyone is either training with Kade or tending to the castle's various needs. Not many people have the luxury of wasting time. There it is again: the faint scrape of the heel of a boot. I turn around to see no one. In my panic, I open another door and run down the hall and up the stairs.

My stalker loses me.

I admire the decorations in this place, how they differ from where I'm from. Everything was steel and diamonds in Sloane castle. Kade's home uses a lot of bronze, gold, and sapphires. It's elegant, unlike how I first imagined Soloman castle. It's not as sophisticated as Sloane castle but it has a stylish appearance.

I keep playing hide and seek. There is no eluding myself. I give up on seeking refuge in the castle. It's dinnertime. I should find Kade. We haven't been apart for too long, but I miss him. My inhale is interrupted. It's bizarre. The more time I spend with him, the more I find myself missing him. I regulate my breathing and start walking back towards the foyer.

There's a creak. Who is following me? Thinking about the last time someone followed me and what they did has me on high alert. I walk like nothing is wrong. Then I run. I dash through hallways and take stairs two at a time. The echo of another pair of shoes on the ground urges me to go faster.

I fall over my feet. My ankle buckles and I'm on my knees. The person stalking me is approaching. I close my eyes, but it doesn't stop the silent tears. "Pardon me, my lady," it's Finn. I look up at him shyly. Why is he lurking in the dark, following the lady of the castle around? He helps me to my feet. I cross my arms and wipe away my tears. They pass my lips and they get caught in my teeth.

"I'm sorry for scaring you," he starts and gestures for us to walk to the dining hall together. "Lord Kade thought someone should keep an eye on you. I didn't mean to frighten you, but I knew you would refuse me."

Finn speaks the truth. I deny most of the help I'm offered. It's not something I can take freely. I nod, and we walk the rest of the way in silence. Kade means well, but I don't want someone watching every move I make. It's unnerving. After Francis pointed out the things I don't notice I see it every day: Kade looking at me like there is no one and nothing else around.

The food smells wonderful. A mix of herbs and spices we didn't have in Syrosa. It's quite robust. The meals they prepare are grand. Thankfully, they don't give me three servings anymore. I run my hand across my hip. It's not as bony. My wrists aren't as thin and my face is fuller. Finn guides me over to Kade and takes a seat across from us.

"Did you have a good day?" he asks as he wraps his arm around me. I nod, but notice Finn's eyes shift. Darius and Jibril are chatting with Mirai. They sit at the table in front of us. Marisol brings me a moderate portion and winks. She knows what I like. Kade and Finn are making conversation while I nibble my food. I eat slowly and watch the festivities of the dining hall.

Men drink wine and the maids dance with a few of them. Francis is sitting up straight and discussing something with the gardener. The servants bring plates of food and pick up empty dishes. Kade's people make the most out of every night. I suppose expecting the worst brings them closer together.

I'm daydreaming as I chew on bread with cilantro baked into it and don't notice Darius and Jibril join us. Finn greets them first. Kade and Darius begin speaking about defenses and the use of cannons. Jibril and Finn utter a couple sentences at each other, but their attention is on their dinner.

"You and your wife seem happy," says Darius. His clear voice draws me out of my thoughts.

"We are," says Kade. His enormous hand is holding a fistful of curls. He brushes my bangs out of my face, as though he wants Darius to see me better. I feel naked.

"I heard Kathryn Sloane asked for her back," says Darius. Finn and Jibril pause mid-bite.

"She implied Ama might want to return to Syrosa, but she doesn't," says Kade. He pulls me closer so I'm leaning on him.

"The queen is relentless. Good thing the desert lines the border into the northeast or she might try to take her," jokes Jibril to lighten the mood. Kade's expression remains neutral, but his voice constricts.

"I wouldn't let that happen," says Kade.

The men at the table eye each other and nod in agreement.

"No, Sir. None of us would let that happen," says Finn. The air changes the way the scent of the wind is altered when it's about to rain. Have they expected my mother trying to regain control over me? She couldn't, anyway. Kade would have to divorce me. Then again… I'm not sure Kade wants this marriage. My mother essentially forced him into it.

QUEEN OF BROKEN HEARTS

27

My new dresses are in. Marisol is excited to show me them. She fawns over their fine fabric. The green one has gems sewn into the bodice. It looks lavish and expensive. I hold up the dusty red one and Marisol squeals in delight. This one has gold thread stitching and white lace at the elbows. The most interesting one is twilight blue. Kade picked this one.

Marisol lifts it up and runs her hand over the white and silver embellishments. The seamstress sewed a thousand little stars into the bodice and sleeves. It's extravagant but not pretentious. I put it on and stare at myself in the mirror as Marisol laces up the back.

Is blue his favorite color? Does it remind him of night skies or the ocean? Kade has seen everything, been everywhere. What does he see when he is staring right through me? Marisol twists my hair and pins it up. She leaves my bangs and a few curls to frame my face.

"You are so pretty, my lady," says Marisol as she toys with my hair and adjusts my dress.

The statement is informal. It reminds me of my sisters. She stands behind me with her hands on my shoulders. Her pleasant smile contrasts with my severity.

"Lord Kade is a lucky man," she says into her reflection, and winks. I wrinkle up my nose and make a face at her. She giggles, which makes me laugh. "The silent princess is not only beautiful, but she's sweet, kind, and fiercely intelligent. You are more than all the rumors combined."

The maids at Sloane castle detested me. They would whisper I was ugly, my hair was nothing but a pain, and because I'm a mute, I must be stupid.

"Queen Kathryn is known as a callous woman. I'm glad you're not like her. You're a brilliant girl with a compassionate heart," she says and ushers me out of the room. Marisol holds onto me and keeps chatting. She's a good friend to have in the castle. "The other maids were worried you might be mean or prim because Syrosa is known as a wealthy nation with high society nobles. But I knew you would be a kind soul."

We make our way to the foyer. Rupert is at my heels. I bend down to pick him up. Marisol strokes his velvety ears. "I thought someone who couldn't speak must be incredibly thoughtful. A deep person," she says as we walk down the stairs. "Also, anyone who is nice to animals must be good."

Marisol's declaration rings true. I don't believe anyone in Sloane castle liked animals except for me. Well, Margaux fell in love with a beast boy. Of course, she was exiled to the misty forest for it. My mother hated birds. The servants detested the racoons and minks wandering the grounds. Kade is waiting for me at the bottom of the steps. Marisol lets me go and gives me a nudge.

Kade holds out his hand and I take it. "I thought you might like to see more of my land," he says, and I nod enthusiastically. Ever since my first taste of freedom, I've grown hungry for more. I want to see it all. We get Fang and Ari from the stables. I let Kade help me onto my horse because I think it upsets him when I do it myself.

He and I ride side by side. Instead of taking the road to town, we veer off onto another path. This one is grassy and lined with petunias. A hawk flies high above a cypress tree. Its wingspan blocks out the sun momentarily.

I glance at Kade. His eyes are straight ahead, face neutral. The light hits his cheekbones at perfect angles. He appears permanently disinterested, but there is a certain something about him. I find his quiet personality appealing.

I'm four years younger than him, but feel completely immature in comparison. Kade seems capable of anything. My husband's stare is cryptic, and I'm not sure what he sees when he looks at me. Does he really find me beautiful? Could it be possible for someone like him to love a mute girl like me?

We ride through an open field dotted with blue thistles and white roses. The grass is the color of hay from lack of rain. It hasn't rained in four weeks. I miss it. As do the flowers. Fang picks up the pace and Ari stays close by. I hold the reins tightly, but let Ari run as fast as she wants.

Kade stops at the top of the hill. I lose my breath, taking in the scenery. We are standing on a cliff and on the other side are rocky mountains with twin waterfalls. Down in the ravine is a serpentine river the color of sapphires. The two of us dismount and take a break in the shade of a juniper tree. I turn my head back and forth. There is too much splendor for my tiny eyes to gather.

"Do you like it?" he asks.

Kade is at my side. The sparkling waterfalls make a muffled splashing noise on the way down into the river. I nod and Kade's rare but charming smile appears.

"This is Ja'Hira Falls. My father told me two foolish gods fought over the love of a human woman. The battle went on so long they didn't notice the woman had grown old and died. When they realized they wasted their time fighting each other, the sky god asked the earth god to turn him into stone. Afterwards the earth god disintegrated and became nothing but dust, leaving behind a perpetually crying man," he says. Not only is Kade capable of beautiful violence, but he knows stories that cause my heart to swell.

***

Like a delinquent, I sneak into the library. Why am I drawn to the place of my defilement? It's early afternoon. Everyone should be busy with their chores. I take my time running my hand over the books I've read, lingering at the ones I haven't.

It looks like the maids have dusted, swept, and mopped in here. In my absence, they have kept it pristine. I pick up books and flip through them. They blur together. My eyes skip over lines and they jumble together.

I'm a criminal in my own home. A glutton for punishment. I weave through the pine shelves the way I assume a weasel would. That's what I am. A sneaky, devilish creature. There's a sickness in my head. It can't be cured with reason.

The desk glares at me, angry I'm back. Oakwood begs to give me splinters. I run my hand over it. A flash of remembrance. It's fragmented, missing pieces, but I know what happened. The wood is stained not with blood, but with my dignity. If Dax lived, how would he remember me? Would he think of me the way I think of him?

Ironic how the desk faces west out the window. Was he mocking me? Making me look towards his homeland while he had his way with me. What a vile man. I shouldn't be, but I'm furious. I'm angry at the world, my mother, and myself. I couldn't have known Dax's evil intentions, but I can't help but feel as though I could have avoided it somehow.

"What are you doing?"

I jolt at his voice. Kade is right next to me. He is a storm, here in a flash, and gone without a sound. I turn to him, embarrassed. He's caught me red-handed. "Why would you want to be here?" Kade usually asks me easy "yes" or "no" questions, but this time I don't have the answer. I squeeze my hands together and stare at the new boots. They came in today. Made of high quality leather the color of clay.

Kade guides me away from the place where I was raped and he murdered two of his men. I can't help myself and steal another glimpse of the scene of the crime over my shoulder. Why I want to see it again, I can't explain. It holds a piece of me. I want it back.

He doesn't ask any questions, but he won't let me leave his side. Whenever I veer off to make my way to the garden or his room, he's standing right there. I give up on choosing where to go and let Kade take the lead.

First, we go to the stables and check on the horses. He hands me an apple to give to Ari. She snorts, and it makes me giggle. Then we make our way to the field where ten of the men are still practicing their archery skills. I stand in awe at Mirai and how she lands a bullseye three times in a row. She gives me a knowing glance. Kade takes me to the garden and we watch the sunset.

The sky turns orange, the shade signifying twilight is near. I look at Kade to gauge whether night is his favorite color. The air is still. My husband is ambiguous. He could be absolutely appalled by sunsets, and I'd have no clue. We wait for the stars to come out before heading back inside.

Rupert greets me. I pick up my little companion. The weight of him in my arms soothes my nerves. Kade motions for us to head to the dining hall. Everyone is laughing and talking loudly. The drunk mercenaries speak slowly and pound their fist onto the tables. I bring Rupert closer to my heart. It's beating like a hammer.

We sit down with Finn, and Marisol brings us our meal. I eat with Rupert on my lap. He gives me sad eyes, so I give him a bite of my chicken. Kade and Finn discuss matters of the castle, past wars, and other things not concerning me. Eli and another mercenary join us. They are boisterous but polite.

"Good evening, sir," says Eli.

Kade nods but doesn't reply.

"How are you, Lord Kade?" asks the other mercenary.

"Fine. How about you, Avery?" asks Kade.

Avery has bushy eyebrows and a scruffy beard. I tense my arms around Rupert and he nuzzles me.

"Very well, thank you. And how is the lady of the castle?" asks Avery. I smile and nod. Best to mind my manners. I don't want the other mercenaries to hold a grudge against me. Kade keeps his hand on my hip as he sips wine and the other men chat.

It happens gradually. I don't notice until Kade is already drunk. He doesn't guffaw the way Eli and Avery do, but he smiles more. His tone lowers, and he enunciates his words, sounding out each syllable. Finn makes jokes with the men but doesn't participate in the drinking. Their roar of laughter startles Rupert, and he jumps out of my lap.

Alone and exposed, I shrink into myself. Kade is running his hand up my side. It finds its way into my hair. He massages the nape of my neck and runs his palm down my back. Avery eyes Kade's hand travelling over my body.

"The young lady looks a bit shy, Sir. You're making her nervous," says Avery in jest.

It's true though. My face is rosy and my gaze is averted.

"She's tired," says Kade as he rises from his seat. "I'll see you all in the morning." He takes my hand and we head upstairs.

Once we're in his room, he kisses my neck. His hand is in my dress, moving up my thigh. Kade's need for me is different. I think it's because he wants me to forget about what happened. Actually, it might be because he doesn't want to remember.

**

I reach for his side of the bed. It's warm, but he's not here. Upon opening my eyes, I see the sun is emerging from the east. I put the pad of my finger to my lips. Mirai's kiss has left me curious. Did she want to know if the rumors were true? Are there other intentions behind it?

Instead of getting up, I decide to sleep a bit longer. I dream about shiny black hair. There is a wolf. She has two different colored eyes, one blue, one brown. She guides me to a waterfall. At the edge of the cliff is a tall man with a black cloak. I can't see his face, but he calls my name.

"Good morning, my lady," I'm awakened by Marisol's voice. Yawning with ferocity, I sit up and smile at her. "Your hair ribbons came in. Would you like to see them?" she asks. I nod and she opens the box on her lap.

Inside are five ribbons, all unique colors, and textures. Marisol holds up a silky white one. It's crisp and elegant. I reach in and pull out a river green one made of satin.

"Lord Kade picked each one. Do you like them?" she asks. I nod and the bounce of my curls on my shoulders tickles. She hands me the wine colored one. It's made of velvet and has gold flowers stitched on it. Marisol gingerly picks up the sky blue ribbon and stares at it. I look at her and then at the ribbon.

"In my country, there are gorgeous light blue flowers that bloom once in the spring. They die after three days," she says. I think this one must remind her of home.

The last one is made with thick fabric, silver and sparkly. I hold it in my palms as if it were alive. They're pretty. Out of the corner of my eye, I catch Marisol grinning at me. Her eyes get a glint in them.

"Lord Kade manages to say so much without saying anything at all." Her statement rings in my ears. Why can't I hear what he is saying? Marisol is helping me out of bed. It's sudden, but she changes the subject to what dress to wear, how to do my hair, which ribbon would I like to wear first? I sit idly and let Marisol do all the talking and choosing. She settles on the river green ribbon and a dress in a similar shade.

Her talented hands plait my hair and secure it. Marisol is able to tolerate my unruly curls. She lets them slide through her fingers without pulling or tugging. My scalp would hurt anytime the maids at Sloane castle tried to tame my hair.

"Let's get you some fresh air," she suggests and walks me out to the garden. "I'll bring you your breakfast and you can enjoy it by the flowers. Would that be alright, my lady?"

I nod, happy someone knows how to make me feel like I'm not a burden. Marisol seems to enjoy doing little things for me. She knows I don't like to eat in the dining hall unless Kade is there. Marisol can tell when I want to be alone and when I want company.

There is no wind. A breezeless day. The heat beams off the ground, hazy, blurring the edge where the grass meets the sky. I lay back and let the poppies surround me. They lean over me with their smiling faces. I hear them telling each other stories.

"My lady," says a female voice. It's Mirai's low whisper. I sit up and lean back on the palms of my hands. "I wanted to apologize for my forwardness. It was wrong of me to kiss you like that."

The beating of my heart hits my rib cage with excessive force. Mirai keeps her eyes on her boots. She tucks her silky black hair behind her ear in a beguiling fashion. Her smile is childish, a bit mischievous.

"It's just…" she starts and laughs to herself. My ears perk up. What is humorous to her? Does it amuse her to toy with me like this when she already has my husband? "…it's difficult for me to hold back my feelings for you. I'm sorry if this is bothersome to you, but I think it's best for me to be honest."

The still day is warm, and my face is becoming feverish. How could this be? The female mercenary is confessing her feelings for me. I clutch my heart because it might pop out of my chest. The bones surrounding it ache from its pounding.

"It won't happen again. Please forgive me for my actions, Lady Amadeus." I put up my palm and wave it off. Mirai's admission is confusing but doesn't upset me. Does this mean she isn't having an affair with Kade? Being locked up in Sloane castle for twenty-four years has left me inexperienced.

Mirai rises but keeps her gaze on me. I try to keep eye contact with her. Most of the time, I avoid everyone's stare. I try to read her but she is ambiguous. Like a boy. Kade is heading this way from the courtyard. The female mercenary looks at him but returns her focus to me.

"The first time I saw you, I knew you would break my heart. Please don't break his," she says and walks off towards the stables.

LEGEND OF THE SLAY LILY

28

How is it I can be this close to someone yet know nothing about what goes on in their head? Dawn hasn't come yet. I'm up before Kade. His hair is covering his face. This time, I dare to reach out and brush aside his bangs. He's given me more than I've asked for. I sleep next to him every night. But I don't know who he is.

I've spent hours trying to figure him out. Days wandering the castle searching for clues. There are artifacts, stories, and the rare times he shares with me, but when I piece everything together, there are missing parts. I have put together his past. What I've gathered from Francis, Mirai, Marisol and the others paint an incomplete portrait.

I'm wordless and he is reserved. I'm never sure how he feels about me. The people of the castle comment on his adoration for me, but he has never told me loves me or he thinks I'm beautiful. He does kind things for me. It's not clear what for, though. A lot of the time, I think he does what he does out of chivalry, not because he wants to.

A muscular hand reaches for my wrist. "Ama," Kade says my name and I cringe. I worry I've disturbed him. "Finn will chaperon you today and take you wherever you want. I'm going to rest today."

He kisses my palm and goes back to sleep. My chest hurts from my cowardly heart. I'm surprised blood isn't seeping out from my side. Kade trains tirelessly for weeks on end and then sleeps for a whole day. I stay with him a bit longer. It feels wrong leaving him.

I wait until his breath has slowed, and his face is slack. As I leave the room, I run into Marisol. I put my index finger to my lips to tell her to be quiet since he's sleeping. She understands and carries on fulfilling her chores.

Finn is in the foyer waiting for me. "Good morning, my lady," he greets me tonelessly. My chaperon isn't the friendliest, but I trust him. "Lord Kade instructed me to take you on a tour to see more of Tessafaye, if you would like."

I nod, and he guides me to the stables. Finn lets me mount my horse without his help. "You pick where we go. I'll follow," he says.

We ride, and it's exhilarating to be able to choose where we go. Ari's hooves kick up dirt and small rocks. I have no idea what I'm doing or where I'm going. All I know is I'm free. There are fields of grass with sandy trails. Sporadic juniper and cypress trees offer shade. I take paths at my leisure. There is a meadow over the knoll, and I let Ari trot until we get there.

Opulent blooms cover the ground. Pink flowers with red spots are prominent. They are mixed with minuscule white blossoms. There are orange flowers with blue leaves. Tessafaye is made up of mostly desert and is accommodated by scattered lush fields. I admire the plentiful blossoms and find myself staring at the field of flowers stretching to the mountains.

"This is called The Path to Paradise," says Finn as he gestures to a trail leading through the field. The horses make their way through exotic flowers. I can't stop craning my head to look at everything. As we continue down the path, I smell water. Rock formations create jagged shadows.

Paradise is a deep blue lake surrounded by boulders and palm trees. The water sparkles under the afternoon sun. Salt and aquatic notes tickle my nose. Finn dismounts and so do I. Ari and Finn's horse find a modest patch of grass to graze on. We step closer to the deep blue, and Finn shields his eyes from the sun.

"This is Lake Zahar. My grandfather told me the goddess who lived here lost her daughter to the king of The Underworld. She cried endless tears, enough to fill the crater," says Finn. He too knows poignant stories. We walk around the lake and I smile the whole time because I'm alive.

There are six red lilies with black stems underneath a palm tree. Their rich color is eye-catching. They stand as tall as me. The flowers are bigger than my hand. It startles me when Finn plucks one.

"This is a slay lily," he says and gives it to me. "They only grow in Tessafaye. It's from all the bloodshed that's taken place on our land and for our land. Beautiful sacrifices spawned a glorious country."

Red is violent. It's also stunning. The flower is quite magnificent. Showy and bold. It doesn't care if it is too much. I pull the stem through my braid to keep it in my hair. Finn permits me to go where I please until the sun is about to set. "We should head back," he says.

I'm tired but jittery. Happiness is open fields filled with flowers. Freedom tastes like vanilla and honey. I nod and Finn leads us home. My eyes are on the desert in the distance. Sensing someone looking at me, I turn and meet Finn's gaze.

"There is no forest here like your land, but the desert possesses a divergent kind of beauty."

I agree. The dark woods of Syrosa were full of secrets. In Tessafaye I'm drawn to the vast dunes.

The horses' hooves run to the rhythm of my heart. Steady but fast. We near the castle and are greeted by Francis and Marisol. Finn takes Ari and his horse back towards the stable. My hands are covered in dirt. They are red from holding the reins. I'm proud of myself.

Marisol is glad to see me. "You must have had a good day, my lady," she says and guides me upstairs. "I've drawn you a bath. I figured you would like one after your adventuring." The tub is full of pink and purple petals. It smells heavenly. I remove the slay lily Finn gave me before I sink into the hot water and submerge myself. When I break the surface, Marisol is gone. She knows I like my privacy.

After the bath turns cold, I return to Kade's room. He's still in bed. It's not good for him to run himself ragged. Kade is wealthy enough after marrying me and winning the war he doesn't have to work this hard. Tessafaye won't need to fight another war for decades. I sit next to him and rest my hand on his shoulder like it belongs there.

"Did you and Finn go out today?" His voice is groggy. He speaks into the pillow. I nod and hand him the slay lily. "You saw Lake Zahar." I nod again and he hands the flower back to me. "I'll show you everything there is to see. Give me time," says Kade and he smiles.

I lean down to kiss him. This causes Rupert to bark and paw at my leg. He gets jealous if I show Kade affection. It's cute and makes me laugh. I pick him up and he squeezes himself between Kade and I.

"Rupert doesn't like me kissing you," says Kade as he pets the small, white, and brown dog. I scratch under Rupert's chin with one hand but keep the other on Kade's shoulder. Rupert accepts this and drifts off to sleep. "I wouldn't like anyone else kissing you either," he says. Mirai comes to mind. Does he know about that? Her curvy lips touched mine.

I hold his hand until he falls back asleep. My restless feet beg me to wander the castle. It's not against the rules, but it feels improper. Rupert is snuggled up next to Kade. I'll leave him be. Out in the hall the lanterns are lit, but it's dim. For whatever reason, I go back to the library.

First, I rummage through the books. I pick two to read tonight while Kade is sleeping. It's relaxing to sit by the fire while my dog and husband dream nearby. This must be what it's like to have a real family. I haven't thought too deeply about it, but we are a family of sorts. He gave me his last name.

The bleeding occurs monthly, undeviated by what I've been doing with my body. I don't think I can get pregnant. This doesn't disappoint me, but I worry Kade is expecting it. All my life I've been told to do what my husband says and bear him an heir. My circumstances are unusual, but lucky.

"What are you doing up so late, my lady?" I drop my books at a male's voice. It's not Kade's. Darius steps out from the shadows of the shelves. "My apologies. I didn't mean to sneak up on you."

He kneels down and retrieves my books for me. I stand awkwardly and hold out my hands for them. Darius grips onto my books for a second too long. I back away, feeling threatened. The mercenary holds up his hands to show me he isn't trying to hurt me.

"It's okay. I only wanted to look at you for a minute longer. You always keep your head down in the dining hall," he admits. I move my curls to see him better. Darius' stare isn't full of lust like Dax's. His jasper gray eyes hold innocent curiosity.

"When Lord Kade told us the silent princess of Syrosa was to be his bride, we didn't know what to say. He's never shown an interest in a woman. Refused every girl who threw herself at him," says Darius as he steps closer. I stay still like a noble lady and let him hold my chin. "I think he was waiting for you."

My sternum reverberates from my pounding heart. The desk I was ruined on is behind Darius. He catches me glancing at it. His wavy hair sits on his shoulders. Turning his head slightly, he looks at the place of my violation.

"Those bastards made me sick. Treated every woman like they owned them. They would harass Mirai, but she didn't tell Lord Kade. She regrets not speaking up." Darius' words bounce around me but are difficult to absorb. "Lord Kade can't atone for the actions of others," he implies my husband is burdened by his guilt of the situation. "Please take good care of him, my lady." Darius exits the library. Manly footsteps disappear down the hall. I hang my head and hold my books the way a woman would hold an infant.

BEAUTIFUL VIOLENCE

29

I stand by the window and watch the men train. The clanging of metal is abrasive. I can't help myself, though. Jibril steps up to fight Kade. They are both skilled, tactical, and calm. Kade knocks him off his feet with an unexpected sweep of his sword.

Next is Finn, who is strong and strategic. They spar with each other for quite some time. In the end, Kade takes him down but isn't as harsh about it. Darius and the other men step up one by one. Kade is hardest on Eli, a sign he doesn't forgive his friendship with Dax.

The mercenaries take partners and fight in hand to hand combat. Knuckles are torn and lips are bloodied. Kade punches his opponent in the chest and nose. Thick ribbons of scarlet liquid stain their shirts.

The youngest mercenary is Margaux's age. He has short chestnut brown hair. It's his turn against Kade. I lean out the window to watch the two of them engage in beautiful violence. Kade eggs on the young mercenary who throws the first punch. He misses and Kade socks him in the shoulder.

Dodging the warlord's second punch, the young mercenary lands a hit to the side of Kade's face. His fists are half the size of the other men's, but it's the first time I've seen a man strike Kade. In retaliation, Kade grabs him by the shoulder and punches him in the chest twice before throwing him aside. The young mercenary holds his stomach and coughs.

It sickens me to be addicted to witnessing such brutal acts. There is an alluring factor to these altercations. I want to see their pain. It arouses a sense of connection. They don't cry, but I do. I feel it for them.

Men are emboldened by their rage, their fury. I wish I was a boy. Being born a female has taught me to forget myself for the sake of others. I have let men tug on my wrists, sniff my hair, and make me cry. A mute girl should take whatever is thrown at her. The lesson I learned.

If I were a boy, I could hit my friends and get drunk on wine. No one would tell me it was wrong. I wouldn't be intimidated because I'd be confident. Kade stands the tallest among the other men. It must be nice to be the leader.

"Lady Amadeus?" Mirai is whispering my name. I scoot away from her. She is standing a few inches behind me. Her feet must hover because I never hear her walking. I step back from the window, embarrassed I've been caught. Mirai isn't deterred and watches the men dust themselves off.

Kade helps Avery up. Both of them have blood on their cheeks. I think Mirai is watching the men, but I turn to see she is staring at me. "I thought you might like to write something for him," she says and hands me her notebook. Mirai goes back to gazing out the window.

The runaway princess escaped her marriage to a tyrant. What if I ran? I don't want to go, nor do I have somewhere to be, but I wonder what kind of person I am if given the choice. Her father didn't care about her happiness. My mother didn't think about mine. We might have more in common than I originally thought.

The curve of her mouth attracts my attention. Her kiss isn't something I crave, but it's constantly on my mind. I hold the paper and pencil, dumbfounded. My silly girlish thoughts aren't useful. I try to push them aside.

Thank you for showing me more of your land. Tessafaye doesn't have a forest, but it doesn't need one. The desert is wondrous. I didn't know the dunes could be so pretty, especially at dusk and dawn, when the sand sparkles.

Don't tease, but I was worried there might not be any flowers. I think I like the ones here better. They don't bloom in Syrosa the way they do here.

The poppies and tiger lilies you got me are lovely. I wish there was something I could give you?

* * *

I tap Mirai's shoulder and hold out my note. It makes me blush, giving her my private thoughts. I resist the urge to keep my head down. Mirai scans my script and her teeth peek out from rosy pink lips.

"Thank you, my lady. Your thoughts are appreciated," she says. Mirai slips out into the hall, but I'm entranced by the happenings outside where the men have their brawl. The skin on their hands is torn open, oozing red liquid, smearing it on their shirts. Hard faces lined in stubble are covered in blood.

Avery tries to punch Kade in the mouth, but Kade catches his fist and returns the favor. The mercenary turns to the side and spits up blood onto the lush grass. I can smell the musky scent of it. It hits the ground and evaporates from the heat. Gore didn't appeal to me a year ago, but Kade grins, teeth drenched in his own blood, and signals for the men to take a break.

***

The rains have come. Flowers drink it hastily. The dying grass will perk up. I haven't done it in so long but I steal away in order to stand in the rain. It comes down in steady streams. I like it better when it pours.

It's the middle of the day but dark gray. I run through the bright orange maze of tiger lilies. Rupert was sleeping by the fire in Kade's chair. It doesn't bother me to run by myself. I dance in the petunias and poppies. It brings me joy to have the heavens rain down on me.

I sneak into the stable and say hi to Ari. She likes the rain, too. I pet her snout and she softly neighs. Fang is eying me like I'm not supposed to be here. He has a piercing stare. The black stallion and Kade have been through everything together.

Frolicking around the castle, I enter the courtyard. Looking for mercenaries, I find none and bolt to the juniper tree. I press my back to the trunk and take another peek around. No one is out but me. A sound of thunder can be heard in the distant north. Rain comes in sideways and sprays my face.

Half laughing, half crying, I make my way back to the garden. Palm trees wave and bend from the harsh wind. My hair blows back and forth over my shoulder. White jasmine tinges the air and I inhale thoughtfully as I run back through the tiger lily maze.

The sound of thunder covers up his voice, but he's got a tight grip on the crook of my arm. He shouts my name after the lightning strikes and the thunder passes. I cower, not sure if from my husband or the threatening sky. "You're going to catch your death out here," he says and begins walking me to the castle.

This time I tug. This perplexes him and he stops. "Come on, I don't want you to get sick again," he says.

Black hair is lifted from the intense gale, revealing his face. I don't know how to explain the art of standing in the rain. Kade is focused on me becoming ill. He isn't well versed in art, poetry, or other aristocratic things.

I don't know what comes over me, but when the lightning strikes, I tug again and free myself. Kade is startled by the fact I've broken his grasp. The thunder distracts him and I take off through the winding row of flowers. He calls my name, but I lose him around the corner. I step into the tall lilies and blend in. My red hair and green dress camouflage me. Kade runs past but doesn't notice me lurking in the stems.

Stepping out from the dark green leaves, I run the other way towards the courtyard. I don't know why I'm hiding from him. He will catch me eventually, but there is something thrilling about eluding my husband. Do I seek punishment? Or do I simply want to know how long he will give chase?

In the bleak gray mist, I'm able to evade Kade. It pleases me to watch him look for me. He keeps calling my name. Two perfectly enunciated syllables lost to the whipping of the wind. Kade searches for me and I slip past him using stealth. I slink by him like a slippery weasel. His head turns this way but doesn't land on my silhouette as I try to remain out of sight. I use the shadows to my advantage, leaning against the walls of the castle, tiptoeing despite the booming storm.

I sneak through shadows and shrubbery. Across the courtyard is the juniper tree. The bitter berry scent coats the air here. My boots have mud splattered on them. So does my dress. Lightning crashes into the dunes and I make a run for it. I don't make it, though, because Kade is right next to me. He snatches me up like I weigh nothing.

"Why are you running away from me?" he asks ruefully. I feel sorry for him. He doesn't understand and neither do I. Critical spessartite eyes wear me down. I point to the sky. While Kade looks up, I kiss him.

Does he know what I'm trying to say?

"You like the rain," he states as he did before when he found me on the balcony.

We stay in the courtyard, our clothes soaked, and let the water fall into our hair. Kade walks towards the castle, but not in a hurry. This time, he contemplates my love of the raindrops and tries to see who I am through them.

Kade holds a substantial pile of hair in his hands. "Your curls remind me of liquid embers," he says. We go inside and Kade dries my frizzy locks. He removes my rain drenched dress and covers me up with my robe. Rupert barks at our feet, trying to make sense of what's happening. The three of us sit by the fire. Tessafaye is hot midday but chilly at night.

I'm reading my book. Kade sits in his chair and I've settled down on the floor with Rupert at my side. I stroke his velvety dog ears. Kade suddenly stands and I wince. He kneels and presses the back of his large hand against my forehead to check for signs of fever.

"Are you feeling alright?" he asks. I bundle the robe around myself and nod. Kade studies me and I smile for him. He could use one. It stresses him out to shepherd me.

THE THIN LINE BETWEEN LOVE AND HATE

30

There is a commotion downstairs. Someone is here. But who? I throw
my hair up and secure it with the emerald green hair ribbon. Anxiety
flushes my cheeks, bringing out my freckles. I pause, checking my face
before taking the stairs two at a time.

"I already declined the Tsar's offer," says Kade.

"Just sign the papers, Kade," says a familiar voice.

It's my mother. Queen Kathryn herself stands in the foyer in a
shouting match with my husband. I stare up at him and then
concentrate on my mother, golden hair with mean brown eyes. She
tries to approach me, but Kade steps in the way. He backs up until he
can reach behind him and grab my wrist. I lean into him and peer out
from under his cloak and am met with her soulless gaze.

"My dear daughter, how I have missed you," she coos at me. Kade's
glove squeaks as he tightens his grip. She notices this and her eyes
shift from his face to mine. "I was just telling Kade you couldn't
possibly want to stay here. I've come to take you home," she says with
a sneer.

I shake my head in protest. There is no way I'm going back to
Syrosa. I'd rather be banished to the desert.

"That's not going to happen," says Kade. He stares her down,
attempting to suppress her wrath. My mother's mouth is a lopsided
grin, wicked and dangerous.

"The Tsar is giving you such an opportunity. You'd be free of my afflicted daughter and I'd have my family back. All you have to do is sign," she sings and holds out the divorce papers to Kade. He presses them back into her hands.

"I told you I don't want a divorce."

"Come on, Kade. Don't be stubborn. She has a young knight waiting for her back home, anyway. Isn't that right? Mason misses you," hisses my mother. She is trying to rile up Kade. If she can't have me, then she is going to turn my husband against me.

"It doesn't matter. She's my wife now," Kade's steel words cut through my mother's ruse. She balls up her fist and bites her lip.

"It must be embarrassing having a ruthless reputation soiled by the fact your wife is a dumb girl." The corners of her eyes rise with her smile. Kade has an irritated tremble in his wrist. She knows this has gotten to him and it opens Kade up for her rage. "Not to mention the fact she's been ruined more than once," says my mother with glee. I open my mouth in horror at the things she spews at me. "I heard what happened here. Under your watch, no less," she says and Kade loses his temper.

"Get out of my house!" he roars. I cover my ears. His voice booms above me.

"I tried to do you a favor, Kade," she lashes out, but she makes her way to the door. Francis is glaring at her. "Don't complain when you don't want her anymore."

I prickle at her insult.

"Leave Tessafaye and never come back. If you do, I'll slit your throat. I mean it, Kathryn," says Kade. My mother howls with laughter on her way out.

"Threats from the young warlord, how seductive. Amadeus, does this inspire lustful thoughts in you?" cackles my mother.

I hide at Kade's side and bury my face in his shirt. He says nothing else, but I know he is watching her exit the castle, a grimace on his handsome face.

Francis closes the door and audibly sighs. My mother can be ten people at once, unpredictable, a ferocious creature. The Tsar granted Kade a chance to divorce me, but he didn't take it. The idea of being abandoned by Kade is a dagger, shredding me to pieces. I've become too attached for my own good.

What will I do if he doesn't want me anymore? I choke on my thoughts. Would he toss me aside and take another wife? Am I replaceable? Kade could have any woman. I see the way they look at him. To believe I'm special makes me a fool. But for now, I'd rather be a fool than a miserable, lonely girl. Kade pulls away and kneels down to embrace me. He wipes away my tears. Soft leather grazes my cheekbone.

"Don't listen to her," he says. I want to ignore my mother's unbridled anger, but I can't. It has been ingrained in me. A part of my brain goes off like the ticking of a clock. Kade can tell I'm not listening. He unties the ribbon and ruffles my hair. "Hey, look at me. I'm your husband now. She can't do anything to you."

As long as Kade remains my husband, he is my guardian, the one who is responsible for me. I want to trust I am safe, but low in the bottom of my heart is the apprehensive beating. Not being my mother's charge means the warlord is my ruler. It seems unwise to trust a killer king, but he gives me refuge from the place where I lost my family and myself.

Kade rises and towers over me. I shudder at the change in the atmosphere. It's cooler and a severe wind comes in from the west. He places his hand on the back of my neck. "Is the young knight waiting for you? Be honest," says Kade. I recoil at the question and shake my head. Mason might have defended me, but I never did what my mother and sister accused me of. I didn't sleep with him or even give him a kiss. All I did was wrap my arms around him after I saw his black eye.

"Really?" he asks. I nod and Kade searches for the cue of a lie. To make up for my skittish behavior, I brave his stare and look into his deep-set eyes.

"Did you love him?" Kade asks, but focuses on his boots instead of looking at me. I put one hand on his shoulder and stand on the tips of my toes to place the other on his chiseled face. He waits for my response and grins when I shake my head no.

***

The morbid suggestion grows rapidly, tangled in my thoughts. Disturbing images and ideas come to mind. They choke out my rational brain like porcelain berries. Vines suffocate the other parts of myself. I keep thinking about suicide.

Stop, that's wrong. It would be unfair to Kade and Rupert. Or am I lying to myself? I'm a burden Kade shouldn't have to carry. Wouldn't it be better for me to die so he could live? I cry at random throughout the day. Marisol, Francis, and Kade are concerned about my well being. Wild thoughts run rampant, like feral beasts.

If I did do it, how would I do it? I speculate about the ways I could meet my death. Do I dare shoot myself with a gun? I could drown myself in the tub. The most reasonable form of dying, I realize, is jumping off the walkway to the tower. It's the second highest point of the castle besides the roof.

Great, I have a plan. It shouldn't quell the nervous bubbling in my veins, but it does. I keep it a secret. The private plans for my demise must not be shared. Don't be too obvious. Everyone thinks I'm unstable as is.

I'm glad Kade didn't believe I had a young knight waiting for me. At least I think he believes me. My mother has a way of painting me in a distasteful light while representing perfect motherhood. Only she could love me. Naturally, a mute girl needs to be with her family.

Perhaps it would be righteous of me to die. Why should Kade be subjected to this marriage? He might be a ruthless warlord, but he is kind enough to tolerate me. The time we spend together isn't dreadful. We eat together, sleep together, ride our horses, watch the sunset, and some days he shows me the riveting landmarks of Tessafaye.

The cliff where he took me to Ja'Hira Falls is a focal point in my fantasies, where I'm jumping into indigo water lined with rocks. I jolt at my sick idea. What causes these thoughts to invade my space?

"Excuse me, my lady," says her hushed female voice. I spin around, caught with horrible thoughts pouring out of the top of my head. Mirai stands upright and stiff, like a boy. "I thought you could write something for Kade."

I nod and pull at my hair with nervous frustration. The notebook is thinner. Kade must be keeping the notes I give him. It pacifies my jealousy, but I don't like Mirai as the translator. I sit in the chair by the window and twirl my hair, thinking of something to write. Mirai leans on the windowsill and looks out at the dunes.

"Living in Sloane castle with Queen Kathryn must have been a harrowing experience," she says to the breeze. Short black hair stops at her chin next to her beguiling lips. The sun's light reflects in her inky black locks. She fiddles with it and tucks a strand behind her ear. "I didn't like the way she spoke to you. Neither did Lord Kade. He's absolutely furious about it. Assuming she could convince him to divorce you so she could take you back. What a pitiful attempt at reclaiming you," she scoffs, the way men do, throaty and harsh.

The admission lands on the paper lightning fast. I don't realize what I'm doing until I hand it to her.

My mother stopped loving me when my father died. I have his hair, his skin, and eyes. Everything to remind her of what she lost. Once she got rid of me, she lost my sisters. I'm all she has left.

Mirai's delicate features soften even more. She looks disturbed by my message. Her eyes scan the page once before facing me.

"I heard you were her prized eldest daughter. Do you mean to say you were not treated as such?" she asks. A hearty laugh in my belly has me gasping for air.

The novelty of a mute princess wears off rather quickly. My suitors found it unappealing, and my mother grew increasingly agitated by my affliction. My sister Adrian had at least ten men waiting for her hand, but the tradition of the oldest daughter entering marriage first interrupted this. They despised me.

"I thought you would have lived a luxurious life in Syrosa. I'm sorry, my lady. You didn't deserve to be a victim of their cruelty," says Mirai. My finger has an indent in it from holding the pencil. I haven't spoken this long with Mirai. Hopefully, I didn't reveal too much. The female mercenary wears me down with her bewitching two toned eyes and I look away. "Lord Kade is troubled by what happened with the westerners. He wants to know if there is anything he can do."

My mother has a way of making everyone around her insecure, whether she is around or not. She can be five, ten, twenty people and no one I recognize. Here in my thoughts, even when she's on her way back to Syrosa, where there are red poppies instead of golden ones.

* * *

Kade, you defend me with such honor. Thank you. I've almost forgotten the dogwood and lavender of Syrosa. It doesn't rain as often here, but that's okay. Every day, I look forward to seeing you. I find myself drawn to the sparkling desert. The stars shine brighter in Tessafaye.

Mirai's eyelashes twitch as she reads my note. She approves and sticks the notebook back in her pocket. "I'll give this to him straight away," she says. I wait until she's out of sight and I can no longer hear her footsteps to cry.

TO EARN A MEMORY

31

My sleep is disturbed, sporadic, and at inconvenient hours. I'm tired most of the day. But then I can't relax in the evening. Rupert and I pace around the castle. I read and walk around aimlessly. I end up falling into deep slumbers accompanied by dreams transformed into gruesome nightmares.

Tonight snuck up on me. One minute I was reading a love story between a poor man and a duchess, next I'm in a gloomy world of despair. My mother is dragging me into Sloane castle. The maids and servants have red eyes. They glare at me. I notice they have antlers.

I'm able to scream in my dream. It does no good. My mother shows me my father's casket. His freckled skin matches mine. We are part of the same starry sky. I go to touch him and he opens his eyes. They are hollow. He keeps saying he wants to go to war. The blackness of the sockets swallows me up.

Penelope waves at me, blood in the corners of her mouth. She's laughing at something, I don't know what. Blood stains the palms of her hands and crook of her elbow. Adrian is throwing me on the ground. She stands over me, telling me I'm worthless. No one will ever love me. Then Margaux steps up beside her. The baby in her arms is deformed and sopping wet with afterbirth. I let out another inhuman scream as I cover my face.

"Ama, wake up," whispers Kade. I'm thrashing in the bed, not sure where the dream stopped and when reality took over. "You're with me, it's okay."

It's raining outside. A stormy night. The moon is full, illuminating the dunes and tops of the cypress trees. Severe winds whip through the tops of the junipers. The raindrops tap, tap, tap rhythmically on the balcony. Petals drip in ecstasy from the long awaited shower.

Kade has his fists wrapped around my arms. I stop fighting him and he lets me go. My breathing is labored. I reach for my forehead, damp curls dripping in sweat. In my frenzy, I rip off my chemise and rush out onto the balcony.

Stormy clouds douse Tessafaye in heavenly rain. I cup my hands to catch it. Like sand, it goes right through my fingers, but I want to feel it, anyway. My nudity no longer brings on a sense of humiliation. The opposite reaction has stirred in me. I like when the mercenaries look at me. What pleases me more is seeing Kade watch them as they stare. They think I'm dimwitted, but I notice everything.

I run my hand from my sternum to my belly button. Places only I, Kade, and Dax have touched. To share something intimate with my husband and my rapist grows thorny roses in my bed of thoughts. Some girls are empty flower pots. I wish I was one. Kade pulls me into him. His hair is saturated in rainwater.

Big hands press into my collarbone and hip. Kade gazes out towards the west. Does he think about what happened as I do? I can't tell what goes on in his head. His neutral expression holds no clues. Kade coaxes me out of the rain and back into his room.

He dries my hair. Stray curls cling to my body. There is a deadly silence between us. The crackling of the fire is a solitary sound. We sit in the orange glow. Kade hands me one of my books off the nightstand. He brushes my hair while I read. The warlord has a rough touch but is extra careful not to damage a single strand.

"Your hair has gotten long," he says.

I set down the novel. The cover is warm from the heat of my hands. I peer at him over my shoulder. It's silly, but I still feel too shy to look right at him. My hair sits on my hips. I pick a lock up off the floor and examine it.

"You used to keep it short," says Kade, and I give him a confused face. "I saw you many years ago on one of my visits to Sloane castle."

I'm incapable of responding because I'm sifting through my memories. I recall them saying Kade came to Sloane castle over ten years ago. At fourteen, my hair barely touched my top rib. I'd secure it at the nape of my neck with a ribbon or let it hang loose when I wanted to irritate my mother. I put my hand on his and nod remembering who I was a lifetime ago. Not that I'm anyone now, but I used to be a princess with no choices. As Kade's wife, I'm Amadeus Soloman and I get to do as I please.

"I like it like this," he says and runs his hand through it to the bottom. Kade is daunting, tall, and alarmingly handsome. How do I not remember his face? I try to wade through the recesses of my mind and come up empty-handed. "Let's go back to bed."

Sliding next to him, I find my cowardly heart catching up to me. Knowing a nightmare is minutes away has my body tense. Kade detects the reverberation in my chest and speaks into the top of my head. "I don't want you to worry so much."

My nervous antics must be tiresome. I chide myself to get it together. Kade massages my shoulder and holds me close enough for me to discern the beating of his rugged heart. Sleep is unreachable because I ruminate on how Kade remembers me, but I don't remember him.

***

In my arms is Rupert. He is having a late morning snooze. Under the juniper tree, I contemplate everything. The weight of silence is heavy, but not everyone can feel it. I've torn myself away from watching Kade train the mercenaries. It's unhealthy, the desire to witness such violent acts.

It's like Dax poisoned my mind with his filthy thoughts when he violated me. They couldn't belong to me, but they do. I rock Rupert and hold him over my heart. A small shrew darts from the shade of a thorny shrub into the hollow of a thin tree. The shape of silence is whole and resounding.

"Good day, my lady. Are you and Rupert enjoying the beautiful weather?" asks Francis. He approaches in his slow and graceful way. I snuggle Rupert and nod. "Are you doing alright? You haven't asked for anything in a while."

Men seem to think I want items: dresses, jewelry, more things. I crave something else. It's a fool's request, but I want to be the only one.

Kade may be my husband, but I suspect he spends the day with Mirai. They sit too close, walk around the castle together, and spend more time together than him and I.

Francis eyes me and I touch my heart and nod to show I'm fine. He doesn't believe me. My acting skills are diminishing. "You don't seem happy, my lady. Please, let me help you."

I manage to stop my body from shaking, but the tears won't be deterred. Francis sits across from me and waits patiently for me to wipe away my tears. I choke back the next wave. He runs his fingertips through the grass. It crinkles as it contacts his hand.

Marisol and Mirai try to be my friends, but I miss my sister. So much about me has changed. I wish I could share it with her.

He reads my note and rubs his chin. Francis takes a deep breath. His leathery hands hold the piece of paper like a snake. "My apologies, my lady. I know the loss of your sister was most troubling. Her funeral was held the same day as your wedding. Not a pleasant reminder," he says to the ink. I cast my eyes the other way and stare at the ground. "Your mother didn't make it any easier," says Francis. I nod again but refuse to face him. He reaches for me and sets his hand on my shoulder.

"I was shocked to hear him threaten Queen Kathryn like that," chuckles Francis. My eyes widen–the elderly steward finds this humorous. "Lord Kade has worked hard to get rid of his bad habits and cool his temper. I saw a bit of the old Kade." Francis must have fond memories of the young warlord growing up because it makes him smile. I grin in return.

"This is your home now," says Francis as he stands. He dusts himself off and smooths his hair. "If you want it," he finishes his sentence as he walks off towards the castle.

Rupert squirms in my arms but remains asleep. Eli, Avery, Finn, and three other men cross the courtyard. I catch Eli taking slower steps. He wants to look at me. I get the obscene sensation of power. The one power I have over them. Finn is psychic and pushes Eli to keep him walking at a faster pace. Their manly footsteps march in unison. I keep my eyes on them. Finn turns to me, but no one else does. I hide my blushing face in the shadow of the juniper.

How sick I've become. I hold Rupert below my chin and nuzzle him. His velvety ears relieve me of some of my anxiety. I close my eyes and think about what I've seen, the places I've been, and where I may go.

He's shown me his world. I didn't think so at the time, but he saved me from mine. I'd have surely died at my mother's or sister's hand. If not them, then one of the knights. Someone was always mad at me there. Nothing I did was good enough. I messed up Sloane castle's perfect reputation.

Kade could have divorced me, but he chose not to. I don't know his opinions, thoughts, or values. What would cause the young warlord to refuse such a grand offer? The possibility of him wanting me chills me to the core. I wished on a star before my sister died. My wish was to be loved.

I'm a burden no one should be subjected to. As much as I want to be loved, I don't think I'm worthy of such a thing. Years of mistreatment has shattered my psyche. I can't determine what's acceptable and what isn't. Whatever sickness Dax had, now I have it, too. My nightmares are accompanied by strange infatuations and demented daydreams.

The breeze has aquatic notes in it from the river. I recall Ja'Hira Falls. The tragic but wonderful story Kade told riveted me. I don't want Kade to be stuck with an odd mute girl. He belongs with someone like Mirai. Rupert wakes and runs off. I'm alone, but I already was. Now I know what I need to do. The next time it rains, I'm going to kill myself.

DEATH OF A TIGER LILY

32

Everything is radiating warmth and sparkling. Since my decision, I'm light as a feather, weighed down by nothing, not even silence, which can cause fractures deep in the bones. I run around the castle like a maniac. My hair moves across my back and shoulders.

For some reason, the thought of knowing I'm going to die soon makes me feel pretty. I play with my hair and run my fingers over my freckled cheekbones. The tip of my ring finger grazes the bridge of my nose. Kade put this ring on me over a year ago. It's a thick gold band, simple but well made. I never noticed how shiny and pristine it is until recently.

Food tastes better, the flowers are valiant in their beauty, and the urge to connect with others comes frequently. I want to walk in the garden with Marisol or follow her around while she does chores. She speaks to me like I'm her sister.

Some days I stay by Francis' side while he makes arrangements around the castle. He tells me stories of his youth, other countries, and sneaks in tidbits about Kade growing up. I don't know why, but I've been hungry to know who the man I've been married to is since I'm going to leave him soon.

He deserves to be with someone of his choosing, not a mute girl who was forced on him. Kade's been good to me, despite who I am. This makes me determined to rid him of me. The rumors about the young warlord being ruthless are true. But nobody talks about his heart.

Once I'm gone, he'll be free to do whatever he wants. The same gift he gave me all those months ago.

The weather has been fair. Not too sunny, not too cloudy. No rain though. I don't mind. Gives me time to say goodbye to everything and everyone. I laugh to myself, thinking about how I'll miss the men whose names I didn't learn. Mirai's two toned eyes fly past my face like a bat. I stumble at the thought of her. Will she and Kade rejoice when I'm gone?

I'll miss her, too. She might be my husband's mistress, but she wiped away my tears. There was the day she kissed me. I lean against the brick wall. It hits me hard in the ribs. I gasp at what Mirai said to me, "The first time I saw you, I knew you would break my heart. Please don't break his."

Perhaps I should reconsider. I stop my skipping and slow my pace, leaning on the wall to steady myself. The thought of being a burden to everyone here forever is making me woozy. No, I can't possibly stay and risk hurting everyone more.

The sun is setting. A patchwork sky of blue, pink, and orange runs together into one indigo night. I head downstairs to meet Kade. It would be immoral to have him look for me when I'm plotting my demise. The meal the servants are preparing smells amazing. Cumin, coriander, and ginger rise from the kitchen.

I turn the corner and run into Kade. "Were you looking for me?" he asks. My hands reach for his. I nod and smile at him. This seems to cheer him up. Kade's charming grin appears on rare occasions, but I've been trying to get him to smile.

In the dining hall, I soak up the lively atmosphere. How every day is a feast. Some men treat every night like a celebration. Finn remains stoic and collected. He and Kade chat about the horses, the castle, and the other mercenaries. I taste each bite thoroughly and gaze out at the rowdy men. Rupert begs for scraps at my feet. I scoop him up and give him a bite.

"She treats the dog like a baby. Look at the way she holds him," teases one of the men. His eyes are half closed; he's so far gone. Eli glares at him, but the man doesn't notice.

"Lady Amadeus is good with animals. Unlike some people," says Jibril in a haughty voice. I don't think he likes this man. Finn makes eye contact with Kade, who has grown alarmingly quiet.

"I think it's precious. Hey, when are you and the princess going to have one, eh?" asks Avery. He gives Kade a playful punch in the arm. By the way he slurs his words, he must be drunk. I cringe, knowing Kade is upset. His hand is in a balled up fist sitting on the table. It's been bloodied, broken, and right now it's thirsty.

Kade hasn't brought it up, but I knew people would talk about it. The fact I've been here for this long and haven't gotten pregnant must embarrass him. I cuddle Rupert closer to my chest and keep my head down. His fist lifts off the table. Instead of a smack, I feel an arm around me.

"I like it being just us," says Kade as he pulls me closer to him. Finn eyes the man who mocked me and Avery. Eli takes a nervous bite. Filling his mouth is better than speaking at this time.

"You two have plenty of time. No need to rush," says Finn. He rescues the conversation and Kade agrees.

What they don't know is Kade and I aren't careful by any means. By the way Finn is looking at us, I suspect he knows, too. Rupert hops out of my arms to beg from Marisol. I lean into Kade as I finish my food.

This is another sign I should die. I look up at my husband. He glances at me but focuses on what Jibril and Finn are saying. They go back and forth about preparations for the changing season. A draft in the castle causes a shiver up my back. Kade wraps his cloak around me. Somehow, he can pretend I'm not completely useless.

***

The sound of a growing storm wakes me. I look out towards the dunes. Purple clouds come in over the mountains. The moon is half full and I hear wolves howl at it. Kade is sleeping, but as soon as I put my lips to his, he brings me to his chest. Big hands are in my hair. He touches me everywhere. I know this is our last time, but he doesn't. Can he taste the lies I can't speak?

I wait for him to fall back asleep. He has his hands on my stomach and collarbone. His grasp loosens and I attempt to slide out of bed without waking him. I throw on my chemise. There's no point in dressing up to kill myself.

The fire is low. It's cold at night. I throw on more wood. Rupert is sleeping in Kade's chair. I kiss the top of his head and his ears twitch.

Saying goodbye is much harder than I thought it would be. I tiptoe back to Kade. His chest rises and falls leisurely.

His palm is resting on my side of the bed. I put my hand on his. He doesn't stir. Risking my chance, I lean down and kiss him. Anise on my lips is the last thing I want to taste before I die. I want to run my fingers through his hair but can't bring myself to do so. It will hurt too much.

I sneak to the door. As I open it, the wood creaks. I peek over my shoulder. Kade hasn't moved. Rupert kicks his legs while he dreams. Tears run down my face as I wave to both of them. Goodbye Kade. You gave me more than I deserve. This way, you get everything you desire. You can have it all: my family's wealth, give my dresses to Mirai, and your other mistresses if you want. I'm grateful to you. You were the first person to give me freedom. Now I'm going to set you free. I love you.

Rain falls in steady streams. It looks like it's not moving. I stay in the shadows and avoid the well-lit areas. Servants and maids are most likely sleeping, but mercenaries have nightmares. They tend to get up and wander around as I do.

The abandoned tower is one of the highest points of the castle. I head there. No one else is roaming around. I pass by a vase full of tiger lilies. They are fresh. Marisol must have put them here.

Throbbing in my temples tempts me to throw the glass container filled with flowers. The sickness is corroding my heart, burning the soul inside me. I step out onto the ledge. This tower hasn't been used in months, even before I came here. This was my hiding place when I was afraid of my new home.

The wind has picked up. A harsh gale nearly knocks me over. I hold myself steady and ponder the decision I'm about to make. There is nothing honorable about selfish death, but hopefully Kade will understand I'm doing this for him.

This is rationally the only way to repay his kindness. I try to talk myself out of it, but it's no use. What do I have to offer Kade? All I do is sully his reputation. The men who have defiled and ridiculed me have been punished, but I feel like I'm the one who did something wrong.

My feet are bare, my hair is down, and my hands are raw from gripping the bricks. I pull myself up to stand closer to the edge. Rain droplets mix with my tears in my mouth, creating a sad girl elixir.

What the knight said to me echoes in my ears, You're pretty when you cry. I sob at the memory. He wanted to see me in pain. What is about my torment that turns them on? I wince hearing what Kade once said, I like how you look when you read.

My husband isn't one of those men. He is someone completely different. Fighting monsters has made him stony and cold, but not arrogant or cruel. I was lucky to be married off to someone as gracious as him. He must have felt the opposite. What do a mute princess and a young warlord have in common?

I bite my lip and teeter in the wind. This is it. Tonight I'm going to die. Clouds break and I can see the stars. The wish I made with Penelope stuns me. I can't move. Jump, Ama, I tell myself. I wobble and put out my arms. Taking a full body breath, I smile while I cry. Now I'll be with my sister and the man I love will be free. I go to step off into nothing, ready to see the other side, when muscular arms wrap around my waist.

"Ama! What are you doing?" shouts Kade. He's shirtless, and his hair is drenched in rainwater, or maybe it's sweat. "What's wrong with you?" he asks, anger straining him.

I put my arms up defensively. My cowardice has ruined me once again. Kade drags me back inside with a furious grip. "Is being with me really so bad?" he growls. I shake my head. He gets as close to my face as he can without our noses touching. Dune colored eyes glare at me.

"You think you're too good for me," says Kade in a gravelly voice. I shake my head again. He looks me up and down. I cover my mouth to keep in my ugly sobs. "Then what is it?" he asks. I open my mouth, but of course nothing comes out. "Do you think I deserve this?" he yells at me.

I step back and cover my face with my arms. Adrian used to say it drove her crazy, how I would act like she was mistreating me. Kade has the same wild look in his eyes. "Why would you do this to me?" he asks and lunges at me. I try to dodge him, but he grabs both of my wrists.

"Haven't I given you everything you asked for? I gifted you the library. I've shown you the holy landmarks of my country and bought you everything money can buy. Why would you leave me like that?" he asks.

Kade's booming voice and grip on my wrists brings on a hazy whirl of anxiety. He is talking to me, but my vision blurs. "Ama? Ama, are you alright?" Penelope is standing behind him. She waves at me and walks out the door. I reach for her, but satiny blonde hair disappears into the dark hallway. My eyes are forced closed. I can't tell what's real and what's not.

LOST AND FOUND

33

Birds sing to one another to alert their friends and family that they made it through the night. I did, too. In my hysteria, I thought dying would be better than being a burden to Kade. Now I'm morose and mortified. Rupert lays at the foot of the big bed. Fur lined blankets engulf me. I pull them close to my chest and smell them. The fragrant anise scent clings to the covers.

The thrill of death aroused me, and I couldn't control my impulse to jump. Good thing Kade stopped me. What if I succeeded? I guess it wouldn't matter because I'd be dead. My husband would be without me. Rupert kicks his little legs and wags his short, curly tail. I don't want to leave either of them.

I cry out my doubts and my shame. How selfish of me to worry everyone. Surely no one will trust me now. The lady of the castle is mute and apparently she's a lunatic, too. I lay on my curls and let them fall off the side of the bed. Hot tears cascade down my face and burn the sensitive skin of my neck.

Kade comes in and I sit up. Rupert wakes from his slumber. My dog stares at me and so does Kade. I don't know what to do and I open my arms to him. Footsteps thud, thud, thud like my heart. He stands before me but pauses. He ignores my embrace. I put my arms down.

Desert sand eyes burn through the pine green forest. He kneels but doesn't return my affection. I don't blame him. It doesn't stop it from hurting, though. Kade keeps his eyes on me but pulls a notebook out of his pocket. He hands it to me. "Will you write me something?" he asks. This question...I was not expecting this question. Shaky hands remove the pencil and paper from his hands. They are mine, but don't feel like they are attached to my body.

Do you love me?

It's completely ridiculous, but I ask him a question as well. We've been married for over a year and I've been wondering the whole time. I cringe at my loopy cursive. Mirai has read my notes to him for months. I should be able to handle this rejection. After all, I've been rejected at least a hundred times.

Kade pries it out of my hands. Tight fingers have wrinkled the edges of the paper. I keep my head down in shame. My husband is illiterate, but this brings no peace of mind. He stares at the four words for a long time. The birds stop singing. A gust of wind lifts the curtains and stings my face as it hits my tear stained skin.

"I've loved you for a long time," he says. I'm disarmed by Kade's reply. It hits me harder than my mother ever did. Analyzing Kade, I notice he is wearing a smile. "Seneca took me to visit Syrosa after I turned eighteen. I was an overindulgent delinquent at the time. It was raining, and I was irritated about accompanying my father. As we neared Sloane castle, I saw a splash of radiant red vibrant against the green and gray. It was you."

I sit up, but my elbow is trembling and unable to support me. Kade joins at my side and sits next to me on the bed. He toys with a lock of hair. "You were wearing a white dress and holding a bouquet of poppies. The clouds were emptying buckets of rain, but you were smiling in the garden facing east. I couldn't stop looking at you," says Kade, and he turns away sheepishly. "You probably don't remember, but you waved at me. I had my helmet on. You wouldn't have seen my face."

I reach for him, and he holds my tiny hands in his. For the entirety of our marriage, I assumed what he did was because I was his responsibility. Not because he loved me. What a skinny little fool I've been. I saw the signs but closed my eyes to the possibility someone like Kade could ever care for an odd mute girl like me.

Kade reaches into his breast pocket and hands me five hair ribbons tied in a knot in the middle. I turn it over in my palm. It takes me a moment to understand. These are the hair ribbons I thought I lost over the years. The lavender one I wore every day when I was fifteen. An aquamarine one, Penelope let me borrow. I run the tips of my fingers over the blood red ribbon. I see it through fresh eyes. Ones that have seen beautiful violence.

Twirling the royal blue one, I grin at myself. I thought I lost this one to Adrian. For years, I was convinced she stole it. Now I know who the true culprit is. The last one is my favorite shade of green. This is the one I thought was carried away by the wind.

"I'm the boy who broke into Sloane castle to see you," he admits.

I clutch the bundle of hair ribbons to my chest. How something can touch me softly but break me asunder astonishes me.

On the nightstand by the bed is my rainbow crystal. Kade holds it between his index finger and thumb. He scrutinizes it before speaking. "I'm also the one who gave you this."

I hold the hair ribbons in my open palms like a live rabbit. It's undeniably sweet. I can barely comprehend their meaning. My good luck charm was gifted to me by Kade. I thought someone left it for me. Never would I have guessed it was the warlord's son.

"My father knew instantly I wanted you. He told me for me to win your favor I'd have to work twice as hard because I wasn't born a noble. After that day, I started taking my training seriously. I began fighting in my father's wars and taking on jobs of my own. The rainbow crystal is from the southwest caves where I fought a pygmy dragon by myself. It reaped me a high reward from the people of Via'soune-Latos," says Kade. I realize why his smile is charming. It's because it's a boyish grin on a man's face.

"I detested watching the way the men treated you. Forgive me, but I sat in on their arrival a handful of times. I came so far to see you and when I heard the maids whispering about another prince or duke coming for you, I couldn't leave until I saw them."

I get the warm wave of shame and it burns me out like a fever. Kade saw the men belittle me, call me names, and refuse to marry me for various reasons. What torture it must have been to see the one you love be auctioned off to the highest bidder.

"In my youth I was full of rage, a hot-tempered kid from the slums. I had to stop myself from throttling the men who made you cry," he says, gritting his teeth. "I know it was painful for you to be rejected, but I was relieved every time one of those bastards stormed out. You couldn't have known the deserts I crossed, the valleys I trudged through, the forest I wandered, and the armies I fought to get to you."

Kade takes back his bundle of hair ribbons, trinkets of his affection. He has kept them close to his heart for a decade. Who would have guessed the young warlord of Tessafaye would be a romantic?

"When your mother asked for my assistance in the war and offered your hand in marriage to me, I thought I was dreaming. I had to remind myself periodically my prayers had been answered," says Kade as he brushes my bangs from my forehead. I can't stop staring at him. My childish curiosity has me wide eyed and fully enthralled. Kade lets his arm fall. "I thought by the way you've been acting you might feel the same," he says and shrinks away from me. "But I understand if you don't."

He's not one to be shy, but he is quiet. Kade hardly speaks and I'm perpetually silent. He holds me hostage where I witness beautiful violence. I sit on my knees and wrap my arms around Kade's neck. He smiles as I kiss him over and over again.

"Does this mean you love me back?" he asks. Kade's eyelashes tickle my face. I lean back and nod. The stern face of the warlord is replaced by a juvenile expression.

"Good."

***

The sound of a desert poppy blooming is a fuzzy unfurling of petals. Lapis blue skies are clear. Sunshine caresses the earth. I no longer envy the sun's beauty or wholeness. The moon is mystical, magical, powerful in the realm of the unknown. She doesn't need to be full to shine bright.

Rupert rolls in the grass next to me. He paws at low-flying butterflies. They flutter around my crown. I can see the dust come off their wings. I pick poppies and embellish my hair and clothes with them.

I wonder if my father can see me. Does he know how often I think about him? Sometimes I think he must have heard Kade's prayers and sought a way to bring us together. Penelope did say we would be happy, and she was right.

"There's my wife," says Kade as he joins me. He sits too close and Rupert becomes immediately jealous. I pick him up for a snuggle. This makes him feel better, and he runs off to chase after a grasshopper.

Kade rests his large palm on the crook of my neck. "If it were up to Rupert, I'd never get to be this close to you," he says and kisses me.

I hand him one of the gold and black poppies, reminding me of him. The desert is vast. It can be cool and dark, but it's beautiful.

Francis and Mirai walk by us. Their grins are stretched above their chins. Kade smiles and waves to both of them. I nod and touch my heart. Mirai takes notice of this and winks at me.

"Mirai is the one who has been teaching me to read. I used your notes as references," says Kade.

I clutch my arm in shame, thinking of all the times I cursed Mirai for being nosy and sleeping with him. She wanted us to be able to communicate. I thought Francis had been teaching Kade, but it was her.

I sit up so I can see my husband better. His face is neutral, but in his eyes, I can see Kade is content. I scoot closer and put my hands on his shoulders. Kade puts his arms around me and laughs. "Did you think I wouldn't find a way to talk to you?"

My face flushes. Not many people have gone out of their way to understand me. Kade moves my hair to one side and ignores my shyness. "We're going to be together for the rest of our lives. I want you to be able to share everything with me," he says. I embrace him and smile into his neck.

Over Kade's shoulders, I watch the mercenaries march across the yard. Darius and Jibril seem pleased to see the young warlord carefree. He hasn't been training as hard. The men and I are thankful. Kade sleeps in and we watch the dawn turn into day together now.

Finn stands out with his blood red cloak. The scar by his eye makes him appear a distinguished mercenary. I wave at him and he waves back. Besides Kade and Francis, Finn is the only man I've trusted. He is an upstanding person who doesn't drink or take part in crude banter. It makes sense he is Kade's closest friend.

Kade pulls me into his lap, which, of course, embarrasses me because the men are watching. Avery whistles and shouts with joy while waving at Kade. Eli nudges him and he stops hollering when

Finn turns around and gives him a deathly stare. Kade kisses me hard in front of them.

"How much do you love me?" he asks. I take out my notebook and look at him slyly as I scribble my message. Kade tries to take the piece of paper from me, but I hide it behind my back. My game doesn't last for long, but it's fun to play. He unfolds the wrinkled note.

I love you more than rain.

"I almost gave up on my dream of having you. Everyone thought I was a madman. Maybe I was. I'm glad my father encouraged me. I knew it would be worth it," he says and holds onto me. "My love for you has won countless wars and slayed numerous monsters. After I fell for you, the world was a different place. One where I'd fight to the death to get closer to you."

We stay in the garden since he took the entire day off. I instruct Kade to lean back into the flowers. One can hear them better this way. The wind is high and lifts our hair as it zigzags through the grass. He rests his head in his palm and the other on my hip.

The resounding beat of his heart drums into me. Desert sand eyes are on the sky's transformation from day to dusk. The shape of silence is a shimmering circle. Kade's hair is disheveled from the wind. I brush his bangs out of his face and he kisses my palm.

"I love you, Ama," says Kade. I point to my eye, then my heart, and place my hand on his chest. "Good."

Here I can be myself. I can read all day. My dog keeps me company and we have fun running around the courtyard. I wander the castle and feel no fear of punishment in my own house.

The desert is a wondrous but dangerous place, much like my husband's heart. Kade and I were meant to be. I got my wish. He was in front of me this whole time, but I couldn't see until now, a silent discovery.

THE END